CAPE COD
KISSES

Love on Rockwell Island
Book One

Bella Andre

&

Melissa Foster

ISBN-13: 9780986135835
ISBN-10: 0986135836

Cover Design: Natasha Brown

BAYSIDE BOOKS, LLC
PRINTED IN THE UNITED STATES OF AMERICA

Note to Readers

For the past year we have been having the most wonderful time writing about the loyal, loving, and super-sexy Rockwell family—and we couldn't be more excited about finally getting to introduce you to everyone in Rockwell Island!

There's nothing we love more than creating big family romances that you can disappear into and become a part of. Quinn Rockwell and Shelley Walters' love story made both of us laugh, cry...and sigh with happiness. We hope you love Quinn and Shelley as much as we do!

Happy reading,
Bella & Melissa

PS. Trent Rockwell is going to be the next Rockwell to find love in *Cape Cod Promises*—a seriously yummy romance with the woman he's never been able to forget. Be sure to sign up for our newsletter so we can let you know as soon as the newest books in our *Love on Rockwell Island* series are released!

www.LoveonRockwellIsland.com/Newsletter

Chapter One

SHELLEY WALTERS STOOD on the porch of the Rockwell Resort honeymoon cottage, gazing out at Cape Cod Bay. Silver ribbons of moonlight reflected off the dark water, dancing with the motion of the tide.

She stepped from the porch onto the beach with a bottle of champagne in one hand and her cell phone in the other, and dug her toes into the sand. She was a lightweight when it came to alcohol, but she liked carrying the bottle instead of a glass. It felt more celebratory. More fun.

A cool breeze brushed her dress over her thighs.

This place is perfect for a honeymoon. Seven full days and six nights of pure, unadulterated bliss.

Her phone vibrated with a call. *Taryn,* her cousin and closest friend.

"I was just about to text you to let you know that I'm finally here," Shelley said as she sank down to sit in the sand and sipped the champagne. *Mm. Those Rockwells don't skimp on a thing.* While researching places to honeymoon, Shelley had learned that the Rockwell family had owned the resort—and the island—for generations.

"How great is the island?"

Shelley pictured her cousin in her design studio, her long dark hair pinned up in a messy bun with a pencil securing it in place and a wide smile on her lips. With most women, Shelley felt like an accessory. *Rochelle Walters, sole heir to the diamond dynasty Walters Enterprises.* Her name carried weight in the social circles she worked hard to avoid—and that others clawed their way into. Luckily, Taryn didn't care one whit about wealth or social status.

"The honeymoon cottage is just as cute as the pictures online." Shelley sighed dreamily as she looked out over the water. "And it's right on the beach, with the most amazing view of the bay."

"I'm so glad you decided to do this for yourself, Shell. You're my hero for even thinking up something as great as a solo honeymoon, let alone actually doing it!"

Shelley loved running her coffee shop, the Creek Café, and she wasn't so overly stressed by it that she'd needed time away from her everyday life. But after watching what felt like half the single women in Maryland get married and then hearing all about their fabulous honeymoons, she'd decided she wanted one. A honeymoon, that is, not a marriage. She had yet to see a marriage where the husband and wife loved each other more than they loved material things and the idea of being married, but the honeymoons sounded spectacular.

Shelley had always followed her own path through life, letting gut instincts and her heart lead the way. So, having thrown societal norms out the window long ago, she threw caution to the wind yet again, stopped waiting for Mr. Right, and booked a solo honeymoon.

Over the years Taryn had supported all of Shelley's whims, like moving to Maryland, buying the coffee shop, and refusing any monetary help from her parents. In fact, Taryn had made the beautiful, strapless, lacy dress that Shelley had on tonight, and she was glad she was getting to share some of the joy of being on Rockwell Island with her cousin.

"Coming in on the plane, I got a spectacular view of the whole island. It's like paradise. I saw two marinas, a lighthouse, and lots of little ponds."

"Kettle ponds probably," Taryn said excitedly. "They're common around the Cape."

"The Cape," Shelley repeated. "I've always loved the sound of that." She couldn't stop smiling. "There are also miles of beaches and several pools at the resort. The Rockwell Island Resort is big and fancy, but the staff is so warm and friendly that it isn't snooty, like all those over-the-top resorts my parents dragged me to when I was growing up."

"I can't picture your parents ever vacationing anywhere near Cape Cod," Taryn agreed.

"Only Aunt Marla would," Shelley said.

Shelley's best memories from childhood were of her weeks spent in Eastham, on the Cape with her aunt—the perfect break from the exhausting jet-set life her parents lived. One that truly had no place in it for raising or nurturing a daughter. Especially not a free spirit like Shelley. But with Aunt Marla, Shelley had spent wonderfully lazy hours looking for sea glass and meandering through the small towns. They'd cooked meals over outdoor fires and had gone fishing at the spur-of-the-moment. Aunt Marla had been the polar opposite of her sister, Shelley's mother—spontaneous rather than rigid—and Shelley missed her aunt every day since she'd passed away five years earlier.

"Sometimes," Shelley admitted in a low voice, "I used to pretend that I was actually her daughter."

"Anyone would have," Taryn said, as supportive as ever. "Marla was such a wonderful person."

Saltwater spraying from a wave crashing to the shore helped bring Shelley back to the beach she was sitting on. It should have been easy to push the uncomfortable thoughts of her parents away, given that she'd been doing it forever. She'd had to in order to break free from their grasp and live her own life. And yet she couldn't deny that it still hurt to realize she'd never fit in with the two people on earth who should have loved her most of all.

"So..." Taryn said, and Shelley knew what her cousin was going to say even before the words, "give me the lowdown on the hunky male options," left her mouth.

Just then Shelley spotted an older man being pushed in a wheelchair down the beach by a tall, exotic-looking blonde. A golden retriever padded alongside them. *Perfect*. Teasing Taryn was more fun than trying to convince her cousin that men weren't all they were chocked up to be.

"Actually," Shelley said, "I see one of the local men right now. He's got a golden retriever, and he's heading up the beach."

"And?" Taryn sounded excited. "I need more details."

The old man said something that caused the blonde to stop pushing the wheelchair. He patted his legs, and the dog put its fluffy paws on his knees and stuck its muzzle toward him. The man held its head with both hands and kissed it on the top of its snout.

"Aw, that's so sweet," Shelley whispered.

"Sweet?" Taryn made a sound of disgust. "Sweet is not exactly alpha material. I was hoping you were going to say how sexy he was."

Shelley laughed. "No, definitely not sexy. But he just stopped to kiss his dog, and it *was* really sweet." She watched the woman turn the wheelchair around and head back the way they'd come. "Anyway, I'm here for a solo honeymoon, not to scope out the hunky island men, remember?"

It had been ages since Shelley had been close with a man. Most of the guys she met reminded her of her father—all business. Finding someone who wasn't afraid to live life *and* had a mind of his own was like playing an impossible game of Where's Waldo? She was done with that whole disappointing scene.

"Come on, Shell," Taryn replied, clearly undeterred. "No one on Rockwell Island knows you, so why not cut loose, meet a guy, and get a little wild for a night or two? You usually throw caution to the wind, but not when it comes to guys. Why not live a little?"

"Because all the men I've ever met wouldn't know how to go with the flow if a good time came with a map." Shelley sipped more champagne. "Besides, I *am* cutting loose. The resort left champagne in my cottage, and it is delish. I think I'm going to take a walk on the beach now and dip my toes in the water."

"Okay, but be careful of sharks."

"I'm almost positive that sharks don't swim in the bay, but if I meet any on land, I'll definitely let you know."

"Steer clear of those, but promise me you'll have some fun. Go skinny-dipping or do something crazy, okay? And if a great guy does happen to come along, at least *think* about giving him a chance."

After hanging up, Shelley took another sip of champagne. She probably should have eaten dinner, but it was almost nine p.m., and she was far more interested in exploring the island than eating. She watched the woman and old man move farther down the beach, and then she headed off in the opposite direction.

The last thing she wanted this week was to think about men. A solo honeymoon meant Shelley could enjoy the things she wanted, *exactly* how she wanted them, without being told where to go and what to do by anyone. Taryn knew that, but she still had hope that the right guy was out there somewhere.

Shelley wasn't holding her breath.

But skinny-dipping? That sure sounded like fun...

QUINN ROCKWELL PACED across the plush carpeting in the resort suite with his cell phone pressed to his ear and his other hand pinching the bridge of his nose as he listened to his business partner lay into him about leaving Annapolis.

"We're on the brink of the merger of a lifetime, and you leave town with nothing more than an e-mail telling me you'll be in touch?"

Richard Bailey had been Quinn's business partner since day one. After graduating from Stanford, he and Rich had set out together, bound and determined to build a shipping empire to rival all others. Rockwell Bailey Enterprises, RBE, was a leader in the industry, and the impending merger with Capital Freight Management would solidify their untouchable stature. Both Rich and Quinn wanted this merger, and they wanted it bad. But for Quinn,

8

it wasn't just building the business that was driving his crazy hours and laser focus on the merger. He hadn't talked with Rich about the feeling he'd been fighting lately, that he was spinning his wheels running their company. They were more successful than ever, and he should have been happier, more satisfied with his life. Quinn hoped this merger would bring back the excitement he'd felt in the early days of building RBE.

"You know this is a huge inconvenience to me, Rich, coming back to the island where I grew up." And couldn't wait to leave. "I'm not here because I *want* to be."

"I still don't get it. Your bullheaded grandfather demands that you and your brothers drop what you're doing and run back to appease whatever whim he's got going, and even though you're thirty-four years old, for some reason you still go."

After getting caught in an evening meeting and missing his flight, Quinn had to charter a plane to get to the island. It was almost midnight, and he was in no mood to defend this trip to Rich when he hadn't wanted to take it in the first place.

"My grandfather had another heart attack a month ago. I don't know what he's got up his sleeve, but family comes first." *Always.* "Even crotchety, old, stubborn family."

Quinn's grandfather, Chandler Rockwell III, owned the Rockwell Resort and employed more than half of the island's workforce. He wasn't known by his family or his staff for his warm demeanor. But that didn't mean Quinn would ever disrespect him.

"At least you made tonight's meeting," Rich relented. "I'll have those documents ready for signature by this time next week, but you need to go over the reports as soon as possible."

After agreeing to compile information for Rich to take to Monday's meeting and get back to Maryland in time to sign the documents in person, Quinn ended the call and loosened his tie. Needing to go for a run to burn off some energy, he threw his leather duffel up on the bed and pulled out his jogging shorts. He was as much of an exercise junkie as he was a workaholic. He believed in keeping his mind and his body sharp, and even though he was tired after a grueling sixteen-hour day, he was going to go for that run.

He changed into his shorts, splashed water on his face, and glanced up at his reflection in the mirror. For a moment, it was like looking into his grandfather's eyes—serious and way too stressed.

Quinn shook his head to clear that strange thought, stuffed the keycard into his pocket, and headed out the door just as his eldest brother, Trent, came out of the suite next door.

"I thought I heard you." Smiling, Trent embraced Quinn.

The Rockwell men were all over six feet tall and broad shouldered. Trent, Quinn, and their younger brothers, Derek and Ethan, all resembled their father, with thick dark hair, an angular nose, and a strong jawline. Quinn and Trent shared their mother's baby blues, while their brothers and their sister, Sierra, inherited their father's dark brown eyes.

"Got in late. Hope I didn't wake you." It had been a few weeks since Quinn and Trent had been able to find a couple of spare hours away from their demanding jobs to meet for dinner in New York, where Trent lived and ran his legal practice.

Trent raked a hand through his hair. He was still wearing his suit pants but no shirt. "I'm not even close to heading to bed yet." He eyed Quinn's shorts. "Going for a run? At midnight?"

"Gotta work off some steam. Want to join me?" Quinn and Trent had often run together as teenagers and when they were home during college breaks.

"Thanks, but I've got at least another hour of work to do on these briefs, and we've got the meeting with Chandler in the morning."

They always called their grandfather by his first name when speaking to each other, since he wasn't warm enough to be considered *Grandpa*, and he'd never have allowed the endearment anyway. Chandler demanded that they refer to him as *Grandfather*.

"Now that you've reminded me about Chandler, I think I'll make it a six-mile run instead of five." Quinn blew out a frustrated breath. "Did you hear anything more about why he's made all of us come back here?"

"Sierra said she thinks it has to do with the resort, but I couldn't get ahold of Dad. He's going to meet with all of us tomorrow afternoon." Trent checked his watch. "You'd better go if you're set on running."

"Right. We'll catch up in the morning."

Quinn's legs felt like they'd been caged in place for too long as he headed out for his run. It took a while for his limbs to loosen up and his body to remember it *liked* to run.

He took off down Bay Road, running parallel to the water. Stars dotted the sky, and moonlight basked the road in a soft glow. Finally, he found his groove and ran at a good clip for the first few miles, mentally working through his meetings from earlier in the day and trying to ignore his agitation at being summoned to the island.

Like always, he ran down a path by the trees, heading for Mill Cove. If any place on this island could help him clear his head, it was the secluded cove where, as a kid, he used to escape when he felt the island pressing in on him.

Rockwell Island was large in size but had always felt like it was small on choices for Quinn. He knew if he'd stayed on the island, he'd have been railroaded into running the resort, like his father had. His grandfather had not been pleased when Trent, Quinn, and Derek had left the island to build careers elsewhere, or when Sierra and Ethan had followed their own career paths outside of the resort, even though the two of them had returned to the island to live after college.

With the encouragement of their parents, the five of them had all found ways to avoid falling under the scrutiny of Chandler as the latest Rockwell Resort employee. Their father, Griffin, however, had not been so lucky. He'd worked at the resort his entire life under the controlling and often demeaning eyes of Chandler. Although Griffin practically ran the resort now, Chandler still refused to acknowledge his son's vital role in the resort's success.

As Quinn neared the water, the temperature dropped and the sounds of the bay infiltrated the chaos in his head. A welcome distraction, although still not loud enough to drown out thoughts of work. He ran along the wet sand, close to the shoreline, his heart beating hard and fast as the boulders that marked the entrance of the secluded cove came into view. The soles of his running shoes pounded against the dense sand as he rounded the massive rocks, and there, nestled between a thick tree line on one side and a rocky outcropping on the other, was Mill Cove.

He smiled as he slowed his pace, fixing to stay awhile, maybe think through some of the work he had to prepare for the meeting with Rich later that week. Each footfall became less pronounced as he neared the edge of the cove, the water shrouded from the moonlight by thick, full branches and sharp boulders.

Quinn was bending at the waist, placing his hands on his thighs to catch his breath, when splashing sounds caught his attention. He shifted his eyes to the water, listening intently.

A soft feminine laugh filtered into his ears, and he turned toward it, taking a step forward and nearly tripping over an empty champagne bottle.

Great. It would be just his luck to stumble upon a couple making out in *his* cove.

He caught movement near the water's edge and squinted, bringing the gorgeous curves of a naked woman into focus. She was facing away from him, her fingertips dragging along the surface of the water, flinging it into the air every few seconds, accompanied by that feminine laugh.

All alone in the water, she turned in the iridescent light of the moon, revealing a silhouette of her full breasts, the lush curves of her hips, and her long dark hair.

Quinn stood stock-still, mesmerized by her beauty and the sweet sound of her laughter. But when he shifted and stepped on a piece of driftwood, she immediately looked toward the sound of wood cracking.

For a split second their eyes locked. *Sweet Lord, she was beautiful.*

And then with a gasp of surprise, she was suddenly submerged beneath the water, the waves covering her head to toe.

Chapter Two

QUINN SPRINTED INTO the icy water and scooped the woman up in his arms, incredibly thankful that he had been there when she went under.

Holding her close, the first thing he did was make sure she was breathing okay. Thanking God that she was, he asked, "Are you okay? Are you hurt?"

She looked up at him in confusion. "What are you doing?"

"Saving you." His heart was still pounding way too hard as he strode out of the water with her in his arms. That split second when he'd thought she was drowning had been terrifying.

"Saving me?"

She pushed wet hair out of her eyes, and he nearly stumbled as a direct ray of moonlight illuminated her high cheekbones, full lips, and eyes that managed to look both intelligent *and* seductive. She truly was the most beautiful woman he'd ever set eyes on.

"I was just having fun skinny-dipping. At least until I realized you were standing there. That's when I dropped down under the water so you wouldn't see me naked. Besides," she said as he finally realized she was trying to push out of his arms, while also trying futilely to cover up her lush curves, "how do I know you're not the one I need saving from? Some guy skulking around the cove after midnight grabbing naked women out of the sea."

"I'm not that kind of guy," he promised her, even though he was losing the battle of trying to ignore the feel of her bare breasts against his chest, the sweet scent of her naked skin, and the fact that her voice fit the rest of her perfectly—warm and full-bodied. "I would *never* hurt a woman. I swear I'm just trying to help you."

But he knew if he really wanted to prove to her that he was a good guy, now that they were out of the water, he needed to let go of her naked body. Deliberately not letting his eyes wander over her curves again, he finally set her down.

"Do you remember where you left your clothes?" he asked as he turned around to give her privacy to go find them.

"Of course I remember."

Quinn assumed by the distant sound of her voice that she'd walked a short ways up the beach to find her clothes and was now getting dressed.

"I might be a lightweight," she continued, "but I didn't drink *that* much champagne tonight. Besides, you're *supposed* to have fun and be a little wild on your honeymoon. You can turn around again now. I'm dressed."

Quinn turned, and holy smokes, the strapless minidress she wore was now drenched and nearly translucent, doing absolutely nothing to hide her curves. He tried to shift his eyes away, but *Jesus*, it was hard. She was *that* sexy.

By the time he was finally able to make himself look away from the wet fabric over her naked curves, he was stunned by the expression on her face. Not fear, anymore. Not confusion, either. Instead, it looked like she wished she were back in his arms again. The night was cool, but in that moment the heat between them easily trumped the evening breeze.

At least until his brain finally registered what she'd just said.

"Honeymoon?" None of this made any sense. Why was she out here by herself if it was her honeymoon? And if she'd just gotten married, then where had the desire he swore he'd seen in her eyes come from? The only thing he knew for sure right now was that some guy was going to try to kick his ass when he found Quinn out here on the beach with his wife, when all Quinn had been trying to do was make sure she was okay—or at least that's what he'd started out doing. "Where's your husband?"

His questions, especially the word *husband,* seemed to sever the heated thread between them. She waved a dismissive hand and made a face. "Husbands are *totally* overrated. Plus, you don't need one for a solo honeymoon."

Solo honeymoon? He'd never heard that one before. She was surprising him at every turn. Sexy *and* interesting was a combination he hadn't come across many times in his life.

"You're not married?"

She shook her head, but even just that small movement sent her off-balance. She was still as good as naked, and he'd hate for some other guy to find her like this—a little tipsy and too damn gorgeous for her own good. No question about it, he wouldn't be able to sleep if he didn't see her home safely in one piece.

Quinn didn't know if this was his lucky night or if he was being punished for some unknown sin. But given that he would never dream of taking advantage of a woman out having fun skinny-dipping by herself in the moonlight, he was putting odds on punishment. Especially since even though he now knew she wasn't married, he was only on the island for long enough to get through tomorrow's meeting.

But at the same time, he'd never been this drawn to a woman before. Or been so intrigued. Maybe tomorrow, some how, some way, he could track her down and—

Just then, he realized there was a scrap of material floating near the water's edge. A scrap that looked like super-sexy lace panties.

"Are those yours, too?"

She followed his gaze, and her cheeks pinked up as she went to retrieve them. "Thanks. I would have been sad to lose my favorite pair."

Great. Now he was going to have to work like crazy to stop thinking about both her skintight, see-through dress *and* the panties she'd just picked up. Already, though, he was failing on every front as desire continued to simmer hotter inside of him by the second.

"I'd like to make sure you get home okay."

She didn't respond, simply started heading up the beach. He kicked something else and bent down to find a cell phone half buried in the sand. Looked like she'd forgotten more than just her favorite pair of panties.

"Where are you staying?" he said after he picked up her phone and slipped it into his pocket. He spotted the empty champagne bottle and picked that up too, and then caught up to her.

"The honeymoon cottage at the resort." She looked to the right, then the left, then stopped walking. "I'm not going the right way, am I?" The sudden laughter underlying her words gave him the sense that the alcohol was beginning to sink in big-time now.

Even her laughter was sexy. "Nope."

Quinn found himself wishing the honeymoon cottage wasn't quite so close by. He wasn't ready to say goodnight to her just yet. Not anywhere near close to ready.

"Well," she said as she turned around and headed in the opposite direction, "I suppose since we're on an island, I would have gotten there eventually."

Quinn felt his lips twitch. She was like a sweet—and breathtakingly sensual—ray of moonlight on what had been a bleak and chaotic night. He'd never understood how people could allow themselves to float through even one night without a plan, without being completely in control. But in the few moments before she'd seen him in the cove and ducked down in the water to cover herself with the waves, it had been captivating to watch her act like she hadn't a care in the world, so happy and confident.

As they walked past the boulders and followed the surf toward the lights of the resort in the distance, he said, "I'm Quinn."

"I'm Shelley." She smiled at him, another ray of moonlight shining down as she said, "Shelley Walters."

"I've got to ask you, why a solo honeymoon, Shelley?"

"Because dating is a bore, and waiting for a honeymoon might mean I'd never take one."

"Dating is a bore, huh?" He couldn't agree more.

For a moment as she turned to meet his gaze, he swore heat flared between them again. But then, she stopped walking, put her hand on her forehead, and shook her head as if she was trying to stave off the effects of the champagne by sheer will.

Quinn remembered that feeling from his college days when he'd had one too many. He had the urge to put his arm around her, to steady her and block her from the bay breeze. She had to be cold in that wet dress. But before he could, she began walking again, each step a little less steady.

"Guys are all about work, sex, and more work," she continued. "Don't get me wrong. I really enjoy certain parts of that, but..." She trailed off as she focused on stepping over a large rock in the sand.

She had men nailed down pretty well. He couldn't dispute her assessment, but hearing it from her made him feel a little embarrassed because the "more work" part hit so close to home. They walked across the sand, listening to the sounds of the bay, her pace slowing considerably as the champagne fully hit her system. She stumbled over another rock, and he reached for her.

"Whoa," he whispered, pulling her against him before she could fall. "I've got you, sweetheart."

"*Sweetheart.*" She sounded almost wistful. Slightly breathless, too, as if being this close again felt as good to her as it did to him. "That sounds surprisingly nice when you say it. Almost like you mean it." She flattened her palms on his bare chest, fully awakening the desires he'd been trying to push down before he could forcefully bank them. Her words sounded a little more rounded now as she looked up at him and said, "Maybe Taryn is right and an island fling would be fun."

An island fling?

What had he done to deserve this test? Quinn hadn't had an island fling in too many years to count, ever since he'd become so consumed with his business that he came back to the island for only a few hours over the holidays, for family gatherings. But a fling with Shelley? Just the thought of it made him want to cancel every meeting he had scheduled for the next week so that he could focus on learning everything about her. Why she'd come to the island. What made her laugh. And, especially, what would make her gasp with pleasure...

"Maybe you should kiss me," she said, swaying a bit more now. "Just like a real honeymoon."

Hell yeah, I should kiss you. Not because of any honeymoon, but because you're gorgeous...and your laughter is the sweetest sound I've heard in forever.

He knew he wouldn't, though, knew he couldn't when the shock of the cold cove water had worn off and champagne was clearly swimming through her veins. He set the champagne bottle down in case she stumbled again.

"Come on. Let's get you inside." He settled a hand on her lower back in an effort to guide her toward the porch, her skin hot to his touch despite the wet dress.

Before he could step away, she said, "Well, if you won't kiss me..."

The next thing he knew, her body was melting against him and she was winding her hands around his neck...and pressing her full, warm lips to his.

It was pure instinct to kiss her back—how could anyone resist a woman this beautiful? This sweet. This *sexy*.

For a long moment, Quinn was caught up in the heat of their kiss, the smooth dance of their tongues. She kissed him eagerly, tasting of sweet champagne and wicked desires. Her tongue traced his lips and her hands slid into his hair, and he was lost to anything but his need to deepen the kiss, to put his hands firmly on her hips and draw her closer and learn more of her taste, and to drink in more of her little gasps of pleasure as they both instinctively closed the distance between them.

A brisk breeze brushed over his skin, bringing his senses back into focus, and it took every ounce of self-control he possessed to force himself to pull away. He'd already let the kiss go on longer than he should, but *holy hell*, what she did to him was like nothing he'd ever felt before. She'd felt so right in his arms that it knocked him totally off kilter.

He couldn't let her go, though, since she was obviously still not steady on her feet. With an arm around her waist, he said, "You should probably get some rest, Shelley."

She touched her fingertips to her lips and stared up at him, her eyes guileless. And so damned sensual that his hands itched to pull her closer again. "Or we could kiss some more."

He could still taste her on his tongue, could still feel her sweet curves pressed against him. There was nothing he wanted more than to kiss her again. Not one thing on this planet would be better than devouring her mouth again, stripping her wet dress away, tasting every inch of her skin...and getting to learn each and every one of her sounds of pleasure. But Quinn knew it wouldn't be right. Not when her eyes, and her words, were still fuzzy from the champagne.

"Next time we kiss," he promised her before he could think better of making promises to a beautiful stranger on a dark beach, "I want to make sure you remember it."

"How could I forget when it felt so good?"

Her question sent his heart kicking into overdrive again, just the way her kiss had. Knowing better than to try to even answer her question, he simply pulled deep from his control again and suggested, "Do you want me to walk you up?"

She frowned for a moment. "No. Not yet." She looked out at the ocean. "It's so pretty out. I want to sit on the beach for a little while and look at the stars."

It would be safer for both of them if she simply went inside and got into bed—alone. But she'd plopped down on the sand beside his feet. Telling himself the only way to make sure she didn't get back in the water was to stay with her, Quinn grabbed a towel from the porch of her cottage, draped it over her shoulders to keep her warm, then sat down beside her.

"It's beautiful here, isn't it?" Shelley lay back on the sand, looking up at the clear night sky. "One of the most stunning things I've ever seen."

"It really is," he agreed as he also lay back on the sand. But he wasn't looking at the stars.

He couldn't stop looking at her. Her hair was soaking wet, and now sandy, too, but her contented smile and the happy sigh she'd just exhaled, told him that she didn't mind it at all.

She turned to face him. "Thanks for saving me on my solo honeymoon, Quinn. Even if I didn't need saving, it was actually kind of fun. Especially," she added with a sexy gleam in her alluring eyes, "that kiss."

That kiss...

It was one he'd never forget.

She fell quiet, then, for long enough that he realized she'd fallen asleep, the smile still on her lips.

Trying not to wake her, he lifted her into his arms again. He'd never actually carried a woman before, but tonight he'd already had her in his arms twice—and both times had felt damn good.

Carrying her up the cottage stairs, he reached for the door and wasn't surprised to find it unlocked. Not only because the resort and the island were both very safe places, but because Shelley didn't seem like the kind of woman who worried about locking her doors too often.

The cottage was dark, save for a light left on above the sink in the kitchenette. He carried her across the threshold and quickly surveyed the cottage. His brother Derek had remodeled it two years earlier, removing the wall between the kitchen and living room and installing a big bay window, complete with a window seat, opening up to a beautiful view of the water. The hardwood floors were wide planked and still in perfect condition.

Quinn hesitated, debating both about putting a sexy stranger in bed and about wearing his wet, sandy sneakers inside the cottage. His grandfather's voice sailed unbidden into his mind. *Treat this resort like a castle and it will always be one.*

With Chandler's voice grating against his every nerve, Quinn toed off his wet running shoes and then carried her through the cozy living room, past the built-in bookcases and the stone fireplace. When his feet hit the plush bedroom carpeting, he hesitated again, imagining Shelley waking up and being terrified if she couldn't remember who he was.

For the first time in his life, he hoped a woman would stay asleep when he took her to bed. He walked into the bedroom, pulled back the thick, burgundy comforter and plush sheet, and laid her gently on the bed, still wrapped in the towel. She made a seductive little sound as she curled toward him, one arm arcing over her head, the other across her ribs, with her long dark hair spread across the pillow. Noticing flecks of sand on the sheets, he debated changing her out of the sandy dress and into something else from her closet, but he wasn't sure he trusted himself *that* much.

Not when she was his every fantasy come true.

Quinn brushed a strand of hair from her forehead, unable to stop drinking in her incredible beauty. She'd thanked him for being a part of her solo honeymoon, but the truth was that he should be thanking her for saving him from a night of living in his own head, going over and over all the things he needed to accomplish by the end of the week.

What was it about her that had his heart taking notice and his mind taking a reprieve from work?

All he knew for sure was that it felt surprisingly natural to press a soft kiss to her forehead and to whisper, "Good night, Shelley Walters. Thanks for making it a surprisingly good one."

Chapter Three

WHAT WAS I thinking last night?

Shelley squinted at the sunlight peeking in through the blinds and rolled over, burying her face in the pillow, wishing she had a toffee-flavored coffee from her café. She needed a gallon to come out from under this hangover fog. She'd had only a couple glasses of champagne, but for a lightweight like her, that was easily more than enough. She kicked her feet to get whatever was scratching them off, but every kick abraded her skin. As she flung the covers off and found a smattering of sand in the sheets, pieces of last night started to come back into focus.

Quinn.

Pictures came to her, one after the other, of the most beautiful man she'd ever set eyes on—

blue eyes, dark hair, and a gorgeous chest—along with a vague memory of the two of them walking across the beach to her cottage, where she put her arms around his neck and—

Oh God.

I kissed him!

She bolted upright, eyes wide as the memory of a perfect—and shockingly hot—kiss suddenly hit her as clear as day. The delicious taste of his mouth, wonderfully sweet and fiercely possessive all at once. How he'd gripped her hips and pulled her closer, so close that she'd gasped at the pleasure of being pressed up against such hard, hot muscles. She'd never experienced such an intense, sexy kiss before, one that she'd never ever wanted to end.

But had it ended? Or had their kiss turned into so much more?

She'd been skinny-dipping when he'd found her, but the rest of it was a little too vague for her peace of mind right now.

She might have been considering getting a little bit wild last night...but this was *way* too wild, even for her.

Holding her breath, she looked down at her thighs and closed her eyes as she slid her hand up her hip under her dress to feel for her underwear.

Oh no. I'm not wearing any.

No, no, no.

Scanning the room for clues, she jumped from the bed. Her head throbbed and the room swayed. She grabbed ahold of the bedpost for stability. She never drank much, and a hangover was not something she was used to dealing with. Nor did she *want* to deal with it.

Following a trail of sand into the living room, she tried to put the pieces of last night together. She touched her hair, which was a sticky, sandy mess, just like her dress. She had nothing on beneath her dress. But she didn't have any recollection of his body over hers or his hands on her skin.

Shelley looked at her hands, the memory of his firm chest against her palms finally resurfacing. Surely if they had gone to bed together, she'd have some memory of more than one incredible kiss and her hands brushing briefly over hard muscle. Something told her that making love with Quinn was something no woman could ever possibly forget. Not when one look, one touch, one kiss had been enough to melt her insides.

No amount of champagne could have made Shelley forget her breathless awareness to him. She'd never felt anything like it before, a *wanting* that had instantly taken her over right from the first moment she'd set eyes on him. Wanting that shook her even now with its intensity as she replayed the previous night with greater and greater clarity by the minute.

She opened the front door and inhaled the chilly sea air. *Too bright.* Shading her eyes, she crossed the deep porch and sat down on one of the rocking chairs beside the small painted table. When she'd arrived at the cottage, she'd imagined having breakfast at this table, but food didn't sound at all appetizing right now.

Her eyes finally landed on a bottle of Motrin, a carafe of orange juice, and an envelope with her phone lying on top of it.

She picked up the bulky envelope, peeked inside, and felt her cheeks heat up as she withdrew her thong. Her hand instinctively covered her face, and she didn't know if she should laugh or cry. She was almost afraid to read the accompanying note...

> *Solo honeymooner,*
> *Thought you might want these—*
> *especially the Motrin. I found your*
> *favorite scrap of lace in the sand*
> *again and didn't want to chance it*
> *getting lost. Enjoy the beautiful*
> *day, and don't worry—apart from*
> *our one kiss, I was a perfect*
> *gentleman when I tucked you in.*
> *Q.R.*

With a shaky hand, and feeling relieved, she set the note on the table. But when she started to head inside to take the Motrin, she realized he'd also brought back her empty champagne bottle and left it for her at the other side of the door. He'd placed a candle in the neck of the bottle, melting it around the edges to secure it in place.

She was touched by his simple, lovely gift— and so grateful that he'd made sure to let her know that he'd been a perfect gentleman. Even if a part of her suddenly couldn't help but wish he hadn't been *quite* so much of a gentleman. With a huge smile on her face, she downed the Motrin, then immediately texted Taryn.

I might be reconsidering my island fling options.

Her phone rang a second later, as she'd known it would.

"Something happened last night, didn't it? Tell me everything!"

Shelley told Taryn about Quinn finding her skinny-dipping, their walk back to the cottage, and how they'd shared one seriously hot kiss.

But instead of whooping for joy the way Shelley had expected her to, Taryn asked, "Did you see a wedding ring?" Her cousin had clearly gone into protective mode.

Shelley knew she never would have hit on a married man in a million years. "No."

"And you really don't think he tried anything last night?"

"Nothing I wasn't *begging* him for." Perhaps embarrassment should have swept over her at the memory of the way she'd thrown herself back into Quinn's arms in front of the cottage. But Quinn had been simply irresistible in the cove in the moonlight. And she wouldn't give up her memory of the kiss they'd shared for anything in the world.

"Congratulations, Shelley." Her cousin laughed, clearly delighted now. "You are finally turning into a normal girl."

"What is that supposed to mean?"

"Just that you're so freaking picky when it comes to guys; it's nice to see you easing up a little. I say go for it. Be safe, use condoms, and all that, but the beauty of having an island fling is that you're away from everyone. No one will ever know about it, and your parents can't judge him if they don't know him. I mean, if you had a tryst anywhere near home, God only knows what Sheila and Margo would let slip if they found out, right?"

Sheila Lavington and Margo Burland were two women they'd gone to school with. Both had married for money, keeping in the same social realm as their parents. They'd given up everything in their lives other than attending charity events. Shelley didn't even want to contemplate their snooty looks if they found out she'd been skinny-dipping. Shelley was supposed to be bred of the same cloth as the Lavingtons and the Burlands, and God forbid she do anything so frivolous.

Shelley glanced down at her lacy minidress, her sandy feet, and remembering her thong, still outside on the table with the champagne bottle and note, said, "We're *so* not cut from the same cloth." The thought made her giddy with delight. Although not anywhere near as giddy as Quinn's kiss had made her feel.

"Forget them," Taryn said. "The big question is, what's your plan for the hunky guy who ran into the water to save you?"

Suddenly she remembered what he'd said to her right before they'd sat down on the sand outside her cottage: *Next time we kiss, I want to make sure you remember it.*

A wicked thrill rocked through her at the memory of his sexy promise. "Well, if he's as gorgeous in the light of day as he was beneath a full moon, if I do end up seeing him again, I just might let things take their natural course." And let him make good on his promise to her. "Even though I don't know how long he's here, or his last name, or anything."

"All the better," Taryn insisted. "Remember, island flings don't need to be complicated. The less info revealed the better."

"You're really good at this, T. If I were you, I wouldn't let your brothers get wind of your affinity for quickie affairs."

Taryn groaned. "Can you imagine? I'd be locked in a chastity belt and put in a high tower. It's surprising that they don't sit on my doorstep and guard me."

"Well, at least they care. You could be like me and live a life where your family is totally disinterested in anything you do."

"Oh, come on. Give them some credit—your parents are really good at chastising you when you go against their social graces. Which is pretty much all the time." Taryn was laughing, but when Shelley didn't join her, she stopped and added, "Hey, I'm family, and you know I love you."

"My parents do, too, in their own weird way, I'm sure," Shelley said, even though sometimes she wondered if that was really true. "Anyway, I'll let you know. Thanks for being there for me to bounce this off of."

"You mean to *brag* to, don't you? Shelley Walters has never needed permission for a darn thing in her entire life, and you and I both know having an island fling with a hot guy you met while skinny-dipping is no different."

Shelley grinned. "I should be worried about how well you know me. Gloat, gloat, gloat."

After they ended the call, Shelley showered and dressed, feeling a little lighter on her feet. The Motrin had finally kicked in, and her talk with Taryn had not only diminished any embarrassment that might have come, but helped make her feel excited about the possibility of being even naughtier during her vacation.

She didn't need approval for an island fling, but she did need the extra bolster of confidence, given that the sexy man whom she had tried to seduce had already seen her naked. Not to mention that she'd never actually had a fling and she wasn't sure she'd be capable of pulling off something so intimate that was meant to be, well, meaningless.

Still...she wasn't against trying. *Especially with Quinn.*

An hour later, she was one hundred percent again as she strolled down the beach toward the main resort buildings to see about breakfast. The beach by her cottage was empty, save for a few gulls feeding on unlucky fish, but the closer she got to the resort, the more people milled about.

When she had first chosen the Rockwell Resort for her trip, she'd had a little niggling worry that she might not like staying in such a fancy resort. She had been raised to hobnob with the best of them, but she didn't like the pretentious act that so many wealthy people wore like banners. The Rockwell Resort boasted an expansive private beach, and it was one of the few resorts that had a significant number of online reviews. It was the only resort where the reviews spoke of the intimate feeling of the resort and the friendliness and efficiency of the staff, in addition to the exquisite location and amenities. In the end, it was the reviews that had sold her on visiting the property.

The resort was very impressive, with a patio on the beach meeting a sweeping stairway that led to a terrace, where guests were enjoying breakfast at glass-topped tables. She stopped to admire the view of the two tiered pools farther up the property to the right and the surrounding gardens bursting with colorful blooms and verdant plants. The main building stood just beyond, with one wing running adjacent to the terrace, the other built at a ninety-degree angle behind the pools.

When she'd first seen the size of the resort, the pools, the beach cabanas, yachts, sailboats, and other amenities, she'd worried that maybe she'd made a mistake. The last thing she wanted was to take a vacation in a place that would feel more comfortable for her parents than for her. But from the moment she'd walked in the front doors, she was warmly welcomed with smiles and small talk from the friendly staff, and by the time she was done checking in and had been escorted to her cottage by a sweet concierge, she'd known she'd made the right choice.

She turned away from the resort to take in the view of the bay one more time before heading up for breakfast. It was a lovely morning, clear and crisp, without a cloud in the sky.

"Chugger!"

She turned at the sharp command and noticed the fluffy golden retriever she'd seen last night bounding toward her. The exotic honey-blonde was pushing the old man in the wheelchair in the same direction.

Shelley crouched to pet the puppy, who was full of wet kisses for her.

"I'm so sorry," the woman said as she brought the wheelchair to a stop. "He usually doesn't run off like that."

"That's okay. I love dogs." Shelley smiled, admiring the woman's lovely Mediterranean accent. Greek ancestry was her guess.

The older gentleman in the wheelchair patted his thighs, as he'd done the evening before, calling Chugger up for another kiss. "You're a good boy, aren't you?"

The man's eyes were dark, reminding Shelley of the coffee beans she worked with on a daily basis at her café. The top of his head was balding, the hair on the sides silver, as was his beard, while his salt-and-pepper mustache and thick black eyebrows clung to younger years. His brows angled up at the edges, reminding Shelley of Sean Connery and giving him an even more serious look. Fine lines mapped his forehead and defined his eyes, while deep grooves ran from his nose to the corners of his mouth. Dressed in a crisp white dress shirt and dark trousers, he was remarkably handsome for a man of his age, which Shelley guessed to be somewhere in the neighborhood of his early eighties.

"Are you staying at the resort?" the woman asked. She was tall and slim, with a regal but friendly face.

Shelley wondered how the woman managed to push the wheelchair through the thick sand so easily. Was she his granddaughter? Young trophy wife?

"Yes," Shelley replied. "I'm staying in the honeymoon cottage."

The old man shifted in his chair, and the woman settled a hand on his shoulder as she asked, "You're on your honeymoon?"

"Actually, I'm not married. I'm on a solo honeymoon." She tried to sound as if it was something people did every day. "This trip was a gift to myself."

The old man's hand stilled on the dog's neck as he lifted serious eyes to Shelley. His gaze was careful and assessing, as if he was considering how what she'd said about taking a *solo* honeymoon fit with her image. But then, just that quickly, he turned his attention back to petting the dog.

Shelley stiffened, realizing just how quickly she'd been dismissed.

"Now, that sounds like a fun idea," the woman said with a warm smile that instantly put Shelley at ease again. "I'm Didi Kostas, Mr. Rockwell's private nurse."

Mr. Rockwell? Shelley hadn't expected to meet—or rather, be alternately ignored, then scrutinized, then dismissed by—Mr. Rockwell. She'd read about him online when she was researching the property and knew that Chandler Rockwell III was a very impressive man. He'd taken over the family business after graduating from Harvard Law and had dedicated himself to it ever since.

Shelley tried not to act surprised or impressed. After all, she hated when people connected the dots between her name and her own wealthy family.

"I'm Shelley Walters. It's nice to meet you." Shelley dropped her eyes to Mr. Rockwell, hoping to introduce herself to him as well, but he didn't deign to look her way again.

"It's a pleasure meeting you, Shelley," Didi said. "Well, we'd better get going. Mr. Rockwell has a meeting this morning." When she patted his shoulder, he finally—and somewhat reluctantly—met Shelley's gaze again and offered her a curt nod before they headed off.

Shelley watched them for a moment, then turned back to take one last look at the bay before tending to her growling stomach, wondering how such a standoffish man ran such a warm and friendly resort.

Warm and friendly.

Her mind traveled back to thoughts of Quinn. She'd felt warm in his arms last night. Safe and warm. And *wanton.*

She smiled as the word unexpectedly passed through her mind. She'd never thought herself the *wanton* type before. Not until last night when every inch of her had been vibrating with desire as Quinn's mouth devoured hers and his hands possessed her like he never wanted to let her go.

Did he live on the island? Or was he here on a vacation? Or on business? She had so many questions and nothing but time on her hands for the next week.

She headed toward the resort, hoping to run into the man she couldn't forget.

Mysterious, sexy Quinn.

Chapter Four

QUINN STOOD IN his grandfather's massive office in Chandler's private wing of the resort, flanked by Trent and their brother Derek as they waited for their grandfather to arrive for their meeting. Ethan, their youngest and quietest brother, was looking out the window at the beach.

Quinn had been unable to get the image of Shelley playing in the waves, the sinful feel of her mouth against his, or the sexy sound of her gasp of pleasure as he'd dragged her closer in the heat of passion, out of his mind since last night. No matter how hard he'd tried to immerse himself in work after arriving back at his suite, his mind had continually drifted to her. He'd never had difficulty focusing on work before, and he hadn't known what to do with the energy—or the desire—meeting Shelley had instilled in him. He couldn't exactly go for another run, and he couldn't focus on work, so he'd ended up taking a cold shower, then lying in bed...still thinking of Shelley.

And still wanting her, just as fiercely as he had when she'd been in his arms.

He'd finally fallen asleep a little after four, and he'd awakened again soon after with the sound of her laughter playing through his memory and the sweet taste of her still on his tongue. But it was her smile, and the way her eyes had radiated happiness like beacons in the night, that had brought him down to her cottage at the ungodly hour of six in the morning to deliver a hangover remedy.

He'd been compelled to also leave her with a reminder of him that wouldn't be easily forgotten. Because he sure as hell hadn't been able to forget her.

He'd grabbed the candle and a pack of matches, and he'd sat on her porch while he'd made the champagne bottle into a candleholder just like he and his siblings had done when they were kids, under the watchful eyes of their mother. It had taken twenty minutes, but he hadn't minded a second of it. It was such a strange feeling, wanting to do something like that instead of picking up where he'd left off with his work the night before like he normally would have.

Now, though they were about to meet with their grandfather and it was sure to be a tense meeting, he was surprised by the smile on his face from just thinking about Shelley. Unfortunately, in a few minutes he'd need to push those thoughts away and focus completely on the issue at hand, whatever the hell that was. Yet again he wished his grandfather had been less cagey about why he'd needed to have Quinn and his four siblings back on the island today for this meeting.

Quinn eyed the bandage on Derek's forearm. The most adventurous of them all, Derek was an adrenaline junkie at heart. His love of risk came second only to his love of creating things with his hands. Derek was a custom builder and stonemason and ran a very successful business in Boston. He'd gone on a caving expedition with a group of his buddies last week, and one of his spring-loaded camming devices failed. He'd caught the sharp edge of the wall with his forearm, leaving a four-inch gash that had to be stitched up.

"How're the stitches?"

Derek shrugged. "Barely notice them."

Quinn shook his head, knowing it had to be throbbing. But given that Derek had injured himself so many times, Quinn thought his brother was probably telling the truth that he didn't even notice the stitched-up gash.

"Where'd you stay last night?" Trent asked Derek. "They said you never checked in to the suite Chandler booked for you."

"I wasn't going to let him pull all the strings." Derek flashed a crooked grin. "I stayed at my cabin." Years ago he'd bought a rustic cabin in the woods, and he clearly preferred roughing it to staying in plush luxury that came with strings attached.

"Your cabin?" Ethan laughed. His thick, wavy hair was unkempt from an early-morning fishing expedition. He ran the biggest fishery in the area, and lived and breathed for life on the water. "That thing isn't fit to live in. There isn't even a bed."

Derek rolled his eyes and paced. He got restless if he stayed in one place for too long. "Unlike you pansies, I don't mind sleeping on the floor in a sleeping bag." He peered down into the hall toward Chandler's office. "Where is he? First he mandates that the three of us return to the island, pulls Ethan off his boat, totally negates Dad—who has given his whole life to this frigging place—and Sierra by not even inviting them to the meeting. And now he's late?"

"I saw him from the window coming up from the beach a minute ago," Ethan said. "He's on his fourth private nurse, Didi. From what I've seen, though, she's got a strong will. He fired his last three nurses within days of hiring them. So far she holds the record for lasting the longest, and she shows promise of being able to put up with Chandler."

"Well, good luck to her." Derek checked his watch. "So you think it's true what Dad told you this morning? That Chandler's going to try to get us to take over the resort?"

Ethan nodded. "He said that's his hunch."

Quinn exchanged an incredulous glance with Trent. As the two eldest, they'd taken the brunt of the heat from their grandfather's disappointment in their avoidance of the family business, buffering the others. But there wasn't enough buffering in the world to take the sting out of Chandler's stern demeanor.

"He can't seriously think we're going to walk away from the businesses we've busted our asses building so we can take over for a man who treats his own son like garbage, can he?" Fire ran through Quinn's veins. "And even if he did think that, why would he come to us? Dad runs the show here. We all know that."

"Damn right," Derek agreed. "Without Dad this place would have tanked ages ago. He cleans up all of Chandler's messes, and I'll tell you what. He's a better man than me, because there's no way I'd be able to put up with Chandler for all these years. Dad's a saint."

Trent crossed his arms over his white dress shirt. His hair was perfectly combed, his suit pressed, his shoes shined. He obviously expected to leave the island after the meeting and be back in New York in time to get on with his law practice. He'd always been the voice of reason, the peacemaker, and Quinn could tell by the way he was looking at them that he was already slipping into mediator mode.

"I'm concerned about why Sierra and Dad aren't here, too," Trent said. "But we should hear Chandler out, play it cool, and then figure out our next step as a group. There's no need to get up in arms while he's in the room. The man just had his second heart attack. We don't need to be the cause of a third."

Quinn heard voices in the hall and motioned for the others, alerting them just before Chandler appeared in the doorway in his wheelchair, with a tall, attractive blonde standing behind him.

Chandler's face was stoic as his dark eyes moved over each of them. "Trent. Quinn. Derek. Ethan. Please, have a seat." He gripped the arms of the wheelchair tightly as Didi brought him to the head of the large conference table.

Even from the confines of the wheelchair he sucked all the air from the room. Not to mention that he had the audacity not to introduce Didi. Chandler hadn't changed in the months since Quinn had last been home. He wore the same brittle frown as he always had.

Trent smiled at Chandler's nurse. "You must be Didi. Ethan speaks very highly of you. I'm Trent."

"Trent, it's a pleasure." Her Greek heritage was evident in the inflection of her voice. Her eyes flitted to Derek, lingering for a moment before dropping back down to her charge.

Trent leaned down and hugged Chandler, who remained rigid, hands glued to the cold metal chair. "Grandfather, it's nice to see you. You look well." While Chandler always insisted on being formally addressed, their grandmother had been warm and affectionate and had loved being called *Grandma Caroline*. Quinn had never understood how the two had ended up together.

Chandler grumbled something indiscernible as Trent followed his command and sat in one of the leather seats across from where Derek and Quinn stood, waiting their turn to properly greet the man who had never seemed to welcome or want affection. Their parents had raised them to always respect their elders, so they showed their love to family whether they asked for it or not.

Quinn greeted Didi, then placed a hand on his grandfather's forearm and gave it a gentle squeeze before leaning down for a brief embrace that was not returned.

"Grandfather."

Chandler only nodded in return.

Quinn sat next to Trent while Derek held on to Didi's hand just a little too long as he shook it. "Didi, it's a pleasure to meet you. I'm Derek."

As her cheeks flushed, Chandler gruffly told Derek to sit down, while Quinn, Trent, and Ethan all stifled smiles. Derek and Ethan said quick greetings to their grandfather, then took their seats, giving him the floor.

When they were all seated, Chandler said, "Didi, the papers," in his gruff, deep voice.

"Yes, Mr. Rockwell." She moved with grace as she handed each of them a thick document before returning silently to her place behind Chandler's chair and professionally averting her gaze to the window.

Derek's eyes trailed Didi around the table, and Quinn had to nudge his brother's knee beneath the table to bring his attention back to the document before him.

Quinn quickly scanned the document, anger brewing hotter with every word he read. He could tell by the tightening of Trent's jaw and his grip on the papers that his peacekeeping brother was doing all he could to remain calm.

"Grandfather." Trent's tone was harsher than usual but calmer than anything out of Quinn's mouth would have been. "What exactly is your intention with this document?"

Chandler held his chin high, his dark gaze steady, unflappable. Clearly, his second heart attack hadn't softened him one bit.

"The terms are clear," Chandler said. "You and your brothers are to move back to the island and take over the resort. Rockwell Island will be your primary residence for at least ninety-five percent of the next calendar year. If you choose not to accept the terms of this agreement, I have a multinational business lined up to purchase the resort. They will overhaul the island, making it into a high-rise mecca, complete with their own staff."

Derek smacked his palm on the table. "You can't give us an ultimatum and expect us to upend our entire lives and our businesses in an instant and threaten to sell the property that's been in the family for generations if we don't do exactly as you say." He rose and paced as he asked, "And what about Dad? What about Sierra?"

Chandler's expression didn't change; nor did he respond.

"Why now?" Quinn asked. "Why the four of us?"

"I'm eighty-four years old, and my health has not been as strong as it once was." Chandler's tone was even and emotionless. "You are my heirs, and the resort should be your responsibility."

"With all due respect, Grandfather, our father is your heir. He's the one who should inherit this business." Ethan's voice was as calm as their grandfather's. He was the strong, silent type and was usually willing to yield to his grandfather's unreasonable demands out of respect. His speaking up should show Chandler how strongly he felt about their father being passed over, but that assumed Chandler would care.

Their grandfather narrowed his eyes. "That's my decision, and it's been made."

Derek's narrow-eyed expression mirrored their grandfather's. "Only you would expect me, Trent, and Quinn to give up everything we've worked so hard to build even though you know we can't just walk away from our businesses for a year and expect them to survive. Quinn has a shipping empire that mandates daily oversight. Trent has an entire legal practice to run. And I have more than a hundred employees, contractors, and clients depending on my masonry and building company."

Trent cocked his head and set his elder-brother stare on Derek, indicating that he needed to get control of himself.

Derek turned away from them all, muttering a curse. One Quinn agreed with wholeheartedly.

"I'll be reading over this document with a fine-tooth comb this evening," Trent said in a remarkably even voice, one Quinn knew he'd honed from years of being the best lawyer in the business. "What is your deadline on our decision?"

"One week from today, seven a.m." Their grandfather clutched the arms of his wheelchair again. "Didi."

"Yes, sir." Her soft, apologetic gaze swept over the brothers—"Gentlemen"—before she wheeled their grandfather from the office.

Chapter Five

SHELLEY HAD BREAKFAST at the resort and spent an hour reading through brochures of the amenities the island had to offer while staff members stopped by to give their two cents about places to visit and things to do. At her coffee shop, one of her favorite things to do was talk with the customers. Anyone could see that the resort staff felt the same way. Another hotel guest struck up a conversation about sailing lessons, which Shelley immediately signed up for. By midafternoon she was having fantasies about what it would be like to live on the warm, friendly island full-time.

After breakfast she set out on foot to explore the nearby town, silently thanking Quinn for the Motrin. She followed a group of window-shopping tourists along pristine sidewalks lined with manicured flowerbeds to the town center. The town center had a turnabout with a courtyard in the center, complete with iron benches, tall trees, and a dark, cedar-sided tourist information center.

Already enthralled by the island, Shelley went inside the information center to make sure she didn't miss anything Rockwell Island had to offer. A gray-haired woman smiled up at her from behind the information desk, where she sat with a phone pressed to her ear. There were even more brochures here than there were in the resort, and on the wall to the right, a mass of photographs were thumbtacked to a corkboard, immediately drawing Shelley's attention. There were pictures of children holding up handmade signs announcing various events: the Rockwell Wine Festival, a book fair, a 10K race, and more. Other pictures included photographs of men and women with large fish and wide smiles, and quite a few wedding pictures, too.

"Hello there." The woman moved from behind the desk and joined Shelley by the pictures. "I call this our brag wall." She had warm, deep-set gray-blue eyes, and her face was mapped with lines that told of lots of sun and smiles.

A brag wall for the town? I love that.

Shelley scanned the wall, then focused on a picture of a lanky teenager on a sailboat. His eyes looked strikingly familiar. "Are these island residents?"

"Why, yes. I call all the youngsters here on the island my grandchildren. I think I have hundreds now." She laughed. "See this handsome man with the large fish? That's Ethan Rockwell. I've known him since he was yay high." She held her hand up just above her knees. "And Quinn on his sailboat? That's one of my favorites." She pointed to the picture of the lanky teen Shelley had been admiring.

Quinn grew up on the island. Shelley's pulse quickened all over again from memory of the kiss they'd shared. She worked to pay attention as the woman pointed out and named several more residents, but she couldn't take her eyes off the photograph of Quinn. His eyes were wide with excitement in the picture, one long arm holding the mast of the boat, the other waving to whoever took the picture. The boy she saw in the picture was a far cry from the broad and muscular man she'd met last night.

A family came into the visitors' center, and the woman touched Shelley's arm. "My name is Eleanor. Please come back and see me sometime. I'll show you more pictures. I replace them every few months, except for my favorites, which stay up for years."

Shelley meandered into Books by the Bay next, where she bought the newest romance novel by her favorite author. Then she stopped into Taylor's Treasures, a souvenir shop, where she bought an island key chain. Farther down the road a cheerful yellow sign with red letters caught her eye. ANNABELLE'S.

Annabelle's was a clothing shop that had hardwood floors and effervescent blue walls trimmed with dark stained wood. There were two tables out front with lovely soft shirts and lightweight cardigans. Shelley happily began to look through racks of pretty summer dresses along the far wall. She'd never been a clotheshorse, but she wanted one of everything in this boutique.

"Hi. Is there something I can help you find?"

Shelley turned at the soft voice and was met with a pretty, petite blonde with big blue eyes and a wide smile. "I'm just looking. But everything is gorgeous."

"Thank you. Some of the clothing is from specialty designers in New York and Boston, but I love working with local designers most of all."

"Are you Annabelle?"

"Yes. I opened the store two years ago, after finishing college." Annabelle glanced around the store with pride in her eyes before straightening a display of scarves on the table in front of them. "I couldn't wait to come back to the island. What about you? Do you live here, or are you just visiting?"

"I'm only here for the week, but I'm already in love with the island," Shelley said. "And I think I'm in love with your scarves, too. They're absolutely gorgeous."

"This one would look fantastic on you," Annabelle said as she handed Shelley a forest-green scarf with light green threading. "They're my sister's designs."

"She's very talented." Shelley wound the colorful scarf around her neck and gave a sigh of delight at how wonderfully soft it was.

"That is definitely your color. It really brings out your eyes. And I have an emerald-green sundress that will go perfectly with that scarf. If you'd like to follow me, I'll show it to you."

As Shelley followed her to the back of the store, Annabelle said, "Since you're here for a week, be sure to go to the fireworks display the day after tomorrow. The resort puts on a huge display three times a year. You can see it from almost anywhere on the island."

Shelley took the green dress Annabelle handed her into the fitting room and was pleased to find that the halter top and midthigh length flattered her figure, with the scarf as the perfect accessory for the cool New England evenings.

Shelley felt so beautiful in the dress that she hated to take it off and reluctantly changed back into her shorts. "This dress is incredible. I'd like to buy the scarf, too. In fact, I think I'm going to wear these when I watch the fireworks."

She had just walked out of the dressing room when a very attractive middle-aged blond woman came into the store. Annabelle waved to the woman as she began to ring up Shelley's purchases. "Hi, Aunt Abby. Your new pants look great on you."

"Griff said the same thing," the woman said with a pretty little flush on her cheeks as she looked down at her black linen pants, which complemented her simple white scoop-neck T-shirt and ballet flats. "Thank you for suggesting them. I thought I'd come down and see if you wanted to have dinner tomorrow with me and Sierra?" After Annabelle said she'd love to, the woman pushed her side-swept bangs out of her eyes and smiled at Shelley. "That dress and scarf are just lovely."

"Annabelle has a great eye," Shelley agreed.

"I'm happy to take the compliment," Annabelle said, "but you could wear tatters and you'd be gorgeous."

"I agree," Abby said, "especially with such great hair. My children have thick hair, thanks to my husband, but I wasn't so lucky."

Shelley had a love-hate relationship with her thick mass of dark hair. More love than hate since her teenage years, thankfully, but there was definitely a lot of frustration leading up to that point. She'd spent her youth trying to tame it, to make it straight and shiny, even going so far as to iron it to fit in with the other girls in her parents' social circles. But when she was a teenager she'd given up and decided she was going to own her differences. At first it had been a way to rebel against her supremely prim parents, but it had quickly turned into something more. Shelley had come to appreciate all the ways she was different, from her taste in clothing to her spunky personality and inability to sit quietly and not give her opinion about things she didn't agree with. By the time she was eighteen, she'd given up completely on the impossible task of pleasing her parents and had never looked back.

"I'm Abby Rockwell, by the way."

Shelley smiled and held out her hand. "Shelley Walters."

Abby studied her more closely. "You know what—the more we talk, the more I feel like I've met you before."

Shelley would have remembered this vibrant woman if they'd ever met. "This is my first time to Rockwell Island."

"Welcome to the island."

"Thank you. I love it here already. Although if you happen to know where I can find a coffee shop, I'll be in absolute heaven. I'm dying for a toffee latte."

"We have a diner on the corner of West and Wells. Just down the street to the right one block, then two blocks to the left and you'll find it. They won't have specialty coffees, although they do offer flavored creamers." Abby sighed. "I love living in a small town, but the truth is we could really use a nice specialty coffee shop."

"With homemade pastries and cookies, too," Annabelle added.

Abby nodded. "I know the island book clubbers would love to have another place to meet, and the Tuesday-morning ladies' group could meet there, too. Heck, we're all so desperate for a great café that I'm sure it would be mobbed from the moment it opened its doors."

"Actually," Shelley said with a smile, "I own a coffee shop in Maryland, where we offer more than twenty different types of specialty organic coffees, and baked goods, too." Maybe it was the fact that she was having one of the best mornings *ever*, but she suddenly found herself saying, "I hadn't really given much thought to expanding before, but do you really think a café would do that well here?"

"Absolutely!" Abby said, while Annabelle nodded as well. "In fact, if that's really something you would consider, you should meet my daughter, Sierra. She owns the Hideaway over on Main. She's a chef, and she's always talking about expanding the offerings on the island. *And* she's a coffeeaholic. I bet you two would really hit it off."

"Watch out, though," Annabelle said. "Sierra's a total island girl. She'll convince you to pick up and move here in about seven seconds."

"I'm going over there in about an hour," Abby told Shelley. "Why don't you stop by if you have time and I'll introduce you?"

"I'd love that. Thank you." Shelley could hardly believe how friendly the people here were and how vested they were in the island.

Between the idea of a sexy fling on a romantic island with the hottest guy she'd ever met—why not think positive?—*and* the new out-of-the-blue, but very exciting, possibility of bringing her coffee shop to the island, she was smiling like a fool as she headed out the door to see what else this magical island had in store for her.

QUINN SAT AT a table in the Hideaway with the rest of his family, discussing their grandfather's latest mandate. They'd been at it for an hour already, and between the work he had to prepare for the RBE merger and this nightmare with the resort, his frustration was mounting by the second.

"Trent, honey, stop watching the door. Reese isn't back on the island yet." Their mother, Abigail Rockwell, smiled gently at her eldest son. "She's still out in Oregon, helping her sister with her new baby."

Trent and Theresa Nicholson, whom everyone called Reese, had married a little more than ten years ago, after a whirlwind romance the summer after Trent graduated from law school. They'd moved to New York City, and for reasons that none of the rest of them completely knew or understood, Trent and Reese's marriage had ended before the following summer. Reese had moved back to the island, while Trent had stayed in the city. While it was impossible for them to completely avoid each other when he did come back for short visits to the island, both of them clearly did their best to stay out of each other's way. For the most part, the Rockwells avoided talking about Reese around Trent, but Abby was obviously trying to put him at ease during his time on the island so that he wouldn't be stressed about running into her.

Trent shifted uncomfortably in his seat. "I'm not worried about running into Reese."

Sierra touched Trent's shoulder, her expression empathetic as she said, "First loves are hard to forget."

"Right," Quinn said under his breath. A little brotherly teasing was too tempting to resist. Especially when as far as he could remember, Trent and Reese had never been able to keep their hands off each other. The quickie wedding hadn't surprised any of them. Only the almost-as-quick divorce had.

"Can we get back to the matter at hand, please?" Trent cleared his throat. "We all have businesses to get back to, and the longer we put off our decision, the more power Chandler thinks he has."

"Besides the fact that he can't demand that the three of us give up our lives and move back to the island," Derek said, "there's no way I'm going to take part in anything that demeans Dad by completely cutting him out of the resort he's given his entire career to. And the fact that he totally left Sierra out of the negotiations also rubs me the wrong way."

"I appreciate where you're coming from, Derek," Griffin said as he met Derek's angry gaze and also put a hand over Sierra's and gave it a comforting squeeze. "But the responsibility for the resort, and the island, doesn't have to fall on your shoulders."

"Your father had an idea of what your grandfather was up to," their mother told them. "He wasn't blindsided by this."

"Even so, it's not right." Derek turned his attention to Trent. "Did you read the edict?"

Trent reached into his briefcase and pulled out the document. "Every word, several times over. Look, I know we're all angry and frustrated, but I think we need to focus on the things that matter most. We can't let him sell the property to a conglomerate. Not when so many island residents rely on the resort to earn a living."

"Listen," Griffin said, "you kids don't need to do this. I'll figure out a way to get past his crazy plan so the island and the residents aren't in jeopardy. I'd never let the people here down. The last thing I want is to see the island where we all grew up turn into a haven for big business."

As Chandler's only son, Griffin had always been expected to follow in his father's footsteps and run the resort. Only there was no stepping into Chandler's shoes. Not when he kept his fingers in every nook and cranny of the business, often upsetting negotiations and disgruntling employees and distributors.

Everyone, except maybe Chandler, knew that Griffin worked behind the scenes like an undercover superhero smoothing over relationships and keeping the employees happy. If it weren't for Griff, the resort would have lost its loyal staff long ago.

But Griffin Rockwell had never sugarcoated his father's harsh antics where his children were concerned. Not when they'd see right through any veil of protection he tried to extend. Quinn and his siblings knew that their father had lived a life he'd never wish on them. That was why he and their mother had supported—and encouraged—each of their children to move away from the island, and more important, to create their own successful paths. Sierra and Ethan, however, had always felt such a strong kinship to the island that they had returned right after college.

Quinn knew his father meant everything he said. He'd take one for the family, as he'd been doing for years. But Quinn didn't like the idea of it. Not one bit.

"Dad, we aren't going to leave you in a lurch. Hell, I still can't understand how you've put up with Chandler for so long."

"And I can't believe he's doing this," Sierra said, her jaw clenched so tight that Quinn thought she might crack her teeth. "Not just to you guys, but to me and Dad, too. I'm the only one who goes out of my way to be nice to him, and he completely cuts me out of everything? Especially after having the gall to tell me that my restaurant is a *cute hobby*? As if it's just a holdover until I get married, or like it would be more meaningful if I were a man."

Trent draped an arm over Sierra's shoulder. "One thing is for sure—if we even entertain this situation, we're not doing it unless all five of us are part of it."

"Agreed," Quinn said as his other brothers nodded, as well. "Dad, we're not going to let you take the heat alone anymore. You've held down the fort and sheltered us from his wrath long enough. You and Mom are the reasons each of us got out from under his thumb in the first place. As much as I don't like being forced into anything, it's our turn to shoulder the burden of Grandfather *and* the resort. We'll figure out a way to manage our businesses while working here."

"All or nothing, though," Trent said. "Five of us or none of us."

Ethan nodded. "I'm in."

Sierra sat up a little taller. "I'm all in, too, but I'm not giving up my restaurant."

"Don't worry, sis. We're not going to give up any of our businesses," Quinn assured her. "We're five savvy businesspeople. We can do this, and I'm sure all of us don't have to live here to make it happen. He's going to have to forget the part about living on the island ninety-five percent of the time. At least for me."

"All or nothing," Derek finally relented. "But it's for Dad and the residents, not for Grandfather." Their father held his hand up, silencing them all. Their mother placed a gentle hand on his shoulder. "Griff?"

Their father had such a friendly face that even when under duress he possessed underlying warmth. The warmth showed now in his dark eyes as they traveled slowly over each of his children's faces, his love for each of them as clear as could be. Setting a softer gaze on their mother, he took her hand. Silent, effortless communication passed between them, speaking volumes of the strong relationship Quinn had always admired.

"What you are all trying to do is admirable," their father finally said, "but I won't let you take the brunt of my father's overbearing plan."

But Quinn had watched his father take enough heat from Chandler. More than enough. So even though he wasn't keen on any part of their grandfather's plan, he wasn't about to let his father continue handling this alone. At the same time, he also knew that demanding wouldn't get them very far. That was Chandler's way, not his father's.

"Dad," Quinn said, "let us do this for you."

"There comes a time for power in numbers," Trent agreed. "It's time to finally take Grandfather's power away and lay down some ground rules. It's only a year. We can figure this out."

"Trent, Quinn, Derek, Ethan, Sierra," their father said, "you know how much I respect all of you. The choices you've made, the way you live your lives, the incredible men and woman you are. But Chandler is *my* father. He's *not* your responsibility, and I'm not going to give him the power over each of your lives. If we allow this, he'll treat you like his puppets forever. I'll handle it."

Griffin rose to his feet, leaving no room for negotiation, and Abby gave each of them a kiss on their cheeks before leaving with him.

"That went well," Derek said in a sarcastic voice. Sierra looked miserable. Trent was studying the document their grandfather had given them to find some sort of loophole in their grandfather's plan. And Ethan was obviously dying to get back out into his fishing boat to try to forget about the whole thing.

This had been one of Quinn's worst days in recent memory, and he didn't think anything could turn it around. At least not until he looked up and saw Shelley come through the door.

Last night she'd been the one unexpectedly bright part of his day. If he had any luck left at all, maybe she'd be able to do the impossible and brighten up this one, too.

Chapter Six

SHELLEY WAS EVEN more beautiful than Quinn remembered. In the light of day, her skin glistened with the sheen of a fresh tan. Her dark hair was sexily mussed, cascading in thick waves over her bare shoulders, and she wore a loose, casual spaghetti-strap top with a pair of jeans shorts. Vividly remembering dragging her hips into his and her gasp of pleasure as he'd taken their kiss even deeper, when he saw that her eyes were dancing over the bar like she was looking for someone, he hoped like hell it was him.

"We need to think things over and come up with a game plan, despite what Dad said. Let's reconvene tomorrow morning over breakfast?" Trent suggested.

Quinn was only half listening, though, because Ray Brewster, a guy who'd grown up with them on the island, had just put his hand on Shelley's lower back. Quinn's jaw tightened as Brewster leaned in close and said something to her. Whatever it was, Quinn wanted the guy's hand off Shelley's back. *Now.*

"Quinn?" Trent waved a hand in front of his face. "Tomorrow morning work for you?"

"Sure." He rose to his feet.

"Where are you going?" Trent followed Quinn's gaze. "Oh. Is that her? Cove girl?"

"Shelley," Quinn corrected him. He'd told Trent about meeting Shelley at the cove, although he'd left out the details of the skinny-dipping and the kiss.

Trent laughed under his breath. "Looks like Brewster is making a move. You'd better go claim her."

In his mind he already had. They hadn't done more than walk from the cove to the cottage in the moonlight and share one incredible kiss, but it was a kiss—and an evening—that Quinn knew he'd never forget. Shelley was the only woman who had ever claimed one hundred percent of his attention, and the only woman to ever make him *want* so wildly, so possessively. And though he knew she'd been a little tipsy, he had a feeling that even so, he had seen the real Shelley. Sweet and passionate. Nice, yet a little bit naughty, too.

All day long he'd been dealing with his family and the resort. He'd hoped to get over to the beach to see if he could catch her to ask her out for a drink, but between dealing with his grandfather, his family, and his business, he'd barely had the chance to even take a full breath.

Now all he wanted to do was forget about all of that for a little while so that he could focus on Shelley.

Which meant getting her away from Ray Brewster, for a start. Ray wasn't a bad guy. On the contrary, he was a nice, trustworthy guy— and in a minute he'd be a nice guy who didn't have a shot at Shelley.

Shelley turned as Quinn approached, and when their eyes locked, the path between them immediately blazed with heat, just as it had last night. "Shelley, I was just thinking about you, hoping I'd see you again."

Her breathing visibly hitched at his words and he nearly grabbed her right then and there in front of everyone to kiss her.

"I was hoping to see you again, too, Quinn."

Brewster's hand immediately slid from her back.

Perfect.

"Hey, Rockwell," Brewster said. "It's been a while since I've seen all of your brothers and Sierra in one place. How's it going?"

Quinn had to work hard not to grunt like a Neanderthal as he quickly replied, "Things are great, Brewster. Hope they're good for you, too," then turned his attention back to Shelley.

But when Quinn looked into her eyes again, he was surprised to see that she looked slightly stunned. "Rockwell? As in Rockwell Island? As in Rockwell Resort?"

Quinn was used to women gushing over his familial wealth and the extra-flirtatious giggles and touches they lavished him with when they found out that he was a Rockwell, even if he didn't care for it.

"Yes, that Rockwell." He nodded to the table behind him. "That's my family."

In an instant, the shimmer of desire that had sparked between them when he'd found her in the bar all but disappeared. But before he could even get a chance to ask Shelley what he'd said—or done—wrong, Quinn felt a hand on his shoulder.

"Quinn, honey," his mother said, "in all the hullabaloo, I forgot my purse."

He'd been so lost in Shelley that he hadn't seen his mother come back into the restaurant.

"Shelley." His mother smiled warmly. "I'm so glad you made it."

"Thank you, Abby," Shelley said, although her voice sounded a bit strained now. "Your directions were perfect."

"And I see you've already met Quinn."

Abby applied gentle pressure to the hand on Quinn's shoulder in a way that reminded him of when he was twelve and had won a sailing medal. Before going up to accept the award, his mother had touched him on his lower back, giving him a gentle nudge forward.

But he didn't need a nudge toward Shelley. He was ready to sprint toward her.

Only, somewhere between the look of desire they'd shared when he'd first walked up to her in the bar and when she'd learned his last name, their connection—or rather, *her* connection—seemed to have been severed.

He couldn't believe he was on the verge of losing the brightest part of this whole trip back to the island.

"Sierra, honey. Come here for a moment." His mother waved his sister over. "I want you to meet Shelley. She owns a gourmet coffee shop off the island, and I was thinking it would be great for the two of you to get together to chat about all the possibilities for a café like that here on Rockwell Island."

"It's great to meet you, Shelley, and I'd love to talk about possibilities," Sierra said.

Quinn could see by the silent questions in his sister's eyes that she'd also already noticed his interest in Shelley.

"I'm afraid I have another meeting to go to right now," Sierra said. "But let's be sure to get together soon. I'm usually here at the restaurant, or you can come by my house. I live in the bungalow at the end of Shore Road, right on the beach, and if the light's on, it means I'm home." She jotted down her phone number and handed it to Shelley. "Why don't you give me your number, too?"

Shelley wrote down her number, then handed it to Sierra. "I'm really looking forward to it."

As both his mother and sister headed out of the bar, Shelley took a step away from him as if she were planning to follow them out.

Quinn touched her elbow before she could go, not at all surprised by how electric that one small touch felt. "Have a drink with me?"

Something dark flashed in her eyes, almost as if she was warring with herself for the heat sparking between them. "I don't think that's a good idea."

Not a good idea? Women usually clamored to tie him and his brothers down, and she thought a drink wasn't a good idea? Hadn't she been the one to kiss him last night? And hadn't the kiss blown both their minds?

"How about a walk on the beach, then?"

"Honestly, *this*"—she pointed her finger between them—"is probably not a good idea." She sighed and shifted her eyes away, but not before Quinn saw the struggle in them. "You're a *Rockwell*, and I'm…"

"Not going to hold it against me?" he teased to try to lighten the mood.

A soft laugh escaped her lips—the same laughter that had caught his attention last night at the cove and played again and again in his head in the early hours of the morning. The sweet and sexy sound tugged at his heart in a way that he didn't understand or recognize. But at the same time he couldn't, and didn't want to, ignore it.

Whatever her reason for not wanting to spend time with him anymore, he was determined to change her mind. "I could tell by how comfortable you were in the cove last night that you really love the island, right?"

"Yes, but—"

"Then I promise you're going to *really* love this secret spot that tourists don't even know exists."

Quinn put his hand on the small of her back, hoping she'd let him lead her toward the door. He felt the eyes of his family on them, but he didn't care. He didn't know how long Shelley was on the island, but he didn't want to take a chance that she'd leave without him having a chance to get to know her better.

"Do you really have a secret place that no one knows about?"

Thankfully, some of the tension had gone out of her voice by the time they got out to the sidewalk. He drew his brows together in what he hoped was a serious look and tried hard not to smile as he said, "I really do," in a conspiratorial whisper. "Can I trust you to keep it just between us?"

Her eyes lit with curiosity before she shrugged and said, "That depends how good of a secret it is."

"Oh, it's good." He couldn't keep his gaze from dropping to her mouth as the wild thrill from their kiss hit him all over again. "Really good."

She trapped her lower lip in her teeth, and her eyes widened with excitement.

Oh yeah, he knew just how to get this special adventurous woman's attention.

"Just as long as you don't mind getting a little dirty."

Her lips curved into a mischievous smile. "Are you kidding? I *love* getting dirty."

Their eyes held for a long moment as desire sparked again, fast and hot. He hated to break the connection, but if he didn't, his lips were going to find their way to hers, and even though he was dying to taste her again, he didn't think that was the best way to win her over...*yet.*

Instead, he went for another kind of connection, by slipping her hand into his. She looked down at their hands in surprise.

Has no one ever held her hand before?

It had been a long time since Quinn had held a woman's hand, but he liked the way her fingers fit perfectly between his. Liked it a lot, actually.

His life was so busy that when he did make time to date, it usually included dinner at a fancy restaurant, a few drinks, and then a quick stress-relieving roll between the sheets—at the woman's house—before he made his exit at the end of the evening, swift and on his terms. Dating rarely included getting to know the women very well. Mostly because he'd never met a woman he wanted to take time to get to know.

Until Shelley.

"So," he asked, "are you up for having a little adventure with me today?"

She studied his face for a few long moments, each of which had him holding his breath as he waited for her answer. But then, finally, she smiled up at him, turning his dark day so much brighter as she said, "Take me to your secret place, Quinn."

Chapter Seven

THE MINUTE SHELLEY found out that Quinn was part of the Rockwell family, her stomach had taken a nosedive.

She'd spent her childhood with a father who worked too much and a mother who cared too much about her place in society for either of them to have time for a relationship with their own daughter. Her father had regarded her with the coldness of a business associate, offering a brief hug only when it was socially expected, like at her high school graduation. Her mother had been only slightly warmer, assessing Shelley's outfit and "fixing" her wild hair each morning before the driver took her to school.

Shelley didn't want a lifestyle—or a relationship—like her parents. Which meant that a hot island fling with Quinn *Rockwell* was off the table.

At least, until he'd led her outside and she began to see a playful side of him that her father and her friends' husbands had never shown.

Thinking of the seductive glimmer that had been in his eyes when he'd made the comment about *getting dirty* made her smile. Yes, he was still a Rockwell, but she supposed it couldn't hurt to give him an afternoon to try to prove her wrong about all rich men being self-absorbed and materialistic, could it? Especially considering how good he looked with his white T-shirt hugging his firm, broad chest...and how nice it felt to hold his hand.

Last night she'd been too stunned by being caught skinny-dipping at the deserted cove—and too fuzzy from the bubbly—to fully appreciate just how gorgeous he was. Or how power simply radiated out from him. Despite the fact that he was wearing casual clothes instead of a suit and that she didn't yet know what he did for a living, she could easily imagine him presiding over a boardroom, making multimillion-dollar decisions. He'd been so strong when he'd picked her up out of the water last night, and now his hand was equally strong and unexpectedly gentle over hers as he led her through town.

Upon waking this morning and thinking about what had happened last night, he'd been a mystery to her. Now that she was with him again, she found him to be even more of a mystery than ever—the sexy, powerful man who could be so gentle with her and sweet with his mother and sister, too.

A mystery that she was more and more tempted to unravel, despite her lingering doubts about getting involved with a wealthy Rockwell. Especially when just holding his hand was doing crazy things to her insides...

As they walked hand in hand through town, past the library, a park overflowing with flowers, and a baseball diamond, he asked, "So you own a coffee shop?"

She had to pause to focus for a moment on what he'd just asked her. With his hand over hers all she could think about was pulling him into her for another kiss. But she couldn't, not yet. Not when she still needed more proof that he wasn't just like every other rich, preoccupied guy out there.

"Yes," she finally answered. "My café is in Severn, Maryland."

They stopped to let a car pass, and Quinn looked at her in surprise.

"Severn? You're kidding me. I live in Annapolis. What's the name of your café?"

Severn was only a thirty-minute drive from Annapolis. It really was a small world. "It's called the Creek Café. Have you heard of it?"

"Heard of it? I was there two weeks ago on my way back from a meeting. But I don't remember seeing you there."

He'd been to her shop? She would have *definitely* remembered seeing him. Quinn Rockwell wasn't the kind of man it was possible to forget. "I'm guessing you must have come on a Tuesday. That's the day I work with my suppliers, and I usually do that from home, because otherwise I get too involved with my customers to get any real work done."

They walked through a residential neighborhood with lush gardens and expansive beach houses. The hilly street had an incredible view of the town. By that point they'd taken so many turns that the resort was no longer in sight, but the view of low tide was awe-inspiring.

"It's great, isn't it?" Quinn said, clearly noticing how enthralled she was by the view. "This is one of my favorite views on the island. At high tide it looks like the bay is spilled out before us. Now, at low tide, it's more like the bay has been sucked away, leaving footprints on the sea floor."

"*Footprints.* I love that." And she also loved finding out about Quinn's surprisingly poetic side. One more lovely surprise to add to the others. "Low tide always feels like such a miracle. Just the idea that all that water recedes like it does is amazing. When I was a kid I used to envision a water god that would inhale a deep breath, sucking all the water into his lungs at low tide, and then at high tide he'd blow it out until it refilled the mold it had left behind."

"A water god." He looked as pleased by her imagination as she'd been with his. "That would explain the footprints. When I was a kid we'd skateboard and ride our bikes all over the island. I used to wish there was a ramp big enough to send me flying up over the water."

Shelley was stirred by the wonder in his voice, something she'd never heard in either of her parents' voices, or from anyone in their extremely wealthy social circle—a true love of life and dreams of something other than mergers, takeovers, and investments.

Seeing the hint of nostalgia in Quinn's eyes and hearing it in his voice as he talked about his childhood made her extra interested in finding out more about him. How could a guy from a family as wealthy as the Rockwells have had such a normal childhood, with skateboards and bicycles? What had it been like to grow up on this island? And how could he have ever left it?

Having met Abby, Shelley already knew that Quinn's mother was a far cry from her own cold mother. But since she'd also met his grandfather, she had to wonder how the rather forbidding older man fit into the Rockwell family equation.

"Did you like growing up here?" she asked.

Tension suddenly filled Quinn's grip, and she realized she'd struck a nerve. He was quiet for several moments as they headed down the road, then cut over toward the marina. He seemed to take careful consideration before answering.

"Growing up on an island isn't like growing up in the city. Not that I have that experience to compare it to, but there aren't as many things to do here, and there are limited career choices, obviously."

"But did you *enjoy* it? Spending afternoons riding your bike or your skateboard? Being so close to the bay and growing up in such a close-knit town?"

Instead of answering her questions, Quinn stopped beside the boathouse and looked at her. "You have a way of making me think about things that I'd long ago forgotten."

"A good way or a bad way?"

He stepped in close and caressed her cheek. She barely stifled a moan at how good it felt to be so close to him. Close enough that she could feel the heat of his body all along hers. She wanted to close her eyes and revel in the intimate moment, but she didn't want to miss the intense look he was giving her. A look full of not only desire, but something else, too. Something deep and sweet. "A good way, Shelley. A surprisingly good way."

For a moment she was positive he would kiss her again. And even though she was still torn over his being a Rockwell, she held her breath waiting for the press of his lips over hers.

But he must have read her mind—and the conflicts she was still struggling with—because instead of kissing her the way she could see that he wanted to, he sucked in a harsh breath, then stepped back. "Come on. Let's get to your secret."

But just because he didn't kiss her, that didn't stop him from rubbing seductive little circles on the sensitive skin of her palm with his thumb as they continued toward a boathouse. With every soft caress on her hand, she felt her breath grow shallower, her legs get weaker, and her need for him ratchet up another million levels.

By the time he led her to a shed beside the boathouse and handed her two metal rakes, she was a lust-filled mess. "Would you mind holding these?"

"Sure." It took everything she had to keep her voice from being breathless. Husky. "But what are we going to do with them?"

From the way his dark eyes had dilated and he was running his hand roughly through his hair, he looked just as wrecked by unfulfilled desire as she was. "You'll see."

He snagged a bucket, and then she followed him into the boathouse. Tools and boating equipment filled the high-ceilinged building. Large workbenches lined the walls, with cabinets above and below. Quinn reached into a cabinet beneath one of the work areas, grabbed a towel and tossed it over his shoulder. He took the rakes from Shelley and put them in the bucket.

"Now we're ready," he said as he led her away from the boathouse along the main road.

Yes, she thought. She was so freaking *ready* to kiss him again, it wasn't even funny...

Still, she tried to focus on the secret he was about to show her. "We're either going to build some funky sand castles," she guessed, "or you're going to use the rakes to dig a shallow grave, bury me before the tide comes in, and hope no one notices."

"Sweetheart, if those are the best ideas you can come up with for a rake and a bucket, you haven't spent nearly enough time on the island yet."

Sweetheart. He barely knew her, yet the endearment sounded natural. Just as natural as it had when he'd said it to her last night. Right before she'd thrown herself into his arms and learned just how good a kiss could be. Good enough to turn a girl *wanton.*

"I already love it here on the island. So much, in fact, that I'd like to stay longer."

He shot her a questioning glance. "Are you considering extending your vacation?"

"I don't know exactly what I'm thinking yet, but even in the short time I've been here...I feel like I *fit*, you know?"

"I can't imagine you not fitting in anywhere."

"Oh, there are definitely places," she said softly.

But she didn't want to go into details on her family life right now. She wanted to get to know the real Quinn Rockwell, and if she told him about her childhood and her concerns about wealthy people as a whole, he might try to bend to please her.

She didn't even know why she'd revealed to him that she'd like to stay longer, but once the words were out, she knew they were true. She did feel like she fit in with the easygoing lifestyle here, at least what she'd seen of it so far. She felt relaxed and accepted here, just like she always had with her aunt in Eastham.

Shelley was glad that he didn't push for details as they walked down a side street to a sandy, rutted road that looked like it had seen better days. Every part of her was keenly aware of his athletic build, the firm outlines of his thighs against his khaki shorts, his strong hands engulfing hers. He was just so sexy and confident, and best of all, noticeably lacking the air of self-importance that surrounded her father like a cloud. Quinn felt substantial—not that she needed a big man to protect her, or that she was looking for one, for that matter, but she felt safe with him.

At the end of the dirt road, a hill rose up to meet thick, spiny bushes. "We're heading through there." He nodded to a narrow path between the thorny bushes. "I'll go first to clear away the branches."

"What's over the ridge?"

He grinned, and her heart started pounding faster at the way the expression utterly transformed his face, from handsome to heart-stoppingly gorgeous and carefree.

"Your surprise." Quinn carefully pushed aside the bushes.

He held the bucket in one hand high above the tops of the bushes and used his other hand to hold the branches away from her, oblivious to the way thorns were clinging to his own shirt.

"You're getting pricked!" She tried to pull the branches from his shirt and a thorn stuck in her fingers. "Ouch."

She drew her hand back, and a bead of blood appeared on her finger. When she sucked it into her mouth, Quinn's eyes darkened and the air between them sizzled, causing her pulse to quicken. She couldn't stop herself from imagining what it would feel like to have his mouth on her finger, his tongue licking a lazy path up her skin.

"Shelley."

She'd never heard anyone say her name with that much heat, with that much desire. Her finger fell from her mouth, making a loud kissing sound that hung in the air between them.

The sound was so unexpected, and loud, that a second later they both laughed, momentarily breaking the spell. Long enough, at least, for Quinn to guide her the rest of the way through the bushes. As they climbed down the steep dunes toward the beach, Shelley stumbled and nearly fell down the last few feet.

He caught her and swept her against his chest. *Oh God.* He smelled potent, virile. Delicious. So delicious that Shelley's body immediately heated up and she couldn't tear her gaze away from his mouth. A mouth that had tasted better than anything else ever had.

"You okay?" he asked.

"Yeah." Her response came out breathy and swoony. She never swooned.

What is wrong with me?

Quinn put his hands on her waist as he lifted her off her feet and set her on the sand. And when their eyes caught and sparks flew again, Shelley suddenly realized she'd gotten it backward about something being wrong.

Not only had things never felt so *right* with anyone else, but every moment they spent together having fun this afternoon made the idea of an island fling with Quinn look better and better.

Rockwell or not.

Chapter Eight

"CLAMMING?" SHELLEY LOOKED so sexy with one hand on her hip as she looked from the bucket to the wet sand and then to him in surprise that it took all of Quinn's willpower not to kiss her.

Their outing had started out as a way to spend time with her, but it had already moved way past that. The more he got to know her, the more he wanted her—and the more he liked her, too. Unlike some women who seemed acutely aware of every move they made, almost to the point of appearing calculated, Shelley was clearly comfortable in her own skin and didn't seem to worry about how she acted. And she was obviously not attracted to his family wealth. She'd nearly run from it, in fact. He definitely wanted to get to the bottom of what that was all about, but right now he just wanted to have some fun with her.

And, hopefully, to also make good on his promise from last night to give her a kiss that she wouldn't be able to forget...

"Clamming is my dirty little secret." He grinned at the thought of digging around together in the sand with her for a while. It had been a really long time since he'd done something like this, an activity that wasn't attached to a spreadsheet or a bottom line.

Quinn took off his shoes, and she did the same. Hell, even her pretty painted toe-nails turned him on. Every last part of her was so beautiful, so damn sexy. The sparks that flew between them as he took her hand to lead her closer to the water line were so strong that he once again had to forcefully tamp down the urge to kiss her. He was desperate to feel her curves against him, to hear her gasp with pleasure, and to see desire take her over. But he knew he wouldn't be able to stop at just one kiss, and right now he was determined to show her a good time—outside of the bedroom. So, for now he'd have to be satisfied holding her hand as they walked across the bay floor.

"Clamming has always sounded like a lot of fun," she said. Her words were a little husky, and it wasn't hard to guess that she was right up against the edge of desire the way he was.

"But how can we do it when there's no water? Don't the clams move around?"

Lord knew he wasn't having any easier of a time staying focused on clamming as he told her, "Most people get big rakes, about as tall as you are, and when the tide is still around waist high, they drag the rakes through the bay floor and scoop up the clams. But when my dad taught us how to clam when we were kids, he'd take us out at low tide and make us use our hands to dig them up. The sand is soft on top, but it's hard just an inch or two deeper. It makes for sliced-up fingers from razor clams and fingernails full of grit, but it's actually more fun than using rakes."

"More fun? I'm in. Let's do it that way." She tossed her rake into the bucket.

"You sure? It's pretty messy business. You might break a nail, and like I said, razor clams can cut pretty deep."

"Do I look like the type of girl who cares about breaking a nail?" She stepped in close and went up on her toes, bringing her closer to his height. "And before you answer that, you should know that if you answer yes, I'll work twice as hard to prove you wrong."

Their thighs brushed, and just as his body registered the feel of hers against him, every sizzling, perfect memory of the hot kiss they'd shared came rushing back. He'd tried to refrain from kissing her until he was absolutely sure she wanted him to, but everything she did drew him closer.

"Okay, skinny-dipping girl. Let's put your money where your mouth is."

Shelley had a handful of looks, and Quinn now realized he was cataloging them. Her eyes widened when she was excited. When she was nervous, her lower lip quivered the slightest bit. And when the air between them heated up and her breathing quickened—just the way it was right now—her whole face softened, from her stunning green eyes to her full lips, as if she were readying herself for a kiss.

That was his favorite look, he thought as she stepped in closer. And this time, he couldn't resist lowering his lips to hers.

QUINN KISSED HER slowly, sensually, as if he was discovering her through the kiss and didn't want to miss a single dip or curve of her mouth. Need built inside her by the second as he lingered on her lower lip, his tongue teasing her there before sweeping inside her mouth to tangle with hers.

In a heartbeat, she felt his control snap just as hers did, his hands tangling in her hair even as hers were grasping at his broad shoulders. His muscles were hard and flexing beneath her fingertips, his mouth hungry and hot as she tried to draw him closer.

She'd never known anything more perfect than kissing Quinn while the sun warmed them as they wound limbs tighter to each other and the ocean birds sang above them.

Oh God, how could she possibly resist him— his passion, his intensity? Quinn's kiss wasn't a moment; it was an *experience*...and every inch of her felt blissfully alive.

"I've wanted to kiss you again since I tucked you into bed last night. Wanted to make good on my promise to you to give you a kiss that you'd never be able to forget."

It wasn't only his words, wasn't just the sensuality in his tone that weakened Shelley's resolve. It was the way he looked at her—as if he was unbelievably thankful to be holding her in his arms and kissing her—that made her desperate to experience his glorious mouth again.

"You definitely made good on it," she told him. "Because there's no way I will *ever* be able to forget that kiss. Or this next one, either, I hope."

Going up on her toes, *she* kissed *him* this time, and it was so easy to sink into the strength of his embrace as they both took each other deeper. Part of her wanted to go slow and relish every single second in his arms, but the other part of her wanted to give in to the frenzied rush of passion, the storm of desire that swamped her as she realized just how right Quinn's arms felt around her, holding them close.

As if the intense kisses were overwhelming him in the same powerful way they were overwhelming her, he drew back and touched his forehead to hers, his breath coming fast, his fingers still tangled in her hair.

"I love kissing you, Shelley." He moved one hand from her hair to stroke the pad of his thumb across her lower lip, and she shivered at how *erotic* it felt. "So damn much."

And she loved the sensual way he said her name. For twenty-seven years *Shelley* had sounded like the most normal name in the world, but in one afternoon, Quinn had breathed extraordinary new life into it.

At the same time that a part of her longed to kiss him again and just keep kissing him for the rest of the afternoon, the still barely rational part of her knew she really did need to think beyond the reckless desire pulsing through her. Because while she liked the idea of a fling, in reality, she wasn't a quickie and forget-the-guy type of girl. Besides, for the life of her, she couldn't slot Quinn into *that* place in her mind. He just didn't feel like a fling despite the fact that they'd only just met.

With her heartbeat throbbing in her ears, and her lips still tingling from their incredible kisses, she forced herself to take a step back so that they could spend more time getting to know each other before any of their clothes started coming off.

"I love kissing you, too," she told him, her voice still more than a little breathless from his kisses, her self-control hanging on only by the barest thread. "But we should probably focus on clamming...for now."

"Yes. Right." But he didn't stop looking at her mouth for several long beats, until he finally said, as if he was trying to remind himself, "I brought you here to teach you how to clam. I have to warn you, though, I want to kiss you again so badly that I can hardly think of anything else. So I may not be the best teacher."

She would bet he had plenty of other things he could teach her.

Ohmygod. Stop it.

The problem was that she'd never enjoyed kissing anyone as much as she enjoyed kissing Quinn...and all she could think about was doing it again. And again. And again. Especially when he was still looking at her as if he wanted to devour every inch of her, head to toe.

Clearly, this wasn't just an adventure in clamming; it was an adventure in reeling in temptation as well.

Both of them looked out at the bay for a few moments, and she knew he was trying to clear his head just like she was.

Finally, he cleared his throat and said, "Clams burrow under the sand." He squinted as he visually inspected the sand. "We're looking for spit marks."

"Spit marks?"

"Yeah, that's what we call them. If you fling excess water onto the sand, the drops of water make marks." He curled his fingers so his fingertips touched his thumb, then flung them open. "We're looking for steamers, or soft-shell clams, and when they burrow into the wet sand, their siphon spurts water and makes the mark."

"Sounds like we have to really look carefully," Shelley said as she worked to focus on his instruction and not how sexy he looked as he gave it, "because if you splash in one of these little pools of water, then you can create those marks, and you'd be digging for nothing."

"You're a quick study, aren't you?" He grinned at her, making her feel all swoony again...and hot everywhere she was dying for him to kiss, to touch. "My siblings and I had a good time playing that prank to death. Let's see if we can find some marks."

"How many brothers do you have?" she asked as they moved at a snail's pace farther away from the beach.

"Three brothers, and you just met my only sister, Sierra. I don't know how good a look you got at the rest of my family in the restaurant, but my oldest brother, Trent, was the one in the white dress shirt at the table. He's an attorney and lives in New York. My younger brother Derek was sitting closest to the bar. He's a custom builder and stonemason and lives in Boston. Ethan's my youngest brother. He lives on the island and runs a fishery. He's usually easy to spot because he always looks like he's just come off a boat and can't wait to get right back out on the water."

Shelley had taken only a quick glance at the table when she was talking with Sierra, but she'd seen three handsome men, all very similar in looks, though none were as striking to her as Quinn.

"Do you all get along?"

"Most of the time. We tease each other a lot, but just out of love, you know. And we're all protective of Sierra." He shrugged like it wasn't a big deal, but she could tell by his smile that his relationship with his siblings was *everything.* "What about you? Do you have brothers or sisters?"

"No. It's just me. I used to wish I had brothers or sisters, but wishing doesn't get us very far, does it?"

"I don't know about that. I think we usually are able to accomplish our goals because they're based on really strong wishes, don't you? I can't imagine it was easy to get your café started. Did that start as a dream, or did you stumble upon it?"

He rubbed his chin again, and Shelley realized that was something he did when he was either thinking or listening intently. She liked that he was interested in her life.

"My coffee shop wasn't really a wish or a dream. I'm not much of a planner, actually."

He cocked an eyebrow. "But you planned a solo honeymoon."

"True, but that was just flight and hotel arrangements. I didn't plan a single minute of the week I'm going to be here." A week that suddenly felt way too short. "I think life is more fun when you follow your heart, so that's how I live mine. It's even how I stumbled into my coffee business. Don't laugh, but the reason I moved to Maryland was because I fell in love with a bungalow on Waring Creek. I'd taken a weekend road trip to go to a Renaissance festival and got horrifically lost trying to find the small town it was supposed to be in. Anyway, I found this bungalow for sale, and it was a steal. Since it felt like the right place for me at the time, I took a chance, used the money I'd saved from working during and after college, and bought it."

"Why would I laugh at that?"

"A girl gets lost and buys a house in an unfamiliar state. Some people might find that strange."

"More like going with your gut, if you ask me. Plus, it fits you perfectly."

Most of the people she shared that story with called her crazy, but Quinn didn't seem to think it sounded crazy at all. Warmth spread through her as she thought about how nice it was not only to be accepted for who she was, but to also be respected for following her instincts. She was amazed, yet again, to realize that he appealed to her both as a sexy man she wanted to be naughty with *and* also as a friend. She'd never met a man who could be both a lover and a friend. Not until Quinn. And, of course, it only made her want him *more.*

"So what happened after you got the house?"

"The coffee shop is around the corner from my bungalow, and I would walk there every morning and have coffee. I got to know the owner, this lovely old man named Gus

McGentry." She smiled with the memory of the gentle, smart-witted, grandfatherly man. "He'd run the business for forty years. Never made much of it other than the quaint shop on the corner, but he loved it, and it showed. Especially by how much he enjoyed getting to know the customers. He didn't have family, and I guess we sort of became each other's family."

"Don't you have family?"

"I do, but we're not very close." She deliberately shook that thought away as she continued with her story. "Gus and I used to spend hours talking about life and the dreams he'd had for the business but could never afford to make come true. Although I suspect it was more that he didn't know the right way to go about it, because he picked my brain on a daily basis about what I'd do with the shop. Eventually customers came to expect seeing me, and I spent more and more time getting to know them. Long story short, he hired me, and we spent months working side by side. We'd often talk long after the shop was closed."

She felt a tug of longing for the man who had given her such unexpected joy.

"Anyway, I expect he knew that he was nearing the end of his life, although he'd never said anything to me. He passed away in his sleep and he left the business to me. I'll never forget the day he died. He used to open the doors at five a.m. sharp. He never missed a day during the months I knew him. But he missed that day. When I arrived at six and the shop was dark and the doors were locked, I knew."

When her breath hitched in her chest at the pain of loss she still felt to this day, Quinn brought her hand to his lips and kissed it. "It sounds like you made his life better. So much better, Shelley. You must miss him."

"Yes." She had to clear her throat to push past the lump in it. "We both really enjoyed each other's company, and I miss him a lot. I've always believed that the day I got lost, I was supposed to find the bungalow, because Gus and I were supposed to meet."

"I'm thinking you're right," he agreed in a gentle voice.

She looked up at him and smiled, loving the way he accepted who she was so easily. Her parents had scoffed when she'd taken over Gus's business and had tried to talk her out of running *some old man's dying venture*. She'd never thought they had much vision, and their comment had made her wonder if they had no hearts, either. The Creek Café hadn't been anywhere close to a dying venture, and since she'd taken it over, it had become a huge success.

"Do you believe in fate?" Shelley suddenly asked Quinn.

He paused for a long moment, never once looking away from her face, before finally saying, "I'd like to."

That was good enough for Shelley, so she didn't push for more. But as she continued to walk hand in hand with him on the wet sand, she couldn't help but wonder if fate had stepped in again with the intent of turning her solo honeymoon into something made for two instead.

The question had barely passed through her head when suddenly he was crouching and pulling her down to the sand beside him.

"See these marks? And see this hole?" He pointed to small indentations in the sand. "These are perfect spit marks, and that's where the clam dug down, but this is old. See how the hole is dry and sunken around the top? This is what it looks like when the clam dug down too long ago. That clam is too deep by now and not worth digging for, but hopefully we'll find another one pretty soon."

She smiled at him as they rose to their feet, thinking how much more relaxed Quinn seemed compared to how he'd been when he'd walked up to her at the bar. "It's incredible to think that with all the chaos in day-to-day lives, people actually slow down enough to come here and look for these marks, isn't it?"

"Actually, I think what's really incredible is the way that you connected with Gus at his coffee shop," Quinn said. "But maybe some things *are* meant to be. Especially since it sounds like you found a business you love."

"I really do love it. I know I might seem like a fly-by-the-seat-of-my-pants type of person, but the café keeps me grounded—and lets me fly at the same time. I have all the administrative things to keep up with, like sourcing the best organic beans, and then there's the consistency of the schedule, of course. But it's more than a business to me, whether I'm comforting a customer who needs a shoulder to lean on or chatting with college kids coming in to do homework. I think they see me as the older, wiser sister type and ask for advice."

"You're full of so much passion, aren't you?"

He stroked her cheek again as he said it, and she barely held back her gasp of awareness at how much she liked his touch. *Craved* his touch already, if she was being totally honest with herself. And the way his eyes heated whenever he looked at her made her want so badly to show him *exactly* how much passion she had inside of her.

She couldn't believe how strongly she was drawn to him. Not just sexually—even though the heat between them was off the charts—but because he *got* her.

And yet that, more than anything, was what had her instinctively pushing the idea of a fling even farther away. Because if they got each other this well, this quickly, and he came to mean something special to her this week, how much harder would it be to walk away from him?

Of course, for all she knew, Quinn might be one of those guys who *only* had flings.

Desperate to get ahold of her emotions so that they didn't bloom into something bigger than either of them were prepared for, she said, "Tell me about your work."

"I own a shipping company."

Ah, so she'd been right about the boardroom and the suit. He exuded power, and she could easily imagine how women everywhere must drool at the sight of him in a suit and tie. She had to work really hard to push aside a supersexy vision of surprising him in a boardroom and reaching up to unknot his tie. "Did you always want to do that?"

"Believe it or not, the impetus behind it was because I loved my boats so much when I was growing up, and I wanted to do something that would allow me to be on the water. Little did I know that I would run a fleet of ships and land transport vehicles from an office while my personal boats sit unused." She could have sworn there was regret on his face as he said it, but before she could ask him any other questions about his career, he pointed at the sand. "Look. There they are."

"Spit marks!" Water spurted out of the hole in the sand, and she laughed delightedly. "What do we do?"

"We dig, but I'd better warn you, jumping on the sand makes them burrow faster. You'll never catch it now."

"Oh, come on!" She dropped to her knees and dug as fast and as deep as she could while Quinn stood beside her, laughing. Sand flung right and left as her hands burrowed deeper into the wet channel.

"Oh my God, I feel it." She dug one hand deeper, leaning into the sand as her fingers continued digging, trying to grip the clam's slick shell. "Help me, Quinn!"

But he was already on his knees, and in seconds his fingers were brushing hers, the wet sand cutting into both their skin as they laughed and egged each other on.

"Faster. Come on!"

"Come here, you little bugger," Quinn said through gritted teeth.

Shelley fell back on her heels in a fit of laughter.

"Get him, Quinn. Don't let him get away!"

His biceps flexed with his efforts. He laughed and groaned, then laughed some more as he dug down elbow deep and actually fell over, sinking to his butt on the wet sand.

Shelley fell across his lap in another fit of laughter. They were both covered in wet, gritty sand, but he was making no move to brush it off. She'd never met a man like him, who was as serious as he was carefree, as sexy and powerful as he was gentle and sweet.

When their laughter subsided, Quinn reached for her cheek.

"You have sand..."

Unable to wait another second, she leaned up to kiss him. Quinn immediately drew her closer, deepening the kiss and filling all of the places inside her that had been empty for far too long. His hand slid beneath her hair and he angled her head back, allowing his mouth to claim hers even more powerfully.

Coming together with Quinn felt like an awakening, releasing her preconceived notions about power and wealth and all the hurt they'd caused her over the years, and replacing those memories with hope for something more.

"I think I'm becoming addicted to your mouth." Quinn pressed his lips to hers again before saying, "I'm sorry I got sand in your hair."

"Sand?" Her brain was too foggy to respond coherently. But, still vibrating from the kiss, she was in no rush to remember how to think.

No rush at all, she thought as she pulled him back down to her for another mind-blowing kiss.

Chapter Nine

FOR THE SECOND time in as many days, Shelley had made Quinn completely forget about work and his grandfather's demands about the resort. All he could think about, all he wanted, was her. Her kisses, her laughter, the bright light she shined down on everything around her.

As the tide rolled back in, swirling around their feet, they washed the sand from their limbs and faces. As they dried off their arms and legs with the towel, they couldn't resist the urge to kiss each other again, and then again and again. The sun was starting to set behind them by the time they finally managed to stop kissing each other for long enough to head back to return the rakes and bucket.

The marina came into view, and for the first time in years, Quinn thought about how much he'd loved tinkering with the engines of the power boats and working the masts and riggings on the sailboats. The more he thought about the time he'd spent on the boats, the more he realized he missed those lazy afternoons. He'd come to accept that they were long gone.

But now he found himself wondering: *Do they have to be?*

"Look how pretty the sunset is." Shelley pointed over the bay at the darkening sky, rivers of blue and violet running across the horizon.

"Sometimes I forget how beautiful it is here," he said.

She put her arms around him, and it was pure instinct to gather her in even closer as they watched the sun setting together. Quinn's chest swelled with an unfamiliar fullness. It was easy to imagine Shelley getting to know customers in her café, warmly welcoming them, listening to their problems, consoling them, doling out advice and smiles with complete sincerity. He felt incredibly drawn to her—and he liked the way he felt when they were together.

But at the same time, even as his emotions were flooding in fast, he knew he couldn't let himself pretend that his overwhelming workload—and his drive to be the very best and biggest in his field—weren't there waiting like a viper for him to relax or drop his guard.

"I don't think I'll *ever* forget how beautiful it is here," Shelley said.

As she gazed up at him, he got lost in her emerald eyes, and his thoughts of work fell away again. In that moment, Quinn knew that he'd never be able to forget how beautiful *she* was. No matter how much work he had to do, this afternoon with Shelley would always be special. So special that he didn't want it to end.

"How about we go get some ice cream and then build a bonfire on the beach?"

Ice cream and a bonfire when there was an endless amount of work to be done? *What are you doing to me, Shelley Walters?*

SHELLEY COULDN'T IMAGINE a better way to spend her solo honeymoon than forgoing the solo part, for a little while at least, and spending it with Quinn.

She felt badly now for initially judging him by his family name at the bar when he'd just shown her how different he was from business-only men like her father. And as they walked hand in hand toward her cottage, where they planned to build a bonfire, carrying their shoes and eating their sweet treats, she didn't want the night to end. Every time he kissed her, her body went up in flames. She wanted to ask him to come back to her cottage, wanted so badly to make love with him—wanted a night with Quinn more than she'd ever wanted anything before. But she'd never gone to bed with a man she'd only met twenty-four hours ago, so even though everything about Quinn felt so right, she couldn't quite find the words to ask him for more.

"How much longer will you be on the island, Shelley?"

"The original plan was for five more days after today, but like I said earlier, there's something about this place that's calling to me." Quinn attracted her like crazy, of course. But even before she'd met him, she'd thought Rockwell Island was the prettiest place she'd ever seen. "I'm going to ask Sierra tomorrow what she thinks about the idea of bringing my coffee shop to the island." She breathed in the sweet sea air. "It would be amazing to spend more time here."

"You're really considering moving your coffee shop here? After only a day or two?"

"Why not? I love it here. And if it ends up feeling like it makes sense after I do some more research into it, I figure it will be worth the risk."

"You're not afraid to pick up and leave everything you've built? Everything you know?"

"There's so much in this world to be afraid of. Hackers, contaminated foods, bad drivers. Why would I be afraid to go on an adventure? What's the worst that might happen if I move my business? That it might fail?"

He shrugged. "I don't know. Maybe?"

"I guess I've never been afraid of failure. I don't entertain the *idea* of failure, either. I'd much rather focus on being hopeful and having fun making sure things work out the way I want them to."

"I have no doubt that if anyone can pull off starting a new business in a new place, it will be you."

"Thanks for your vote of confidence." She loved the warmth in his voice. It was as mesmerizing to her as his kisses. "How about you? How long are you going to be here?"

"I'm not exactly sure, but probably just a few more days. I'm in the midst of a huge merger with my own business. Critical meetings are taking place this week and next, so the sooner I get back to Maryland, the better." He paused for a moment and studied her face as if he was trying to decide if he should say more. Finally, he said, "I'm only here because my grandfather wants my brothers and me to take over the resort and move back to the island. But that's never been in the cards for us, so we all have plenty of things to work out. The timing happens to be terrible, since we all have our own ventures to tend to and being away long-term is not an option."

She tried to reconcile his incredibly stressful response to her question with the carefree guy she'd just spent the afternoon with, and it made her wonder about how much of a workaholic he really was.

Thinking of workaholics brought a sudden picture of the old man in the wheelchair to mind. "I met your grandfather on the beach, with his nurse, Didi. She seemed really nice." Shelley held her tongue about his grandfather. Chandler Rockwell had been downright intimidating and unwelcoming. Except with Chugger.

"I just met her today, too," Quinn said. "We'll see how long she lasts."

"Because of your grandfather, you mean? Didi seemed really capable and professional." Shelley hadn't wanted to say anything negative about his grandfather, but the words, "I guess he did seem a little gruff," came out despite herself.

Quinn laughed softly and when he pulled her in closer, every inch of him was so deliciously hard against her that she lost her breath. "Gruff? That's a really nice way of putting it."

"Well," she said, trying to simultaneously get her synapses to start firing normally again while also finding something that was actually nice to say about his grandfather, "he was very loving with his dog, Chugger."

"You saw Chandler with Chugger?" Quinn looked really surprised to hear it. "That's Ethan's dog."

Just then his phone vibrated in his pocket. When he pulled it out and looked at the screen, his brows drew down to a serious slash.

"I'm sorry, Shelley. I really need to take this call from my business partner. I have a feeling it's about that merger I was telling you about."

"Sure," she said with a small smile, a cool breeze rushing over her the moment he stepped away. "Go ahead."

He walked a few feet away and Shelley turned, giving him privacy to take his call. In any case, she was glad for a few moments to think about what he'd said *and* what he hadn't.

When they were talking about how long each of them would be staying on the island, he hadn't made mention of seeing her back in Maryland, which meant he was probably thinking of her as nothing more than a short-term fling—just the way she should be thinking about him.

A fling. She did her very best to try the idea on for size again. *Maybe I can deal with that.*

After all, like Taryn had said, since no one here on the island knew Shelley or her family, this week should be the perfect time and place to cut loose and live a little.

Yes, she wanted him in her bed with a desperation that stunned her. But even as she tried to psyche herself up for her very first fling, she had to work really hard to try to ignore the queasiness in her stomach...and the way the thought of having nothing more than a sexy fling with Quinn stung, smack-dab in the middle of her chest.

TWENTY MINUTES LATER she was still standing by herself, waiting for Quinn to get off the phone. He'd walked farther away, but it was obvious that he was having a heated discussion about the merger as he paced with the phone glued to his ear.

She was reminded of when she was a little girl, standing in her father's office waiting to tell him about how well she'd done on a test in school, or about the part she'd just gotten in a school play. The phone would ring and he'd hold up a finger. He'd never said, *Excuse me, honey,* or, *I'll just be a moment.* He'd just disregard her altogether and take the call, sometimes leaving her standing in his office for half an hour before shooing her silently out so he could finish the call in private. Other times she'd simply left, unnoticed and not missed.

More and more of those same uncomfortable feelings were taking hold by the minute, tightening in her chest, making her feel unimportant and a little lonely. She tried to fight those feelings by remembering how much fun Quinn had been while clamming and what a gentleman he'd been the night before, when he'd found her skinny-dipping. How even after she'd thrown herself at him, and their kisses had sparked like fireworks on the 4th of July, he'd still gone out of his way to make sure things didn't go too far. Plus, she now knew just how much he had on his plate, with the possible resort takeover and his shipping conglomerate.

Ten minutes later, however, when the call didn't look like it was going to end anytime soon, she walked up behind him to let him know she was going to head back over to her cottage and would wait for him there. But just as he caught a glimpse of her out of the corner of his eye, he turned away, as if he needed to make sure he didn't lose focus on his call for even a few seconds.

The pinched look on his face and his complete disregard made her feel so insignificant that tears stung in her eyes.

Again she fought those feelings, trying to give Quinn the benefit of the doubt by telling herself that he was juggling a ton of responsibilities. But she knew better, didn't she?

I'm rationalizing for him.

How hard was it to say, *Excuse me for one moment*, to the person on the phone in order to give the person he was with a quick goodbye, or even an apology for taking so long?

She'd had the most incredible day with Quinn, and there was more heat between them than she'd ever imagined possible—but this was not okay.

She turned on her heel and walked quickly back to her cottage, taking big gulps of the sea air to try to get much-needed oxygen into her lungs. How could she have even *considered* having a fling with Quinn Rockwell, who was one of the wealthiest and most successful men on the East Coast? Was she a glutton for punishment? Hadn't she known enough men like him to know what to expect?

She mounted the steps to her cottage and spied the champagne bottle on the windowsill, but this time, instead of softening her heart, his gesture that had once seemed so sweet only made the hurt from being ignored cut a little deeper.

Shelley had thought that as an adult she was over the hurt of being disregarded, but she clearly wasn't. At the very least, Quinn's behavior was a really good reminder of why she'd planned a solo honeymoon.

I'll have my own damn bonfire.

QUINN'S PHONE BEEPED, indicating the battery was dying. He couldn't afford to drop this call. Not only because there were now four of his business colleagues on the conference line discussing the merger, but because he'd also just learned that a competitor was honing in on Joseph Alger, one of their key executives. They needed to strategize so they didn't lose him. Agitated and annoyed, Quinn sprinted back to his suite in the resort and plugged in the damn charger, continuing the conversation while tethered to the plug.

By the time Quinn ended the call, they'd hammered out several issues that had been looming around the merger, but there were still more on the horizon.

Unbidden, the thought came at him: *There are always more on the horizon.*

Quinn nearly choked as he finally checked his watch and realized that he'd just spent more than four hours on the phone. How the hell could he have been on the call for that long, when it had seemed like ten minutes?

Damn it. He'd asked Shelley to wait, thinking he'd be on the call for only a few minutes—not for four hours. How could he have done that to her?

He cursed as he looked out through the balcony doors. It was pitch-dark, and he hadn't noticed that, either. Studying his reflection in the glass, Quinn didn't like what he saw—a man who had been so consumed with work that he'd been too afraid of losing the focus his business partners demanded by seeing Shelley's smile and hearing her voice to even pause his conversation for five seconds.

He shifted his gaze to his grandfather's wing of the resort. The lights in Chandler's office were still burning bright. *Of course they are.* Because the truth that Quinn could no longer deny was that the more he focused on building his business to the exclusion of all else, the more he became like his grandfather. It had been no fluke that Quinn had seen his grandfather's pinched, stressed eyes on his own face when he'd looked into the mirror last night.

It wasn't easy to admit, but Quinn couldn't ignore this wake-up call. Not when he could too easily see himself in another ten years, alone and so damn focused on his work that no one wanted to be near him.

But the tightening in his chest and the twisting of his stomach over how he'd treated Shelley cut deeper than the thought of becoming unlikable *and* losing his business deal combined ever could.

That guilt was a first, and it hit him like a ton of bricks.

He needed to apologize. Immediately.

Quinn ran out of his suite. He took the stairs two at a time, grabbing a handful of flowers out of a vase in the hallway and bolting out the back door of the resort. The crisp air stung his cheeks as he raced across the patio, down the stone steps to the beach, and sprinted toward her cottage.

As he ran, he couldn't stop thinking about how Shelley reveled in so many things he took for granted. She was not only the sexiest woman alive, she was also so full of happiness, so free-spirited. And she had lit up parts of him, desires in him, that he thought had disappeared forever.

For the first time in his life, he'd been seriously considering more than a fling. He didn't want to lose Shelley's light, that wonderful brightness that had been missing from his life. But at the same time, he couldn't deny the truth that the carefree, relaxed man he'd been on the beach with her this afternoon wasn't at all who he really was.

He stopped running and paced as he tried to untangle his web of emotions.

Shelley sure as hell didn't deserve a guy who got stuck on business calls and was juggling so many demands that he ignored her. Should he set her free to find a man who wasn't destined to become like Chandler?

That thought stopped him cold. Because now that he'd met Shelley, he simply couldn't imagine not holding her again, not seeing her bright smile or hearing her sweet laughter. He refused to think about waking up tomorrow morning knowing today was all they'd have.

Over the past ten years, Quinn had worked doubly—triply—hard to prove himself. He hadn't wanted anyone to think he'd gotten to where he was with his business just because he was a Rockwell. And somewhere along the way, those twenty-hour days, seven days a week, had become a habit. More than that, his workload and endless hours in meetings and at his computer had become his entire life—all he knew and all he could see for himself into the future. Quinn had been only as good as his next deal, only as good as his ranking on the Fortune 100 list. Romance was nowhere on his list of priorities, not even a blip on his screen.

Until last night, when he'd found Shelley at the cove and then spent today clamming with her.

Suddenly, for the first time in a very long time, Quinn could see a different future. One he could have only if he took a long hard look in the mirror, admitted that he didn't like what he was seeing anymore, and then put the work in to change his life. For the better this time.

He'd screwed up, but he was going to fix it, damn it. More than just fix it—he wasn't going to let himself turn into Chandler and end up losing everyone who mattered in his life.

Right here, right now, Quinn Rockwell was going to change.

He knew he hadn't been the man Shelley deserved, and that he'd been a selfish jerk for putting work ahead of her. But there beneath the moonlight, with the chilly air stinging his face and his heart so full of Shelley he felt as if she filled his entire being, he knew that the man he'd been was nowhere near the man he was capable of being—the man he *wanted* to be.

The man he would become for Shelley.

Every step marked with determination, he strode down the beach toward her cottage. The telltale scent of burning wood hung in the air, bringing him back to their conversation before the phone call.

The bonfire.

The ache ground in deeper, fueling his resolve to never, ever let her down again.

Shelley wouldn't have spent the night pining after any man. A woman who took a solo honeymoon would have no trouble having a solo bonfire—and he was bound and determined that she'd never want to have a solo *anything* again.

He would become the man who caused her eyes to light up, not fill with regret. If there was any way she'd give him another chance, he'd make sure to get it right this time.

Somehow, some way, he'd make everything in his life fit together. It might take a hell of a lot of work, but he already knew in his heart that Shelley was worth whatever it took to have her by his side.

But when her cottage came into view, reality sliced him wide-open. The bonfire had been extinguished, and the lights were out in her cottage, too.

He was too late.

He stared at the fire pit feeling as if his hope had been extinguished by a few buckets of seawater. But he knew that wasn't the case. There was no one to blame but himself. He'd killed his chances with Shelley the minute he'd turned his back on her to focus on the phone call.

Quinn looked down at the flowers in his hand, a poor substitution for the apology he needed to say to her face-to-face, so that he could look into her eyes as he told her he was sorry and would never make a mistake like that again.

He walked quietly up the steps to the front porch of her cottage and laid them on the welcome mat, knowing he'd just lost the best thing that had ever happened to him.

Chapter Ten

QUINN WENT BY Shelley's cottage again first thing the next morning, but her curtains were still drawn and he didn't want to make things even worse by waking her up. The remnants of her bonfire reminded him of how strong she was and magnified the fact that Shelley didn't *need* any man.

A long night with little sleep and a lot of heavy thinking had only reinforced his decision—if by some miracle she was willing to give him a second chance, he'd do whatever it took to make it up to her.

Quinn had never needed anyone to make him feel complete. Now, not only did he *want* Shelley in his life, but he couldn't shake the feeling that he needed her there, too. And maybe, if he were really lucky, she would

BELLA ANDRE & MELISSA FOSTER

realize *she* needed *him*, too. Not just because they didn't have a prayer of controlling their attraction to one another, but also because after seeing how much she enjoyed clamming yesterday, he knew she'd enjoy the rest of the unique things the island had to offer: midnight sails, walks in the woods, fishing, the lighthouse—all the things he hadn't even thought of in forever, and only a few of the things he'd let himself give up in order to achieve his success.

After going for a hard and fast run to try to burn through some of his frustration, Quinn showered and dressed, then headed back out to go by Shelley's again, nearly plowing into Trent in the hallway.

"Did you get my message?" Trent wore a pair of trousers and a dress shirt again, which meant he must be planning on going back to New York today.

"No. I didn't check my phone after my run."

"We have a meeting with Grandfather in less than ten minutes. The sooner we get this over with, the sooner we can all get back to our lives."

Quinn shot a look at the door at the end of the hallway, which led outside. *Damn it.* There was no way he'd make it down to Shelley's again and be back in time.

"What's wrong?" Trent asked.

Quinn didn't like lying to his siblings. So instead of saying, *Nothing,* he opted not to answer the question. "Let's go."

SHELLEY WAS DETERMINED to have a good time on the rest of her trip despite having her feelings hurt by Quinn last night.

Deciding to greet the morning with a walk along the beach, she slipped on a pair of cute flip-flops and pulled the front door of her cottage open. The woody, ashen scent of her solo bonfire lingered in the air. Renewed disappointment settled around her, threatening her intent to have a great day despite the fact that this was supposed to be a solo honeymoon anyway. At least until she looked down and realized she'd almost stepped on a handful of pretty flowers lying on the welcome mat.

She crouched beside them, trapping her lower lip between her teeth.

Quinn.

Picking up the bouquet, she saw that the flowers had wilted a little around the edges and their stems were bone dry. Her heart beat a little harder knowing he must have come by last night after she'd gone to bed, after all.

She stared at the flowers for a long moment before deciding to put them in a vase and set it in the bay window beside the champagne bottle with the candle in it as she tried to push past the conflicting emotions stirring inside her.

When she finally headed out for her walk to explore the area in the opposite direction of the resort, she was still mulling everything over.

All night long she'd told herself to nix the idea of Quinn Rockwell. So what if he kissed like a dream? So what if she couldn't stop imagining what his kisses—and his big, strong hands—would feel like roving over her naked skin? She'd tried to convince herself that she'd eventually get over the need that continued to torture her. But now this bouquet had her wondering yet again—was the lighthearted, fun-loving guy she'd spent the afternoon with really *all* about business? Or did he just need a little reminding about how much beauty and adventure there was outside of the boardroom to reclaim that part of himself? And a lesson in manners, too?

And even if he did, was she up for taking that kind of a risk on him...especially if he really did only want a fling?

Shelley heaved out a huge breath, feeling like she was getting way ahead of herself. After all, while the flowers were lovely, they weren't an apology. And while finding them waiting for her this morning did help assuage a little of her hurt, the way Quinn had behaved last night still stung. Stung a lot, actually.

She passed a couple on the beach in front of the resort and then a family with two small children busy filling buckets with sand. Walking down the sandy beach made her think of her aunt and the mornings they'd spent searching for sea glass. What would her aunt Marla make of Quinn? Shelley wondered.

Just then a FOR RENT sign at the top of the dunes caught her attention. She shielded her eyes from the sun, and the cute cottage at the top of the hill called to her. She'd received a text from Sierra, and they'd made plans to meet later that afternoon to discuss the possibility of bringing a specialty café to the island.

Shelley had been toying with ideas ever since. There was nothing tying her to Maryland. She loved her house on the creek, but wouldn't she enjoy living on the island even more? She could even keep the creek house as a getaway if she wanted to. Plus, Taryn lived in Philadelphia, so either way she had to travel to see her closest friend, and wouldn't Taryn *love* visiting her here?

Gus had loved the café and what it stood for—friendships made on a daily basis and doing something he enjoyed—and she was positive he would have understood moving it to someplace as heavenly as Rockwell Island.

Why not work where she could wake up and see the beautiful bay every morning? There was plenty of residential and tourist traffic; she'd seen that for herself. Surely she could sustain a business here as easily as she did in Maryland, or maybe even more so with the resort nearby.

A little out of breath from climbing the dune, she looked around the yard of the cottage. With a little love, the untended gardens could be gorgeous. The house was a typical, moderate-sized Cape-style cottage with dormers out front and a two-story deck out back. She peered in the French doors off the deck, getting more excited by the second. Hardwood floors met white walls and stained wood trim. Furniture was draped beneath tarps, and based on the dust on the windows, she guessed the house hadn't been lived in for at least a few seasons.

She could so easily see herself having coffee right here in the mornings. Taking strolls on the beach, maybe inviting Sierra over for a girls' night. Shelley craved a girlfriend who would enjoy sharing a fruity drink and sitting outside talking about frivolous things, or watching a chick flick and eating pizza in sweatpants and tank tops. Heck, since Taryn was self-employed, maybe she could convince her to move here, too.

Okay, Shelley, now you're just getting ahead of yourself again.

Of course, she usually liked getting ahead of herself. Still, she was prudent enough to force herself to also go over the cons of moving her business to the island. Her parents would loathe this idea, but then again, didn't they loathe nearly *all* of her ideas? And yes, she'd be starting all over with making a name for herself in a new area, but to Shelley that was part of the adventure. She would also have to hire new staff and find local suppliers. But, again, meeting new people was hardly an inconvenience.

She looked inside the windows of the empty cottage again, and for a few moments she couldn't stop herself from imagining sitting on the couch in front of the fireplace with Quinn. He'd be looking over documents, but when he saw her smiling at him, he wouldn't be able to resist tossing his work aside, picking her up with a sexy growl, and carrying her into the bedr—

Yeah, right. She forced herself to cut her way-too-clear vision off at the pass. *He couldn't even look at me when he was on the phone.*

She glanced at the bay and then into the house again, deliberately envisioning herself *alone* on the couch this time. Thankfully, it was just as easy for her to see that picture, and to also visualize padding along the hardwood in her bare feet, a breeze blowing through pretty sheers while she did a puzzle or came up with a new coffee flavor.

She'd never needed a man in her life. Why should now be any different?

But as she walked back down the dune to head back to the marina for the sailing class she'd signed up for yesterday, she tried to ignore the fact that on both the night they'd met and yesterday afternoon out on the beach, Quinn *had* made everything feel different.

Especially her heart.

ETHAN AND DEREK were leaning against the wall outside Chandler's office talking, while Sierra paced nearby. She wore a fitted cream skirt and a peach blouse, and her hair was pulled back in a tight bun. She'd obviously dressed primly in an effort to please their grandfather, because Sierra was an island girl through and through and outside of her restaurant could usually be found wearing flowing skirts and beachy clothes. Even Ethan was wearing jeans and a button-down shirt, which was a step up from his normal fishing gear.

"Who do we want to do the talking?" Derek asked. "I'd be more than happy to give Chandler a piece of my mind."

Quinn practically laughed out loud at that suggestion. "Anyone but you." Derek would be too much of a hothead. And since Ethan saw his grandfather on a weekly basis, after this mess was worked out, he'd still have to see his grandfather every week, while the others could go back to their regular lives off-island, at least part-time. Sierra wasn't even a consideration in talking with the old man, unfortunately, simply because Chandler didn't have nearly enough respect for women. And Quinn knew he was too sidetracked by getting over to see Shelley to think straight.

"I'll do it," Sierra said.

All four brothers shook their heads. "No," they said in unison. Sierra was definitely strong enough to handle going head-to-head with their grandfather on an issue of this magnitude, but the four of them had always protected her at all costs. There was no need for her to take the heat when they were around.

"Why not? I spend the most time with him other than Dad."

"He also excluded you, Sierra," Trent said. "This could get ugly. We don't want to get you in the middle of this mess."

"I can handle him." She settled her hand on her hip and glared at them.

Quinn could imagine Shelley being just as confident and determined as his sister. He draped an arm over her shoulder, hoping to smooth things over.

"Chandler is no match for you, and we all know that," Quinn said. "But you and Ethan have to live near him long after we leave the island. Let us take the hit."

She frowned but said, "Okay, but if I feel like I need to step in, I'm not going to stay quiet in the background."

"My vote is for Trent to do the talking," Quinn suggested, knowing that his brother was the most even-tempered of them all.

With everyone in full agreement, they headed into Chandler's office.

Their grandfather was waiting for them behind his massive wooden desk. Didi stood by his side, professional as ever, with a friendly smile on her lips.

The five of them stood in front of his desk, with their hands at their sides, except Sierra, whose hands fell rebelliously to her hips. They held their heads high, shoulders back, presenting a united front against a one-person firing squad in a wheelchair.

"Good morning, Grandfather," Trent said. "You look well rested."

Chandler's white shirt was perfectly pressed, his tie tightly knotted. Quinn had very few memories of his grandfather wearing anything other than dress clothes, and pristine, expensive ones at that. His hands were folded across his lap, and Quinn wondered how he felt about being in the wheelchair. He had such a commanding presence, whether he was standing or sitting made no difference, but he was a controlling man. Having to rely on anyone, much less a nurse to take his blood pressure and administer medications, had to rub him the wrong way.

Their grandfather nodded, eyeing Sierra curiously, clearly wondering why she was there. "I'm fine."

Trent wasted no time getting to the heart of their decision. "We've read your mandate, and we believe we can come to an amicable agreement as long as you agree to our revisions of the terms."

Chandler's dark brows drew together. "Revisions? Have you done your due diligence already? Looked over the financials, the strategic plans for the resort?"

He was unbelievable, to demand they move here and take over the resort and then question their ability to make their own decision—and Quinn couldn't hold his tongue. "Our reasons for accepting have nothing to do with money. We're not going to stand by while you ruin the lives of hundreds of families that have devoted themselves to this resort and to this island."

Trent cleared his throat, and Quinn belatedly tethered his anger. Chandler's face remained unaffected by Quinn's outburst.

"Would you like to know our terms?" Trent asked.

Their grandfather raised an imperious eyebrow. "Proceed."

"If you want us to run this resort, first and foremost it belongs to all of us. All five, Sierra included. You will not have any say in the direction of the property or the decisions we make about any department or any aspect of the resort. We have final say for one year. You may not give commentary or provide any input, and furthermore, you may not interfere or undermine our authority with suppliers, employees, family members of employees, or guests."

Chandler shifted in his wheelchair. "You expect me to hand over all facets of the resort without a fight?" His tone was gruff.

"Only if you want us to agree to run the resort. The choice is yours." Trent spoke with confidence. "One year. All five of us or none at all. And you're completely hands-off."

Chandler's unyielding eyes swept over each of his grandchildren. His face was as stern as it had been for the last thirty years. "And you will all live on the island at least ninety-five percent of the time?"

Quinn and Derek exchanged an irritated glance. Quinn didn't believe for a second that he would actually need to live on the island full-time to help run the resort for the next year, and he knew Derek definitely didn't. He was fairly certain Trent wouldn't want to stay here either, given the way he carefully avoided Reese whenever he was visiting. Although Trent kept his feelings so close to his chest when it came to his ex-wife that it was anybody's guess what was going on in his mind.

"Ninety-five percent of the time, with the exception of family-related emergencies or other unforeseen circumstances related to our own businesses. For example, if someone has to go to the hospital off the island."

"I will take this under consideration and get back to you by the end of next week," Chandler said.

"Next week?" Derek snapped. "I have a—"

Trent glared at Derek, then returned an even stare to their grandfather. "Our offer is valid for forty-eight hours. Not a second longer." He turned to his siblings, giving them the nod that they were through. "Good day, Grandfather."

They filed out of his office, Derek and Quinn with clenched fists, and stalked toward the elevators.

Ethan placed a hand on Trent's shoulder. "Well played."

"He'll never agree to back out of having any decision-making power," Derek said. "You know he'll come back with another asinine demand."

"I don't think so." Sierra pulled the clips from her hair and shook her bun free. "I think he wants all of you here on the island for some reason. I have no idea why, but knowing him, it's just another warped form of trying to take control."

The elevator doors opened and Jane Moore stepped out. Jane was the entertainment director for the hotel. Her long blond hair was pinned up, and a pencil was tucked over her ear. She carried a clipboard close to her chest. Her white blouse and black pencil skirt made her look a little like a waitress. She was in her midtwenties and had worked part-time at the resort in various positions during high school and full-time since graduating from college.

"Bad mood or good mood?" She nodded toward Chandler's office.

"Is he ever in a good mood?" Derek grumbled.

Jane grimaced. "Our sailing instructor has the flu, and the backup was called off the island for a family emergency. I need Mr. Rockwell's okay on who to pull in for this, because we're really short-staffed this week."

"I'll do it," Quinn said, surprising everyone.

He still had a ton of work to do, but he was too wound up to work effectively right now.

Sailing was exactly what he needed to clear his head of his grandfather's demands—and his frustration over the fact that he still hadn't had a chance to see Shelley again this morning and apologize to her for being such a jerk the night before. He was planning to run down to her cottage again now, but he knew the odds were low that she'd be there when another spontaneous island adventure likely waited. And the longer it took for him to let her know how deeply sorry he was, the worse chance there was that she'd ever forgive him for it.

"You're a lifesaver," Jane said, relief written all over her face. "You'll need to use the second line boat, because one of the guests has already taken out the boat that's usually used for the course. I also hear the rigging is a bit messy." She checked her watch. "The class starts in an hour, so you should have plenty of time to get it under control."

"I'll be down at the dock in time for the class."

With that, he turned to head back to his grandfather's office, but Trent grabbed his arm.

"You're not going back in there, are you?"

Quinn looked his brother in the eye. "Whatever Chandler is up to, he's handling us in the worst possible way by getting all of our backs up. Especially when not one of us would ever let the family down. Someone needs to set him straight and remind him of that fact."

With a nod, Trent let his arm go. "Just try to keep your cool, okay?"

Instead of barreling back into his grandfather's office, Quinn decided to take Trent's sage advice and cool down first. As a successful businessman, he knew anger was like cancer—it spread and did nothing to diffuse a situation, only made it more rotten.

Quinn was drawing in a deep breath and unclenching his hands when Didi's voice came into focus.

"Your grandchildren take after you, Mr. Rockwell."

Quinn shook his head. The poor woman didn't have a clue that opening her mouth about them to the old man was the kiss of death.

"I didn't hire you to talk or evaluate my family," he heard his grandfather reply. "I hired you to heal me so I can get back to work and run this resort."

As if Chandler hadn't said a word, Didi continued. "They're just as tough as you are. Just as determined."

Quinn's eyebrows went up at her retort. *Does she want to be put on the next boat back to Greece?*

"You're right that they're certainly determined," Chandler agreed, much to Quinn's shock. Even more shocking was the undeniable sound of approval in his grandfather's voice.

"And just as devoted to their family," Didi pushed.

She really must want to be fired as soon as possible. Quinn was sure that family bit was going to push his grandfather over the edge, but it wasn't Chandler who spoke next; it was Didi.

"You know they're doing this for your son, don't you? For Griffin and the island residents, not for you."

The old man *harrumphed*. "It's time for you to take my blood pressure."

Quinn's anger and need for another confrontation suddenly diffused, and he turned back to the elevator, replaying what he'd heard over and over in his mind. Didi clearly had a spine of steel, but what had surprised him most of all was the fact that his grandfather didn't refute what she'd said about him and his siblings.

He found Trent in the lobby, talking with Krista, one of the receptionists at the front desk. Quinn waited impatiently for Trent to finish talking, feeling as though every passing second widened the fissure between him and Shelley.

When Trent finally turned to him, Quinn said, "I just overheard something I need to share with you guys. Where is everyone?"

"They're having breakfast in the café. What did you hear?"

"Let's go find everyone else. I'll tell you once we're all together."

The café was bustling with guests eating breakfast and waiters and waitresses, wearing white tops and black slacks or skirts, working efficiently to deliver food on large round trays. Quinn had never worked as a waiter, as many of his friends had when they were growing up. He'd always worked on boats, where he'd soaked up as much knowledge as the captains and deckhands would share. It was during those afternoon and evening hours that he'd learned how to fix engines and check riggings and just about everything else having to do with boats, with the exception of actually sailing.

His father had taught him how to sail when he was a boy, and he treasured those memories. From his very first sail, Quinn had fallen in love with the wind and the sea and the strength of the bay. When he was out on the water, everything felt brighter.

Just like when I'm with Shelley.

Quinn hated knowing he'd wasted his morning dealing with his grandfather when he should have been at her cottage to apologize as soon as she woke up. Even now he was losing time when he could have been running down to her cottage to see if there was any chance that she was still there.

"I thought you were heading down to the dock," Sierra said when he and Trent got to the table where the rest of their siblings were sitting.

"I need to talk with you guys first about something I just heard Chandler say to Didi."

"Before you do," she said, the expression on his sister's face clearly telling him that she wasn't at all looking forward to more discussions about their grandfather, "I've been dying to ask you about Shelley. I'm meeting with her this afternoon to talk about her café. She seems really great. And after you swept her out of my restaurant so fast yesterday, we're all wondering what's up with you two."

Knowing Sierra loved to get the scoop on her brothers' love lives and that she wouldn't relent until he told her something, he admitted, "She is great. Really great." *Really great* felt like the world's biggest understatement when it came to Shelley. "But I completely screwed up with her yesterday, so unless I can find her and convince her to accept my apology today, there's nothing to tell."

"Figures you'd screw things up with a beautiful woman," Derek said, clearly unimpressed as he shook his head.

Quinn shot his brother a narrow-eyed stare as Trent frowned and said, "I've started to wonder if that's how we weed out the ones who matter."

It sounded to Quinn like that was a question Trent had been asking himself a lot lately. About Reese, maybe?

"If she doesn't matter," Trent continued, "you'll let things lie. But if she does matter, you'll grovel yourself back into her good graces. And you'll do anything you can to get her back. And keep her."

Quinn wasn't above groveling, not where Shelley was concerned. Hell, if there was any way he could get her back, he swore he'd do it. But first he needed to tell his siblings what he'd just heard standing outside of Chandler's office.

Ethan was the one who got them back on track. "What did Chandler say that you think we need to know?"

"First of all, Didi..." Quinn was still amazed at the way she'd stood up to their curmudgeonly grandfather. "That woman has a spine of steel."

"Oh no. What happened?" Sierra's smile immediately faded as their grandfather became the focus of their conversation again.

"Didi said something to Chandler about how we're as determined as he is."

"Looks like it's on to nurse number five," Derek said, but he didn't look at all happy about it.

"No, that's just it," Quinn told them. "Grandfather agreed. And when she pushed him further about how we're agreeing to stay on the island and run the resort just to support Dad and the island residents, he didn't refute it." Quinn leaned his palms on the table and lowered his voice. "She also said that we were just as devoted to family as he is." All of his siblings looked as shocked as he still felt. "That tells me two things. Either she knows him better than any of us do, which seems impossible. Or...I wonder if his heart attacks had more of an impact on him than we're giving him credit for. Do you think there's any chance this nonsense with the resort could be his sneaky way of bringing the family back together?"

Derek laughed so loudly the people at nearby tables turned and looked at him.

"You honestly think Chandler gives two hoots about family?" Derek said, no traces of humor left in his voice at all. "When Grandma was around, he treated her like she came third—after the resort *and* after his high school sweetheart left him in the dust well before Grandma even met him."

"Please don't bring Grandma Caroline into this," Sierra said. "She loved Chandler to the ends of the earth, and she never seemed to blame him for treating her like she was his second choice."

"She was a saint," Derek agreed. "But that doesn't make it right. Everyone knew that he never got over Eloise Fisher. He married Grandma Caroline because, for whatever reason, she adored him and he wanted to have an heir. She was probably the only woman who would put up with him. All I'm saying is that I think Quinn's way off base. Chandler wouldn't know about family loyalty if it bit him in the ass."

"Actually," Quinn pointed out, "he did take over the family business, so he obviously knows *something* about family loyalty. I'm just wondering if maybe somewhere over the years he got screwed up in the head"—*and the heart*, he thought silently as he went back to how stupid he had been with Shelley the night before, all because he'd been too focused on work to remember what really mattered—"and forgot how to treat people."

"Maybe you misheard him?" Trent suggested. "Or misunderstood what he meant."

"Maybe," Quinn said, "but I just thought you guys should know what I heard."

With that, Quinn said a quick goodbye to his siblings, then sprinted out of the resort and across the pool area toward Shelley's cottage. But just as he'd expected, she was already gone for the day.

The flowers he'd left on the mat for her the night before were gone now, but for all he knew, she'd thrown them away when she'd realized they were from him. She'd been so excited about the island that he assumed she was off on another adventure. Without him, damn it.

Quinn's heart was heavy, but as he glanced at her cottage one last time, he finally noticed a vase filled with the flowers he'd left for her. She hadn't thrown them away.

His world was a little less dark as he made his way from her cottage to the docks, but *a little less* didn't even begin to brighten his mood.

Accepting flowers was one thing, but accepting his apology—and him—was a whole different program.

Was this how Chandler felt? Riddled with regret for the choices he'd made? And was there any chance that he had been a different man when he was younger?

Quinn wasn't taking any chances of following that same lonely path. He was already on his way to change. Taking the day to teach a sailing class might seem like a baby step, but for Quinn to give up hours of work, it was a giant leap forward. And it was only the beginning.

One way or another, he was going to make last night up to Shelley and win her back.

Chapter Eleven

AFTER GRABBING A croissant at the resort's coffee stand for breakfast, Shelley headed down to the marina for her sailing class.

The wide wooden dock reminded her of fishing with her aunt when she was little. Her father had been beside himself the summer she'd learned to fish, saying that no daughter of his should take part in such a filthy activity. Fishing, in his eyes, was fit only for old men with gray beards and yellow plastic coveralls. Shelley loved her parents, despite everything, but she'd never fit in with them.

The boat for the sailing lesson was at the dock, but Shelley didn't yet see an instructor. Her curiosity getting the better of her, she stepped aboard to nose around a little before they got started. It had been a long time since she'd been on yachts with her family and smaller sailboats with her aunt. The deck was sleek, and the boat was spotless.

She was walking around the cabin when she stopped short at the sight of Quinn, shirtless and leaning over a pile of rope. For a moment, her brain went completely blank as she stared at all that gorgeously tanned, muscle. But then she remembered what he'd done, and as the hurt feelings came rushing back, she made herself shove the attraction down—*all the way* down.

Quinn turned, a surprised smile stretching across his face as he rose to his feet.

"Shelley. I'm so glad you're here." He closed the distance between them until he was so close that she could see a fine sheen of sweat glistening on his skin as he said, "I'm so sorry I took the phone call and I'm sorry I spent so much time on it. I've been wanting you to know all morning just how sorry I am for the way I behaved."

She was stunned to see him on the boat...but even more stunned by his apology. One that seemed very heartfelt. Between his very sweet apology—and his close, shirtless proximity—it took her a few moments to find her voice. "I got the flowers." Her chest clenched as she told him, "They were lovely. Thank you."

"But they weren't enough. I never should have behaved like that. I never should have treated you like you weren't important to me." His regret was palpable. "I came by last night to apologize, but your cottage was dark and I thought you were already asleep. And then, when I jogged by this morning to try to catch you before you went out, your curtains were drawn, and I didn't want to wake you."

His eyes were full of sorrow, but with an underlying hint of hope—hope that cut straight to her heart. It would have been easy to write Quinn off for his family name and extreme wealth alone, and she might have already done just that if he hadn't repeatedly shown the other side of himself—and if she hadn't met Abby and Sierra and connected with their easygoing personalities. If three Rockwells could be that warm and wonderful, didn't that say something about the family as a whole? She didn't want to be judged by her family name, so it wasn't fair to judge them by theirs, was it?

But at the same time, he hadn't hurt her because he was a Rockwell—he had hurt her by treating her like she hadn't mattered last night. Years of that type of treatment from her family wasn't buried as deeply as she'd hoped, and the sting of his ignoring her still remained even after he'd apologized.

Now, despite how wonderful it had felt to kiss him yesterday and how desperately she was aching to touch him again, somewhere in the back of her mind she heard a voice whispering a warning that she needed to be careful.

Knowing he was waiting for her response, with her thoughts in a conflicted jumble, what finally came out was, "I was looking for the sailing lessons. But I guess I'm not in the right place."

He drew his brows together, obviously noting that she hadn't accepted his apology. "You're on the right boat. I'm teaching the lesson."

"You are?" Her stomach apparently didn't get the message about being careful, because it was fluttering like a schoolgirl's.

He smiled and reached for his shirt from the deck. "Yes. The instructor was sick."

Shelley was losing the battle against admiring the sexy sight of the muscles in his back flexing as he pulled his T-shirt over his head, when someone said, "Excuse me?"

They both turned at the sound of the woman's voice. A gray-haired couple waved from the dock.

Quinn touched Shelley's arm, a touch that sizzled through her from head to toe. "I think this is the rest of our class." He took a step away, then glanced over his shoulder and said again, "I truly am sorry, Shelley."

Her heart in her throat—sweet and hot was clearly a *very* dangerous combination, dangerous enough to make her want to throw caution to the wind—she managed a nod.

Quinn helped the older couple up the ramp and onto the boat. Neither of them could have been taller than five feet. Dressed in white slacks and white shirts, with navy blue sneakers and floppy blue hats, they looked like they were ready for a Florida cruise.

"Well, hello, sweetie," the woman said to Quinn. "I'm Georgette Gainer, and this is my husband George."

"Georgette and George?" he said with a friendly smile. "You two were obviously meant to be."

Shelley also smiled at the couple and held out her hand. "It's nice to meet you. I'm Shelley Walters."

"You too, honey. What we usually tell people is just to say, *Hey, GiGi*, and we'll both turn around."

She eyed Quinn and Shelley as Quinn put his hand on Shelley's lower back for a moment to guide her around a coil of rope lying on the deck, then looped her arms into George's.

"George, aren't they a handsome couple? They go together like tea and crumpets."

"Oh, no," Shelley said quickly, even as she tried to fight back the desire vibrating through her at nothing more than Quinn's hand on the small of her back. "We're not a couple. Quinn is the instructor. I'm just here for the class, like you are."

"Oh?" Georgette shared a surprised glance with her husband. "When we saw you two, we thought you were together. I'm sorry. Me and my big mouth."

After helping the older couple put on their life vests, Quinn stepped in front of Shelley to help adjust hers, the apology still evident in his eyes.

When she'd protested that they weren't a couple, his hand had dropped from her back. And she'd instantly missed it. Just as she missed the smile he'd replaced with a frown.

What other man did she know who would have apologized a dozen times inside of five minutes? Shelley knew the dangers of becoming involved—*even for a fling*—with a successful, wealthy businessman. At the same time, however, a part of her admired that he was so driven and interested in his work. When she was doing something she loved, she felt the exact same way.

Plus, for a little while at least, she'd been sure there was more to him than met the eye. Because despite how much pressure she knew he was under, he'd still set his work aside for a while, first for his family and then to take her clamming out on the beach. For a few wonderful hours, she'd had more fun with him than she'd ever had with anyone else.

And when she added in the way his kisses had rocked her down to her very soul and his caresses made her feel utterly wild and wanton? Moment by moment, his sweet behavior on the boat chipped away at her resolve to remain careful.

"One more chance." She said the words softly enough that only Quinn could hear them.

His eyes lit with relief and a renewed desire that not only warmed her from the inside out...but also made her hope she was making the right decision by letting Quinn Rockwell back into her life.

KNOWING HE'D MADE Shelley sad was a terrible feeling. But seeing the light in her eyes dim when he'd been apologizing and she'd been struggling with how to respond? Hell, that had just about killed him.

Thank God by the time he'd helped her with her life vest, she'd decided to give him one more chance.

A chance that he was bound and determined not to screw up.

He powered up the boat and piloted it into the bay. Georgette and George sat side by side holding hands, and Shelley stood at the bow with the wind blowing her hair away from her face.

The more Quinn thought about her initial reaction to his apology, the more he respected her. Shelley's strength did not lessen her femininity—on the contrary, it added a depth that both intrigued him and put him in his place. Her reaction was something he could see his mother or Sierra having, and that endeared her to him even more.

A short while later, Shelley came to sit with the others. "This is glorious. It feels so free being on the water. If I lived here I'd go boating every week."

There was a time when Quinn had gone boating that often, but that was before becoming focused on his career.

"It's not always this smooth," he said. "The bay can be fickle. Calm one minute and stirring up a squall the next."

"But that's the adventure in nature, isn't it? That's what makes it feel like you're just on the edge of being in control. That's what makes it so beautiful."

And it was that outlook that made Shelley so beautiful. In addition to being the sexiest woman he'd ever set eyes on, her beauty radiated from within because she looked at her *whole* life as an adventure. And in doing so, she'd reawakened his adventurous side, sparking memories that made him want to join her in rediscovering the things he'd missed out on over the past ten years. Being with Shelley made him realize that when he'd become consumed with growing his business, he'd left behind the joy in the very things that had driven him toward his success. Great things like the adrenaline rush from being out on the water and the anticipation of finally snagging a clam with his fingertips.

He wished they were alone on the boat so that he could tell her what he was feeling. But not only were they not alone, he also had a lesson to teach.

"The first and most important thing you must know about sailing is the direction the wind is blowing."

Georgette shot to her feet. "I know how to do that." She licked her finger and held it up, then turned her body until the wind was blowing in her face. Her lips curved into a smile. "Here it is!"

"That's exactly right, Georgette," Quinn said. "And if you're ever not sure, there are other clues everywhere, from the direction the clouds are moving, to the ripples in the water, and other sailboats. Even dust or flags can give you guidance."

"That's my girl." George rose beside her and kissed her cheek. "Always on her toes."

Shelley's eyes were soft and warm as she watched the couple be so affectionate with each other. "How long have you been married?"

"Sometimes it feels like forever," Georgette said with a laugh, "but George worked eighty-hour weeks until two years ago, so we actually didn't get much time together until recently."

Quinn didn't miss the faltering of Georgette's smile as she talked about being second to George's job. He couldn't help but think about his grandmother and how she hadn't even been second in line for his grandfather's affection, but third.

"I imagine it's hard to strike a balance," Quinn said to George, the one thought that was hanging heavily on his shoulders after the crappy way he'd behaved last night with Shelley, "but Georgette must have been incredibly understanding if you were as married to your business as you were to her."

Shelley turned her warm—and approving—eyes to him, and he was glad he'd finally gotten something right. At the same time, he also couldn't help but wonder if Chandler regretted how he'd lived his life, never finding the balance between work and love and fun. And if so, did that feed into his bitterness?

Realizing he'd gotten lost in his thoughts again, Quinn made himself refocus on what he was supposed to be doing—teaching a sailing lesson.

"We need to release the boom vang to allow the boom to rise up when the sail is hoisted." Quinn slowed the engine and explained how to hoist the mainsail, carrying out each action as he talked them through the process. "Now we're going to loosen the main sheet, which is the control line that pulls the mainsail in or out, so that wind against the rising sail doesn't cause resistance." He motioned for Shelley and the others to come closer, then pointed to a line sewn into the foot of the mainsail. "See how this piece moves up and down on the groove of the mast? That ensures that you're ready to hoist the mainsail."

He had to let one of them hoist the mast, and he was a little worried about the older couple doing it. Shelley would not only enjoy the thrill of it, but she was also strong enough to handle the weight. Heck, she was clearly strong enough to handle *anything* that came her way.

"Shelley, would you like to hoist the mainsail?"

Her eyes lit with excitement "Would I ever." But then she hesitated for a moment and addressed the others. "Unless you'd like to do the honors?"

"Oh, goodness no," Georgette said. "The two of us together couldn't pull that halyard down."

Quinn was surprised that Georgette knew the nautical term for the rope that raised the sail. As he helped Shelley get into position, he asked the couple, "Have you taken sailing lessons before?"

"We've taken many, but with George's back, he can no longer hoist, and I'm just happy to have the time with him."

"What about you, Shelley? Have you done this before?" Quinn asked.

"I've seen it done plenty of times, but I've never actually done it myself."

"So you've been on a lot of other sailboats before?"

She nodded. "With my parents. But they always hired a crew to handle things like hoisting the sails and piloting the boat, even though I always thought getting to chart the course and control the speed seemed like the best part of sailing." When she realized they were all staring at her, her cheeks flushed as though she felt she'd said too much. "Anyway, I'm just happy to finally get a chance to do it now."

Quinn stared at her for a long moment, his brain rushing to put the pieces of her life together. From what she'd just said, she'd obviously grown up in a wealthy family. Which went a long way to explaining her aversion to learning that he was a Rockwell. He'd met plenty of people like the family she'd described, and it made him want to work even harder to prove to her that he was nothing like them.

Or am I?

Because wasn't he always working so hard that he missed out on things like sailing and hanging out with his family...and having a bonfire with Shelley?

His parents had always made time for each other and for their children. His father sailed frequently and his mother blew glass, and they still went out on dates every week and kissed each other like newlyweds even though they'd been married forever. Whereas, on the opposite end of the spectrum, his grandfather had *never* made time for his grandmother.

And one thing Quinn knew with absolute certainty was that he did *not* want to become Chandler.

The mast hitting his arm brought him back to the present. He reached around Shelley and placed her hands on the rope. "You want to hold it like this."

Shelley hoisted the sail like a pro, then grinned at Quinn. "That was such a rush!"

"You did it perfectly. See how the mainsail is fluttering? That's called luffing."

He wrapped the mainsheet around the winch and cranked it until the mainsail stopped luffing. Then he led them to the cockpit and took the helm. Once settled, he placed Shelley's hand on the helm and asked her to hold her steady while he deployed the jib. She handled the helm like she'd done it a million times—with a sexy confidence that was Shelley through and through—and he knew she must have spent a lot of time watching the crew work while she was on the boats, not just sunbathing on the deck.

"You did a fine job, Shelley," George said. "Maybe one day you'll be able to convince your parents to do more things so they don't miss out like we did." He pulled Georgette into an embrace. "And, Quinn, you're right. I'm a darn lucky man, and my Georgette is probably the only woman who would put up with someone like me."

"Oh, George. That's not true. Remember the way Patricia used to chase you?"

While Georgette and George debated his admirer, Quinn focused on Shelley. He wanted to know more about her, and to apologize about a million more times until she knew exactly how bad he felt. But since this wasn't the time or the place to discuss their relationship, in front of two strangers, for now he simply reached up to tuck a lock of hair behind her ear and ask, "Where are you from?"

Her lips parted, and he heard her breath hitch as if his touch affected her more than she knew how to handle. Lord knew, he felt exactly the same way—he could barely keep his hands off her.

Finally, she replied, "Greenwich is where I grew up, but I spent a lot of my youth traveling with my family to Africa, Europe, Asia."

From most people, that might have sounded like they were bragging. But Shelley sounded more wistful than anything, and given how much she loved the small-town feel of the island, he thought he knew why. "It must have been hard not having a home base as a kid."

She looked at him in surprise, as if she hadn't expected him to have such insight into her emotions. Probably because he'd been such a jerk the night before. "It was. And I'm not complaining, but honestly, as a kid I wanted a more normal life."

"I've never been to Africa, but it's on my bucket list," Georgette said.

Quinn hadn't realized Georgette and George had tuned back into his conversation with Shelley.

"We'll get there, honey," George assured her.

"What's on your bucket list, Shelley?" Georgette asked.

She looked relieved to have the subject diverted from her childhood. "My bucket list? Not traveling to faraway places visiting diamond mines, that's for sure."

Diamond mines?

Wait a minute. Is Shelley one of those Walters?

Walters Enterprises was the most notable of the diamond empires, and if she was related to them, then all of Shelley's aversions to money and overworking all suddenly made perfect sense. Clarence Walters was a starch conservative. He was in all of the high-society pages, but Quinn didn't recall ever reading about his daughter.

Quinn remembered what she'd said about working through college and using the money she'd saved to buy her house. Just as he'd left the island to avoid the family business and strike out in search of bigger, better things, she'd struck out on her own.

Their similarities ran much deeper than he could have ever imagined.

"I think it would be fun to learn to skip rocks," she said. "To paint something that doesn't look like it was made by a five-year-old.

To sing with a choir even though I can barely hold a tune. And I would *love* to spend the night in a tree house. A real tree house, not one of those mini-mansions people sometimes build in their backyards. It's been my dream ever since I was a little girl."

As Quinn listened, he realized that Shelley took nothing for granted, not even the simplest things. He felt as if he were getting a glimpse inside her heart.

When she caught him looking at her, renewed guilt from last night settled on his shoulders. How many times had she been cast aside by her parents as they worked?

Never again, Shelley, he silently promised her. *Never again.*

He'd been right last night when he'd thought Shelley deserved a better man than him—but he'd been wrong to consider, for even five seconds, walking away. He would become that better man, damn it.

For both of them.

During the rest of the sail, George and Georgette happily told them stories of their youth and shared the joy they took in their grandchildren. Shelley didn't offer any more insight into her family, but Quinn already felt like he knew her a thousand times better than he had before they'd set sail.

Back at the dock, Georgette asked Quinn to take their picture, which he was more than happy to do. Then Quinn took out his phone and asked her to take one of him and Shelley.

"Why don't you put your arm around Shelley and pull her in real close so I can fit you both in the picture," Georgette suggested.

Quinn was sure Shelley knew what Georgette was up to, but she smiled up at him as she wrapped one arm around his waist and settled the other on his stomach. Desire ripped through him at the same instant that he felt her breath go, her eyes widening as she looked into his. *So beautiful, Shelley. You're so damn beautiful and sweet.* Her skin flushed as if she could read his mind.

Georgette took several pictures of them before she and George went on their way, leaving Quinn and Shelley alone.

He reached for Shelley's hand as he helped her off the boat, and didn't let go of it as he said, "I'm really glad you came out for a sail with me today."

"I am, too." She looked down at their linked hands, then back up into his eyes. "It was fun, Quinn. Really fun."

"I was thinking of taking one of my boats out tonight. Would you like to come with me? I promise I won't take any work calls."

"It's a leftover hurt from my childhood. I thought I was over it, but now I know I'm not, because it still really stings."

With his free hand, he brushed her hair from her shoulder and cupped the back of her neck. "You shouldn't need to be *over it*. I screwed up in a major way, and you're right to be upset with me. But I'm going to try my damnedest to never do anything that stings again. At least," he added as he drew her closer, "not in a bad way."

He wanted so badly to kiss her, but he didn't know if he'd earned back that right yet. "Can I kiss you again, Shelley?"

She looked surprised by his question for a moment, but that expression quickly shifted into a smile that told him she was glad he'd asked if he could kiss her instead of simply assuming that she was ready to resume things from where they'd left off last night before he'd blown it.

Instead of answering him with words, she went onto her toes and pressed her lips to his in a sensual kiss that sent need rushing through him. A kiss that he wished could have gone on forever.

But knowing he hadn't earned *forever* yet, he made himself draw back and ask again, "Will you come sailing with me again tonight?"

"Yes," she finally said. "I'd love to."

Chapter Twelve

BILLY'S BY THE Bay was a small seafood café located a few miles away from the resort. Shelley and Sierra had just ordered iced tea and salads on the patio beneath a vibrant red umbrella, but Shelley's mind was still tangled in thoughts of Quinn and the magnificent kiss they'd shared on the sailboat after the lesson. They'd agreed to meet later that evening for a moonlit boat ride, and even though she was still more than a little wary of being hurt again, she also couldn't deny that she was excited to see him again.

One more chance.

It was a risk, given his obvious workaholic tendencies, but there were so many great things about Quinn—he was sweet and sexy, smart and funny, and utterly devoted to his family—that made it impossible for Shelley to turn away from him just yet. Not without giving him one more chance to get things right.

"The wind really kicked up this afternoon. Was it this bad when you were sailing?" Sierra gathered her hair over one shoulder and held it tight so that it wouldn't blow all over the place.

Shelley fished around in her purse. "Fortunately it was pretty calm. I know I have a couple elastic bands in here somewhere." She pulled one out and handed it to Sierra, who made quick work of tying back her hair.

"This is why I need sisters," Sierra said. "My brothers would probably take out a piece of rope and try to tie my hair back with some fancy boating knot. Ethan must know a thousand different knots, actually."

Shelley laughed as she also pulled her hair into a ponytail. "Well, I wouldn't mind having a sister *or* a brother. I'd take someone caring enough to tie rope in my hair any day over being cared for by nannies and dragged around like luggage."

She was so comfortable with Sierra already that the words came before she could stop them. She thought about when she'd accidentally mentioned diamond mines on the boat with Quinn and how she'd seen him mentally putting the pieces of her childhood together. He obviously hadn't mentioned it to

Sierra, though, and she was glad he thought enough of her not to share it, to give her the chance to do so at her own pace.

"That couldn't have been fun."

Shelley tried to shrug it off. "It wasn't that bad, just not the same as having a houseful of other kids to play with and parents who were actually around instead of working all the time."

"I thank God every day for my parents. They're so down-to-earth and real. It's always driven my grandfather crazy that none of us play up our surname." Sierra sipped her iced tea. "I probably shouldn't share family secrets, but I feel like I've known you forever for some reason."

"Don't worry. I promise your family secrets are safe with me. And I feel the exact same way about you." Shelley felt so lucky that she had connected with Sierra. Her parents' lifestyle was so different from what most people had been exposed to that she was really glad for the kinship. "Your mom seems really nice. Everyone here does, actually. It's one of the first things I noticed when I landed on the island. Any town that has a brag wall is officially fabulous."

"Eleanor is so cute, isn't she?" Sierra agreed. "She's absolutely the perfect person to run the visitors' center."

"Did you know she has pictures of your brothers from when they were teenagers up on the board?"

"Everyone loves my brothers. Of course, what everyone else doesn't see is what it's like to be their sister. They can be a little overbearing to me sometimes, particularly Trent, Quinn, and Derek, but I try to remind myself that they're only doing what they think is best. And beneath their workaholic sides, they're fun. Especially Quinn. Back when we were kids, at least, he was always the one coming up with crazy plans for all of us."

"I'm not surprised," Shelley said. And she truly wasn't, because she'd seen for herself how much fun he could be.

"Really? You're not surprised to hear that he can be fun?"

Shelley smiled as she told Sierra, "We went clamming yesterday, and then of course he taught the sailing lesson today, which was great."

"Wait." Sierra pressed her palms to the table. "You got Quinn to go clamming? Like *dig in the mud* clamming?"

"He's the one who suggested it, actually. I had no idea how to clam, but I had a blast." She purposefully left out the part where she'd been rolling around on the sand making out with Quinn, of course.

Sierra's brows knitted together as she leaned back and crossed her legs, her long cotton skirt waving in the breeze. "Shelley, Shelley, Shelley..."

"What?"

"Nothing."

But the mischief in Sierra's dark eyes told Shelley there was a lot of *something* in that *nothing*.

On the one hand, Shelley loved knowing that Quinn was different around her than he'd been with other women...but on the other hand, she was also worried about how fast her feelings for him had already grown.

Her mind drifted back to the horrible feelings of the night before, when he'd taken the phone call and ignored her. Then she quickly fast-forwarded to the flowers he'd left on her porch and the deep regret in his eyes when he'd apologized—many times over.

Yet again she tried to convince herself that she still needed to be careful, but she couldn't shake the feeling that they not only generated a shocking amount of heat and passion together, but that they'd also been opening their hearts to each other since day one. And along with opening their hearts came learning, growing, and even sometimes experiencing old wounds as they set boundaries on what was okay and what wasn't.

Wasn't that part of every relationship—at least the ones that lasted?

"Anyway, like I was saying before we started talking about Quinn," Sierra said, as if she could tell that Shelley had grown slightly uncomfortable, "of all my brothers, Ethan's probably the most easygoing. But I think that's because he's the youngest and none of us gave him much of a chance to chime in—we were all such loudmouths. Then again, maybe he just plays that card because women always go gaga for the strong and silent type." Sierra laughed. "There I go, spilling more family tales. You need to act bitchy or something so I stop talking."

"I don't think I'm very good at being bitchy. But chatty? I could do that all day long. All night, too." Although, she didn't want to take up too much of Sierra's time, so she said, "When I met your mom at Annabelle's, she said that you thought an organic coffee shop would do really well here. Do you agree?"

"Oh my goodness, yes! Starbucks tried to come onto the island, but our civic association nixed that. We're really into keeping things local. Otherwise Rockwell Island might become nothing more than an extension of any big city out there."

"I know what you mean. I don't shop at trendy stores, and those restaurants that everyone fights to get in?" Shelley shook her head. "Not me. I'm more about the experience than the notability. I'm proud of sourcing great coffee beans and local bakers for my café, but I think the real reason people come back is because I love getting to know them—talking with them about their lives, their jobs, families."

"That's part of the fun of owning a restaurant for me, too," Sierra said with a smile. "I know when kids are graduating from school, when their plays are. I find out when people get sick and I bring them homemade soups and meals."

Without missing a beat, Sierra leaned forward again to say, "Please tell me you're actually thinking of bringing your café here. And not just because I'm always craving a good cup of coffee, but because I think it would be so much fun to have you in town."

Shelley hadn't been one hundred percent certain before talking to Quinn's sister, but everything just felt so right about being here. It didn't hurt that she also felt like she'd just found a new best friend.

"I like to follow my instincts, and something tells me that this would be a good place for me. The *right* place. A place I can see myself settling in and putting down roots. I've never really had that. I mean, I love where I live now, but I want to find my forever home. A place that my grandchildren will visit and think, our crazy grandma just up and moved here on a whim—and it was the best decision she ever made in her life."

Sierra lifted her glass of iced tea in a toast. "Here's to making great decisions about life, work, and especially love."

And as Shelley clinked her glass against her new friend's, she knew she'd already made one good decision at least—coming to Rockwell Island for her solo honeymoon had been one of the best things she'd ever done.

QUINN SPENT THE afternoon working through the documents for Rich and finally sent them off five minutes before the alarm that he'd set went off. He wasn't about to take a chance of being late for his date with Shelley.

He walked at a fast clip across the marble floors of the spacious lobby. The resort had been redesigned twice that Quinn could remember. The first time his grandfather had gone all-out, with crystal chandeliers and dark marble floors throughout, but the resort had looked more like it belonged in Las Vegas than on the island. Thankfully, his grandmother had finally talked some sense into Chandler. How she got through to the man, no one knew, but within two years of that pricey renovation, he'd had it renovated again, using light-colored marble, stone procured from the island, and replaced many of the crystal chandeliers with iron ones boasting faux candles to give the fancy resort more of an intimate island feel. Dark sofas and settees were replaced with warmer-toned, comfortable furniture.

Thoughts of taking over the resort nagged at the back of Quinn's mind. He didn't want to think about that demon looming over him right now, but as he made his way toward the restaurant, greeting the employees as he went, a part of him couldn't help wondering what it would be like to actually do it. To be in charge of the layout, the offerings, and the success of the family business. Surprisingly, he found it wasn't a terrible thought.

The chef had everything laid out in a corner of the huge kitchen for Quinn as he'd requested. Quinn knew he wasn't the best cook, but he wanted to make the effort for Shelley. He wasn't the type of guy to order dinner out seven nights a week, and the sooner he started proving to Shelley that he wasn't like her parents, the better. If he'd been home, he would have asked her to join him for a glass of wine while he cooked, but with the restaurant working at full speed tonight, he knew that trying to converse with Shelley while working around the chefs would be more chaos than pleasure.

When he was done making dinner, he dropped the food off on the boat, then walked to her cottage. The candle he'd given her in the champagne bottle was lit, its flame dancing in the wind as it swept through the screen. Through the window, he saw Shelley come out of the bedroom wearing a navy miniskirt that revealed her long, lean legs. A white sweater with navy trim clung beautifully to her torso. When she bent to put on a pair of sandals, Quinn had to fight the urge to stare as her neckline fell slightly open, revealing the edge of a lacy blue bra.

From the first moment he'd set eyes on her, her beauty stunned him. Even if he saw her every day for the rest of his life, he knew he'd never stop being awestruck, never be able to look at her, or touch her, without his heartbeat kicking into overdrive.

When he finally knocked, he felt more nervous than he had in years. Shelley pulled the door open, and even though he'd just seen her sixty seconds ago through the window, he lost his breath all over again at her incredible beauty. Loose tendrils framed her face, and she wore a little eye makeup, which gave her already sultry eyes a seductive quality.

"Hi," she said with a smile, her fingers fidgeting with the edge of her sweater. It looked like he wasn't the only nervous one tonight.

He leaned down, intending to kiss her cheek, but she turned her face so that their lips met instead. All day he couldn't stop imagining *this*—the way her body melted against his, the sweet sounds of her gasps of pleasure, the feel of her hair as he tangled his fingers into it.

It took every last ounce of willpower not to deepen the kiss, pick her up, carry her into the bedroom, and let their desires take over. But he'd promised her a boat ride, and that's what she was going to get...even though her hands were fisted in the collar of his shirt and she was kissing him like she wanted to tear his clothes off as badly as he wanted to strip off hers.

Her eyes were hazy with desire and more than a little unfocused as she looked up at him.

"It's really nice to see you again," she whispered. "I hope I'm dressed okay for our boat ride."

"You look beautiful." *The most beautiful woman I've ever seen.*

He loved how her cheeks pinked up at the way he couldn't take his eyes off her. She was so strong that it magnified the moments when she let her defenses down, and though Quinn knew how incredible they would be together if they chucked in their sailing plans tonight and tangled up her sheets instead, he wanted to get to know her better first. To find out about all the things that had led her to be so spontaneous and strong, while also being warm and forgiving.

"Ready to go?"

"I just need to blow this out first," she replied as she went to the window. "The candle you gave me is one of the most thoughtful gifts I've ever received. Well, other than the Motrin," she added with a smile. "When I was little I spent a week at the Cape with my aunt each summer, and she used to buy sparkling cider in wine bottles. I'd pretend I was drinking wine while we sat out on her front porch overlooking the bay at night. Each time we finished a bottle, she'd plant a candle in it, just like you did. Thank you for reminding me of such happiness."

But, yet again, he knew he should be thanking her. Because for the first time in a very long time, he felt happy, too.

Happier than he could ever remember being before.

Chapter Thirteen

LIGHTS OF THE island shone in the distance, and moonlight reflected off of the inky water as they shared the steak dinner Quinn had made, complete with salad, baked potatoes, and a side of vegetables.

"I can't believe you went to all this trouble." Shelley had never had a man cook dinner for her before. Knowing how busy Quinn was, that he'd taken the time to prepare such a wonderful meal made it even more special.

"I loved cooking for you. And I love that you actually enjoyed it, too."

"I really did. It was absolutely delicious." They put the dishes in the cooler he'd brought and sat together, sharing a glass of wine. "It's so thrilling being out on the water at night. If I close my eyes, we could be anywhere. In the middle of the Black Sea or off the Florida coast."

Quinn put an arm around her and pulled her closer. So close that she could feel the heat of his body—and his wonderfully hard muscles—all along her side. "That's one of the things that drew me to boats in the first place." He stroked over her shoulder with the pad of his thumb, awakening every cell in her body with need as he said, "Whenever the island felt confining, the open water felt like it had endless possibilities."

"You've talked about feeling confined before." She knew he must be able to hear the way desire drenched every one of her words, from nothing more than the way his thumb was moving across her skin. The thought of his hands on more of her tonight was so good that she nearly forgot what she'd been about to ask him. "Do you really not like the size of the island?"

"Honestly?" By now, he'd moved his hand up to stroke over the sensitive skin of her neck. Did he have any idea at all how crazy he was making her feel as he said, "I used to feel that way. But since we've been spending time together, you've shaken some of my good memories loose, and now I'm wondering if I've been too critical. I'd forgotten how much I loved boating. I'd forgotten the smell of the bay at low tide. I'd even forgotten about the view from the road where I used to ride my bike. I guess I took for granted the things the island did have to offer, because I was so dead set on striking out on my own."

Now, he brushed his hand over her hair, sending the most delicious shivers of need running through her as he tucked a strand behind her ear.

"What about you? You obviously love the island, but don't you think you'll eventually miss the pace of being back home and running your business?"

His mouth. She couldn't stop staring at his lips...and wishing they were on hers. But, knowing that the biggest and best pleasure would come from a combination of innate heat *and* truly getting to know each other, she forced herself to answer his question first. "I love my customers, of course, but it's not like I wake up and feel like the town of Severn is all there is in life for me. I always knew that one day I'd find a place where I truly wanted to put down roots, and the more time I spend here, the more it feels like this might be it."

"You said you spent time with your aunt at the Cape. Do you think part of feeling so comfortable on the island is because she's nearby?"

"I wish she were still here," she answered softly, feeling the ache of missing her aunt. "She passed away a few years ago."

"I'm so sorry, Shelley." He gently stroked the back of his hand against her cheek, obviously sensing how much she missed her aunt. "Did you ever consider moving to the area where she lived?"

"In Eastham?" She shook her head. "I loved it there, but I know I could never re-create what we had. That was a moment in time, you know? Whereas this island feels like the perfect combination of what my aunt and I shared and something that's all my own. I feel like I fit in here. And I want to make new memories."

When she turned her face to his, his thumb lightly stroking along her jawline now, she saw that the wind had tousled Quinn's hair, making him impossibly sexier, like he'd just rolled out of bed. "What about you? What does your home in Maryland feel like?"

"Nothing like this," was the answer he gave her. An answer that she was barely able to process when he was moving his thumb across her lower lip at the same time. "Nowhere near as good as being with you."

He moved closer and with their lips only a breath apart, heat rushed through her. He looked at her for a long and heady moment, letting her see how much he desired her—and she was positive that he had to be able to read in her eyes that she was just as wild for him.

Shelley was already moving to kiss him when he sealed his lips over hers. Greedily, she took her fill, fisting her hands in his hair, giving in to the fierce *wanting* that had been pulsing between them for days. Desire overrode her every other sense—desire for more of his taste, his scent. The feel of his hard muscles thrilled her as he licked over her bottom lip, and she had to sink her teeth lightly into his in response.

He let out a groan that echoed off into the night sky, his body crashing down upon hers on the padded bench, and she'd never loved anything as much as she loved his heat coursing down the entire length of her. She felt white-hot on the inside, like all of her could just melt around all of him and that every moment in Quinn's arms would be perfect. Beyond perfect. As perfect as the feel of his tongue slicking over hers, consuming her, claiming her as his own.

His hands tangled in her hair as his lips ran a devastating path across her cheeks, then back to her mouth, then down over her chin and the soft underside so that she was arching her neck back even as she began to beg. A breathless *please*, which he immediately answered with a light flick of his tongue against her sensitive skin and then the slight edge of his teeth over her collarbone.

One powerful arm swept behind her, holding her close as his other slipped beneath her sweater to stroke the bare skin beneath it at her waist. With his mouth, he captured her gasp of pleasure at the way his touch turned her inside out, and when she instinctively wrapped her legs around his waist, he groaned again with appreciation. The guttural sound brought her hands beneath his shirt and over his gloriously hard muscles.

"Shell," he said in a heated whisper before taking her in another mind-blowing kiss. He'd never before called her *Shell*, but it felt right. Made her feel even more special.

Somewhere in the back of her mind, questions about whether or not she could actually handle a fling remained. But when Quinn nuzzled in against her hair to take her earlobe between his teeth and shivers of desire racked her head to toe, all of her worries and fears blew away on the night breeze.

Raining kisses over her cheeks and lips, he found her other earlobe, and though she should have been prepared this time, she felt as if fireworks were lighting off inside of her. One gorgeous explosion of color and light after another.

Nothing in her life had prepared her for kisses like these, for wild and sweet, for rough and soft, for bliss that rode through every inch of her, head to toe, all from the touch of his lips against her skin.

Then again, how could she have ever been prepared for Quinn? For her solo honeymoon tumbling upside down until she was here on a boat in the moonlight wrapped all around a gorgeous island man whose smile made her heart swell with happiness, whose hand over hers filled her with such warmth, and whose kisses were pure electricity.

More. She wanted *more!*

But instead of moving faster, instead of reaching for her clothes to strip them away, instead of dragging her hips even closer to his the way she wanted them, he drew back to look into her eyes again. In his gaze she could read his questions—he was afraid of pushing her too fast, too hard. Her heart clenched at the realization that he truly didn't want to hurt her again. Not in any way. Which meant that despite the desire she could feel vibrating through every inch of him, he was waiting for her to give him a signal that she was one hundred percent okay with what they were doing.

She did it first with a kiss and then by saying, "Touch me, Quinn. Taste me." And then she held his gaze and let him see everything she was feeling as she whispered, *"Take me."*

QUINN WAS LOST in sensations. The feel of Shelley's soft, supple body beneath him. The hungry way she devoured his kisses and kissed him right back. The sound of her voice—God, he loved her sexy, heady whispers.

He wanted Shelley so badly that he could hardly remember how to breathe, could barely think straight when he was with her. All he could do was *want* and then want more, and more again. With every kiss he gave her. With every sweet little sound she made as their tongues slicked against each other. With the way his heart swelled when their hands slid together, their fingers linking as they held each other tight.

He couldn't get enough of her, but instead of stripping away her clothes the way he was dying to, he forced himself to draw back and search her eyes one more time to make absolutely sure she wanted this as much as he did.

"Quinn." He loved the way she said his name, in a voice that was heavy with need even as her lips curved up at the corners. There was so much warmth in her eyes as she looked at him, more than just passion—a deeper emotion stirring in their green depths—as she pushed at

his shirt. "I want to feel you against me, skin to skin."

It was the warmth, the emotion, and her smile that told him it was okay to move forward into even deeper pleasure. "I want it, too, Shell. More than I've ever wanted anything else."

He reached behind him and pulled his shirt over his head in one swift move, and when he looked back, her eyes were wide.

"You're—" She swallowed hard as she reached out and pressed her hands to his chest. "You're amazing."

He could feel his heart beating hard and fast for her, harder and faster with every rapt stroke of her hands over his chest. It was heaven—and hell, too, on his self-control—watching her eyes, her face, as she touched him, driving him crazier, making him hungrier for her by the second.

When he couldn't take it anymore, he took her hands in his and lifted them to his lips, pressing kisses to every fingertip and then to the soft skin of her palms. "Now you, Shell. I need to see you, need to touch every inch of you, need to kiss you all over."

"Yes," she gasped out. *"Yes."*

Together they stripped her bare, both of them teasing and tempting as each new soft patch of skin was revealed despite their frantic

BELLA ANDRE & MELISSA FOSTER

need. He had to touch, had to taste every bit of her as she was revealed.

As they drew fabric away, both of their hands shaking now as cotton was thrown across the deck and silk and lace fell to the deck, he ran kisses over her shoulders, her arms, her hands, then back up to her breasts. His tongue left a wet swirl of heat over her nipples, then down to her rib cage and the sweet indent of her belly button.

That first night he'd seen her naked, but though she'd stunned him with her beauty and had been so soft and sweet in his arms, tonight was truly their first time together. Tonight was the first time he was stripping her bare with his own hands while knowing that they both needed each other with a passion that was fierce and unstoppable and beautiful.

So damn beautiful that when she was finally fully naked beneath him, he needed to take a minute to reach deep for his control. But he knew he was just fooling himself to think he could ever be in control with her when she made him want, crave, *need* absolutely everything—body, heart, and soul.

Touching his forehead to hers, he whispered, *"Shelley."* He was so awestruck by her beauty, by her scent, by her bravery—by every single thing about her—that he almost couldn't remember how to form words, could only remember how to say her name.

She whispered his name back, and when she pressed her body to his mouth and hands and hips, he couldn't stop himself from lavishing her skin with feverish kisses and caresses.

"You're stunning, Shelley. The most beautiful woman I've ever seen. *Beyond* beautiful."

She pressed her lips to his chest, kissing a path along his pecs, and when she swept her tongue over his chest, the animal in him took over. Took them *both* over, as their mouths crashed together, tongues slicking, hands groping. He stroked her where she was slick and hot, and her head tilted back with a sexy little noise that short-circuited whatever synapses he had that were still firing.

Desperation rode him, the desperation to take her right then, right there beneath the stars. But even more than that, he wanted to pleasure her. Needed to see her come apart for him. Needed to feel her quiver, hear her gasp, taste her pleasure on his tongue. He wanted her to remember his caresses, his kisses, when she woke up in the morning.

And he wanted her to crave them when she closed her eyes at night.

Quinn wanted to take the time to explore, to arouse, to pleasure her like no other man ever had. He drank in her flushed skin, her tantalizing scent, as he ran his lips from the gorgeous swell of her breasts to the sensitive dip beside the ridge of her hip, over her stomach. She arched her hips up into his hands, into his mouth, but he hadn't had enough yet. Hadn't given *her* enough anticipation, enough yearning, enough desperation yet.

He moved back up her body, feasting on her soft skin, loving her uninhibited response to the slicking tease of his tongue at the underside of her breasts, to the tug of his lips over her nipple, to the gentle scrape of his teeth over her pulse point. Intensity grew by the second, the moon shining brighter above them, the water going darker beneath them, as what was left of his control gave way to need that he wasn't sure he'd ever be able to fully quench. Not even if they had a thousand nights like this.

Following the path of his hands down her torso with his mouth, he traced her hips with his hands, wanting to memorize every lush curve. And when her legs fell open wider, welcoming him, beckoning him, Quinn brought his mouth to the inside of her thigh. She gasped a breath as he teased her with his fingers, and she met each tease with a lift of her hips.

Needing more, wanting to see her so full of desire that she thought she might burst, he slid two fingers into her velvety heat, sinking deep inside.

So good. So, so good.

The blood was rushing so loudly through his brain that he might have missed her sweet words if he weren't so utterly attuned to every breath she took. To every degree that her skin was heating up as she gave herself over to him more and more by the second. To the trembling of her limbs as he took her higher. Took both of them so damn high that he didn't ever want to come down.

Her words echoed everything he was feeling, both of them gasping with the pleasure of their connection. He whispered the same thing against her skin—*so good, so, so good*—and then he lowered his mouth to her sweet, hot center. The first taste of her was pure heaven, and he couldn't stop himself from taking more, and then more still.

When she panted out his name, he nearly lost it then and there on his boat, even with his pants still on. And the way her body responded eagerly to every stroke of his tongue, to every caress of his fingers over her, inside of her?

Nothing had ever been hotter.

Nothing.

BELLA ANDRE & MELISSA FOSTER

She was so sexy, rocking into him as she got closer and closer to the edge, her head thrown back so that moonlight bathed her gorgeous curves in a warm glow. Her muscles tensed and her nails dug into his shoulder as he licked and loved her until her body shuddered, her inner muscles pulsating around his fingers as she cried out his name. Lifting his mouth back to hers, he took her in another hard kiss, needing to brand her as his as she rode out the last of her climax against his hand.

His heart was beating faster than it ever had as her eyes fluttered open, and she looked sated and so incredibly beautiful. "That was..." Her lips curved up into another one of those smiles that made him want to do any and everything he could to keep her smiling. "That was *amazing*."

"*You're* amazing." He kissed her again, intending it to be a sweet press of their lips this time, but he was unable to hold back his passion for her. "Your body's so responsive and you're so damn beautiful. I need to see you come for me again, Shell."

"I need it, too," she said. "And I need to make you feel as good as you just made me feel."

Holy hell, she wasn't the only one who needed that. But as she reached for the button on his jeans, he gently took her wrist.

"Tonight..." He held her gaze, made sure she could see what her pleasure did for him, that he could easily survive on nothing but a steady diet of her gasps of pleasure and the feel of limbs wrapped around him. "Tonight's for you, sweetheart."

And this time he wanted to be right there, watching her, holding her as she found her release. *Needed* to be right there as he laced his right hand with hers and held it up by her head as he used his left to stroke her again. It didn't take long for her breathing to become shallow, especially when he slid lower to take her breast in his mouth, grazing his teeth over her nipple as his fingers entered her.

"Oh...God...Quinn..."

"That's it. Come for me. Let me see how beautiful you are when you're giving yourself to me, Shell." Every word was raw with need. He knew he had no right to ask for this—not yet, not until he'd proved to her that she could trust him always—but he still had to say, "Everything, sweetheart. Give me *everything.*"

Her hips rose off the bench, and her free hand gripped his biceps so tightly he was sure she'd cut deep moons with her nails. But he could watch her come all night long and would gladly carry her marks on his body into the next day.

He held her close, loving the feel of her heart beating against his as both of them worked to catch the breath they'd just lost. Her cheeks were flushed in the moonlight and her eyes were bright when she looked up at him.

"Make love to me, Quinn."

He couldn't speak for a long moment, couldn't do anything but press his mouth to hers and wish their night didn't ever have to end. Wish that there wasn't a real world to return to. And most of all, wish that he'd never hurt her.

But he had, so nothing was simple, not even when desire rode this hot between them.

Every ounce of him throbbed with need as she lay naked beneath him, open and so very trusting and beautiful that it made reining in his desire even more difficult. But Shelley deserved more than a few nights of fun, and he knew he should pull back, give her time to be sure before they went that far.

This was new territory, and it came wrapped in new feelings that scared him and excited him in equal measure. He wouldn't do one more damn thing to blow it, even if slowing down the pace for at least another night was nearly going to kill him.

"I've never wanted anything more than I want to make love to you. But I want you to be sure. To make this decision to be with me with a clear head." With her taste still on his tongue and the heat of her skin still tingling on his fingertips, it was hard to get his synapses to fire all the way. But this was too important to screw up, so he worked to find both his focus and the right words. "This feels real between us. More real than anything I've ever felt, and I don't want to mess that up. I don't want you to wake up tomorrow and regret being with me. I hurt you once. I can't risk doing that again."

"But I'm leaving soon."

She was obviously as desperate to be closer to him as he was to her, making this an even more difficult—and even more right—decision. But what he felt for her was too big, too real, separating tonight from every sexual experience he'd ever had. He reluctantly sat up, gathered her in his arms, and gave her the truth.

"I know. Trust me. I've got the date you're leaving ingrained in my mind. I'm leaving, too, possibly sooner." The light in her eyes dimmed, and he had to pull her closer again. "That's why I want you to be sure. I don't want you to regret being close to me."

"I thought guys loved no-strings-attached flings."

"We usually do, but this...you and me. Do we feel like a fling to you?" He felt like he was already in too deep to turn away.

"No," she whispered. "Maybe it started out that way. Maybe we were both just wanting to have some fun together. But today, tonight, it feels bigger to me, too."

"I'm glad," he said, showing her just how much it meant to him with a kiss that went deep again. But knowing he needed to take her home before he went back on his promise to give her more time to be absolutely sure, he made himself draw back and reach for their clothes. "Are you free tomorrow night around seven?"

"Like I said, I'm not a big planner when I'm on vacation." She smiled and asked, "What did you have in mind?"

"I'd love to watch the fireworks with you at the cove. And then we can see how you feel about everything tomorrow night."

The fireworks were a big event on the island, and Quinn knew his family and the whole town would turn out to watch them at the resort. But he and Shelley would have privacy at the cove.

"I love fireworks," she said just above a whisper. "I even have the perfect dress already."

He pressed her hand to his lips, knowing that if he took her mouth again he wouldn't be able to stop. "Good, then it's a date."

As they sailed back to the dock, Quinn knew he was putting himself in a difficult spot by committing to meet Shelley when he had been putting off his work for so long already—but right now he just didn't care.

Shelley's bright light filled all the empty spots he hadn't known he had. She made him feel something beyond stress and irritation and made him see a world beyond the walls of his office—a world filled with vibrant colors, unbridled laughter, and boundless pleasure.

And only a total fool would miss one single second of the time an amazing woman like Shelley was willing to give to him.

Chapter Fourteen

SHELLEY LAY IN bed early the next morning replaying her date with Quinn over and over in her mind. Being intimate with him had felt so unbelievably good, so natural, so *right*. And yet, when he'd stopped them from going further, despite the fact that she'd been ready to tear his clothes off, she'd felt herself falling even deeper for him.

She could only imagine how difficult it was for him to stop short of making love to her, but the more she thought about it, the more she was glad that he had. Because things between them felt real to her, too. Real and *wonderful*. And not just because he'd known exactly how to kiss her to make her gasp with pleasure, exactly where to touch her to make her sizzle with heat.

Being with Quinn last night had been even more wonderful than she'd expected because he had obviously sensed that a part of her was still wary. It meant a great deal to her that he instinctively understood that until she could fully trust him not to hurt her again, she would need to be careful with both her heart and her body.

She couldn't stop smiling as she hugged her pillow to her chest and replayed his thrilling words: *This feels real between us. More real than anything I've ever felt, and I don't want to mess that up. I don't want you to wake up tomorrow and regret being with me. I hurt you once. I can't risk doing that again.*

And the honest truth was that his pulling back last night before they made love on his boat truly *did* help her get closer to fully trusting in him again.

A tapping sound on her window caught her attention. The pillow fell out of her arms as she jolted toward the sound. When it rang out again, she gathered the blanket around her and bolted upright.

"Shelley?"

"Quinn?" She jumped from the bed in the silk pajama top she'd put on after her bath and pulled the curtains to the side.

His baby blues smiled up at her. "Morning, sunshine. I haven't watched a sunrise on the island since I was a kid. Care to join me?" He held up a small brown bag and two to-go cups. Over his shoulder was a thick blue throw blanket.

Her heart skipped a beat. *A sunrise with Quinn?* What could be more romantic?

Yet again he was proving to her that he was nothing like her workaholic father, who would never have been up before sunrise unless there was a plane to catch or a meeting to attend. Another layer of wariness fell away, replaced with the warmth of trust.

"I'll be right out." She didn't even take the time to change, just stepped into a pair of jeans and threw a cardigan over her top, then hurried out to the porch.

Quinn smiled as she came through the door, his eyes moved slowly over her, lighting sparks all across her skin. "You're so sexy," he said in a raw voice right before he took her mouth in a kiss so full of unfettered desire that he stole her breath completely away.

She grabbed his shirt and tugged him closer, deepening the kiss. She wanted to kiss him all day long, wanted to start at sunrise and just keep on kissing him until it set again. He wrapped one strong arm around her waist, his body heating her from knees to chest and every delicious spot in between.

"God, I love kissing you." He pressed another wild, desperate kiss to her lips. "But if we keep kissing, we'll miss the sunrise."

Sunrise? She could hardly remember what that was anymore, when all she wanted to do was drag Quinn back inside, lock the door behind them...and spend the rest of the day making love.

"Won't there be another one tomorrow morning?"

His laugh vibrated through her, along with the wonderful heat of his body. "I'm trying to woo you, you know, but you're not making it easy."

"I do rather like the sound of being wooed." And she truly did, especially when she knew that Quinn wooing her rather than just thoughtlessly taking her to bed was yet another way of showing her that he could be the man she needed him to be. The man that she deserved. "So let's go see that sunrise, after all."

The sand was cool between her toes, and the predawn air still held the chill of the night, but she was warm tucked beneath his arm. Being with him this early brought back memories of the mornings she and her aunt had watched the sunrise from her aunt's deck. They'd cuddle up under a thick blanket and watch ribbons of color thread through the sky, bringing a new day, and always a new adventure, too.

"There's a house down this way that I'm thinking of renting," she said as they passed the resort.

"You really are serious about coming to the island, aren't you?"

"I'll have to look into space in town for the café and talk to my suppliers, but yes. I think I am."

Shelley pointed to the cottage on the dunes. "That's the house. It's got a gorgeous view, and it looks like it hasn't been lived in for a while. I'm going to call the Realtor today. I haven't been inside it yet, but when I peeked in the windows it looked really nice and open. I like open floor plans. It has a fireplace for the winter and—"

"A beautiful stone mantel," he finished for her as he handed her his coffee cup so he could spread out the blanket. At her surprised look, he said, "I know the house well. When I first opened my business and came back for the holidays, I almost bought it."

He sank down to the blanket and guided her down beside him. She was already addicted to the weight of his arm around her, the feel of his body beside her. She thought about how quickly her feelings had become real. Her memory of the night she and Quinn had met was still a little fuzzy because of the champagne she'd drunk, but the *feel* of that night wasn't fuzzy at all. And since spending more time with him, she *felt* him every time she thought of him, from the way his eyes washed over her skin and felt like a caress, to the warmth of his hands on her. Even the way he called her *Shell* made her heart go pitter-patter. Plus, whenever she thought about how hard he was working to prove himself to her in the aftermath of their one awful night, Shelley could feel herself relaxing into him more and more by the second.

"Why didn't you buy it?"

"My business ramped up faster than I expected, and I knew I'd rarely come home for long enough to enjoy it. I've had my eye on it for a long time, though. It's a fine property."

"I won't rent it if you want to buy it."

He opened the brown bag and handed her a chocolate croissant. He must have been listening to what she'd said on the boat about loving them, even when she thought he was too sidetracked. He scooted closer as they bit into their pastries.

"If you want to be here, Shell, you should rent it. Besides, my business is busier than ever, so I'm in pretty much the same position I was before with it."

Namely, she thought, that he was rarely on the island long enough to be able to enjoy the cute cottage. Reality came back with the weight of a dark cloud, and her perfect morning suddenly felt just a little less perfect with the realization that even if she did decide to fully trust him with her heart, he was going to be heading back to Annapolis soon. Even the chocolate melting on her tongue didn't taste quite as good anymore.

She tried to distract herself from the way her stomach dipped at the idea of him leaving. "How are things going with your grandfather and his plans for the resort? Have you had any resolution?"

"We're still waiting. My grandfather will likely take his sweet time and give us his answer when he's good and ready and not a second before. He gave us his demands and then we gave him back ours. I know that sounds harsh for family, but..." He didn't look particularly happy as he said, "But, unfortunately, that's the way it's always been with him."

She wondered again about Chandler's intentions. Why would anyone want to drive a wedge between themselves and their family? Then again, she thought with a little inward sigh, her parents did it every time they spoke, didn't they?

Still, she couldn't help but try to find a silver lining somewhere in the hopes that she could bring the smile back to Quinn's face. "Do you think there's any way that your grandfather has better, or different, intentions than it seems on the surface?"

"I overheard something that got me thinking that maybe there could be more layers to the situation than the rest of us think. But, honestly, that's probably just wishful thinking on my part. Everything is about control to him. Always has been. And probably always will." He cupped her cheek and brushed it with his thumb. "But I don't really want to talk about the resort or my grandfather, if you don't mind. I'd rather hear about where you are with your big plans to change your life."

"They are pretty big, aren't they?"

"Huge," he agreed, "but you're not the least bit afraid, are you?"

"Not of the idea of starting a new business or moving to a new place." She followed the seam of his jeans with her index finger, thinking over his question. Shelley was comfortable talking about things she loved, but she wasn't accustomed to talking about things that frightened her to anyone but Taryn. No man she'd dated had ever cared enough to ask. "But that doesn't mean other things don't scare me."

"Like what?"

She shrugged, buying time and debating whether she should open up to him in that way.

She felt like she was teetering on the edge of either falling all the way in with Quinn...or backing off from that huge risk.

Clearly able to sense her hesitation, he laced his fingers with hers and pressed another soft kiss to her lips. "I don't mean to push you too far, or faster than you're ready to go, Shell." It warmed her to hear the same sweet nickname he'd called her last night when he was giving her more pleasure than she'd ever known before. "I just want to be closer to you, to get to know you better. I've never wanted that with anyone before, but I can't help wanting to know everything about you."

The sincerity in his voice, and in every wonderful thing he'd said and done since he'd apologized to her on the boat the previous morning, sent her tipping straight toward him and had the truth falling from her lips. "I want that, too, Quinn." She paused as the step she was taking sank in. *Sharing secrets.* It was a big, trusting step. One that she realized felt completely *right.*

"I'm not afraid of normal things, like bad guys or sharks."

"Somehow that doesn't surprise me," he said with a smile. "Want me to take a guess?"

"Sure." She tried to imagine what he'd say, but he'd surprised her so many times already, she knew whatever she guessed would be wrong.

"I think you're afraid of being cast aside, like you don't matter."

Her chest tightened. "How do you...?"

He touched his forehead to hers. "Just from the little things you've said, it sounds like your parents didn't know how lucky they were to have you as their daughter."

She didn't even try to speak. She knew no words could fit past the thickening in her throat. She gazed out over the water to try to deal with how strongly his incredibly sweet— and on-point—words had affected her. Had anyone ever seen into her heart this clearly?

He cupped her cheek and stroked her jaw, both a lover and a friend as he said, "I'm sorry, Shell. I'm sorry for every single time you've ever been hurt. And I'm so damn sorry that I ever hurt you."

She looked up at him, knowing everything she was feeling was in her eyes but not wanting to hide anything from him anymore. "You already apologized. And I've forgiven you, Quinn." And between yesterday and this moment they were sharing on the sand right now, Shelley realized that she truly had. Yet that didn't change how her parents, and everyone in the world she'd grown up in, had always treated her, did it? "I suppose it's silly, isn't it, how I can be a confident businesswoman who's not afraid to start over in a strange place where I only know a handful of people, but am afraid to be ignored, or forgotten, at the same time?" She tried to smile but couldn't quite get her lips to move in the right direction. And she couldn't keep the words from continuing to spill out, either. "How I can have so many friends and yet be afraid of never finding someone who thinks I'm *enough?* Someone who loves me for exactly who I am."

THE SADNESS IN Shelley's voice tugged at Quinn's heart. How could she think she wasn't enough for anyone? She was the brightest light in his life and he'd known her only a few days.

"My mom always says that love finds us when we're busy living our lives, and that one day we realize the person we've just met or the person we've known our whole lives is the *only* person we can't live without." He'd heard her say that a million times, and yet as he repeated the words, it was as if he were hearing them for the first time.

Shelley rested her head on his shoulder. "Your mom is really wise. I like her a lot."

He ran his hand over her hair, loving how soft and full it was and wanting to tangle his hands in her curls as he kissed her while the sun rose and the seabirds began circling the shoreline. "She likes you too, Shell."

And so do I, exactly as you are.

"I'm glad you came by this morning, Quinn."

"I was getting ready to go for a run when I realized that I can go for a run any day, but I only have a few days left to watch the sunrise with you."

"You gave up your run for me?"

She sounded like he'd given up air instead of a sweaty sixty minutes. "You have no idea how special you are, do you?"

She blushed, and it reminded him of how sweet—how *perfect*—she'd looked last night on the boat.

He gently lifted her chin so she had to look at him, and even that one small touch sent his heart beating faster. "Every time we're together you make me think about things I thought I'd left behind ages ago." He had to stroke over her lower lip with his thumb, then had to follow that light caress with a kiss in the exact same place. "You make me see them all differently. That night we met at the cove, I was so pissed about being back on the island and taken away from my business at such a critical time. But then I saw you splashing in the waves, so carefree—"

"And naked. Don't forget naked." She laughed, while heat continued to spark between them, bright and hot. He was so damn glad to see that her smile was back. "That probably helped."

"Naked always helps," he agreed, smiling as he ran his fingers over the gorgeous curve of her neck and shoulders. Wanting her. Always wanting her, even as he said, "But when I saw you playing in the water, it was like my favorite cove, the place I'd used as a brooding ground, suddenly looked different. It was you, so bright and carefree, that turned that cove from a serious sulking spot into a little piece of heaven. That night I was running from everything piling up on my shoulders, trying to figure out how to get off the island as fast as possible, and then...there you were. You're the first person, the *only* person, who has not only obliterated thoughts of work, Shelley, but also made my heart pound like this. It's like everything turned from black-and-white to a kaleidoscope of color the moment I first saw you."

His heart was pouring out of his mouth and he couldn't stop it. Didn't want to stop it. Not when she deserved to know everything he was feeling. "You know what I'm most afraid of right now?" He cupped her cheek in his hand. "Of dimming your bright light. Of you realizing that I'm exactly that guy you *don't* want to be with.

A workaholic like your father and my grandfather."

"Oh, Quinn. Don't you know you're already showing me you aren't that guy? Right here, right now, sharing this moment on the beach with me when we both know you could be holed up in your room poring over contracts and getting ready for meetings. Honestly, I respect how hard you work and how successful you've become. I just—" She drew her brows together, as if she were searching for the right words. "I just want whatever man I end up with to put me on par with work. Not above it, not below, just on an equal level."

"I know I might not be the guy to be saying this when I've never been able to find any sort of balance in my life, but you deserve so much more than to be *on par* with anyone's work."

As if on cue, Quinn's phone vibrated. "How's that for bad timing?" he mumbled in an irritated voice.

She laughed. "Go ahead and answer it. You just spent an hour watching the sunrise with me, and it was like a dream come true. Only better."

He kissed her again, wanting to take his time to drink her in as the light from the sunrise poured over them both, but when his phone buzzed again, he made himself draw back to read the group text from Trent.

"Speak of the devil who looks like my grandfather." He looked up into Shelley's clear green eyes and told her, "Looks like Chandler's summoned us all to his office. He's made his decision."

Chapter Fifteen

HOW COULD ONE text lead to such conflicting feelings?

When Quinn walked Shelley back to her cottage and kissed her goodbye after confirming their plans to meet at the cove that evening to watch the fireworks, he didn't want to leave. More than anything, he wanted to spend the rest of the day with her, exploring the island and pointing out all of the places he knew she'd love. But between his grandfather's nonsense and the four e-mails he'd already received this morning from Rich about the merger, he knew he was lucky to even be able to squeeze in another few hours with her tonight.

He ran his hand roughly through his hair, trying to fit the warring elements of his mind into some semblance of normalcy. He wanted Shelley. Boy did he ever want her. But he had a business to run, and in a few minutes he'd find out if he was going to be set free to run that business—in which case he should be leaving on the next flight out of town rather than going to see the fireworks with Shelley—or if he was going to be saddled with rearranging his entire life to save the resort.

The thought of disappointing Shelley by having to cancel their date tonight slayed him. Her voice sailed through his mind. *You just spent an hour watching the sunrise with me, and it was like a dream come true. Only better.*

But *she* was the one who was better than any dream could ever be.

So he wouldn't disappoint her—or himself, damn it. No matter what happened with his grandfather, Annapolis would wait until morning.

And then after that...well, he really hoped that he and Shelley could figure out how to make a long-distance relationship work. They could see each other when he was in town, leaving her plenty of time to get her work done when he was in Annapolis.

But he already knew it wouldn't be the same as just being able to spontaneously drop by her cottage in the morning to watch the sunrise together, or to be able to make love to her every night after it had set.

Quinn's phone vibrated with a text from Rich as the elevator doors to his grandfather's suite opened. *Just got confirmation about Joseph. It's no longer a rumor. Our competition is definitely pursuing him. Big-time.*

Great. Just what he needed right now on top of everything else, to worry about losing one of their best executives to their biggest competitor.

He texted Rich back before heading toward his grandfather's office. *Find out the stakes. We'll match/beat. Whatever we have to do. Off to talk to Chandler.*

Rich texted right back. *Put your balls in a paper bag and hand them to him—it's quicker.*

Rich was right. Chandler Rockwell had them all in a very precarious position. One Quinn never imagined he'd be in.

Shelley hadn't offered him any advice on the situation. She'd simply been there to listen this morning, which he'd really appreciated. But he knew she would never put up with a situation like this. No, she'd simply change it into a situation she *did* want.

He was still floored at the idea that in just a few days she'd pretty much decided to rent a cottage and move her business. It took huge guts to risk everything by picking up and moving your company and your life. *I've never been afraid of failure. I don't entertain the idea of failure, either. I'd much rather focus on being hopeful and having fun making sure things work out the way I want them to.* Clearly, he could learn a thing or two from her playbook. Seeing his siblings hovering outside Chandler's door, Quinn knew all of them could.

He was about to speak when Sierra put a finger to her lips and pointed to Chandler's office. "Dad's in there giving him hell," she whispered.

"Dad?" His father didn't need to fight their battles. "We told him we've got this covered."

"He's been our buffer for this long," Derek reminded him in a low voice. "Did you really think he'd kowtow to Grandfather's demands now?"

Ethan stuck his head in the group, his expression fierce. People often thought that just because Ethan wasn't always shooting off his mouth like the rest of them, he was a pushover. But that was just plain wrong. In many ways, Quinn often thought that Ethan was the strongest one of them all.

"I say we barrel in and put a stop to this here and now," Ethan said, his normally relaxed voice hard and unwavering. "It's our terms or the deal is off."

"Agreed," Sierra said, already heading for the door.

As the five of them made their way into the room, they heard their father saying, "Your grandchildren are twice as capable as either you or me." Griffin was clearly furious as he leaned over Chandler's desk. "You're belittling their hard-earned successes by using the island residents as collateral for your warped need for control."

"It looks as though those capable adults are here to speak for themselves." Chandler's face was stoic as he watched Quinn and his siblings storm into the room.

Didi stood behind Chandler's wheelchair. Her lips curved up as she watched them take their places behind Griffin.

Griffin turned, catching the eye of each of them, before moving between Trent and Quinn. Trent and Quinn exchanged a knowing glance. Quinn leaned forward and eyed Derek and Ethan, who, without uttering a word, understood and nodded their approval. Sierra's wide grin confirmed that she was all in as well.

"We'd like to amend our previous offer." Trent spoke in his most professional tone. "Our offer now includes the *six* of us taking over the resort. Our other stipulations remain the same. All or nothing."

In all his years of building his shipping empire, Quinn had never felt as proud as he did right then, standing alongside his family with their shoulders squared and their chins held high. The fact that their grandfather almost looked impressed didn't escape him, and suddenly he wondered again if there actually *had* been something to the conversation he'd overheard between Chandler and Didi.

Still, Chandler sat behind his enormous desk like a king on his throne. As he'd previously done, he didn't acknowledge Didi, standing dutifully behind him. He didn't show any signs of emotion, either, beyond the hint of what Quinn had thought might be a smile, and even that was now gone. He simply folded his hands in his lap and nodded.

"Your terms are accepted. I have other things to take care of now, and I would appreciate it if you would all leave me to them."

Without another word, the six of them walked out of the room and down the wide hallway to the elevators. Once out of earshot, Quinn draped an arm around his father's shoulder.

"Way to listen to your kids, old man. We had it covered, you know."

His father's broad shoulders rose with his laugh. "You guys had it covered before you even stepped foot on this island." He embraced

Quinn, and as they stepped into the elevator, he said, "I'm so damn proud of all of you."

"Thanks, Dad." Trent blew out a breath. "Now all we've got to do is divvy up the work and figure out how to run this place."

"I've got to get out on the boat and catch some fish," Ethan said. "But I'll check back later."

"Sounds good." As the tension from Chandler's office began to funnel out of all of them, Trent elbowed Quinn. "Where were you this morning? I saw you leave before sunrise."

"I skipped my run to watch the sunrise from the beach with Shelley."

"Watching the sunrise from the sand?" Derek reached his hand under Quinn's collar.

Quinn swatted him. "What the hell?"

"Just looking for the leash, that's all." Derek let out a deep laugh as he dodged another, much harder, swat from Quinn.

"Did you bring your laptop so you could multitask while you watched it?" Sierra teased him.

"No. Jesus, you guys." He followed Sierra out of the elevator with his brothers in tow. "I am allowed to have a life, you know."

"Sure you are, but you've never wanted one before, that's all." Sierra looked beyond pleased. "I knew Shelley was special."

"Special?" Derek asked. "Wait, you mean you're not just going for the old island fling?"

Quinn slid Derek a narrow-eyed stare and growled, "Watch it." He didn't like his brother—or anyone—talking about Shelley like that.

Everyone looked surprised by his reaction, but fortunately Sierra stepped in by saying, "I've got to get back to the restaurant. When do you guys want to meet again to go over the resort stuff?"

"The fireworks show is tonight, and your mother won't allow me to miss that," his father said.

Derek mimed holding a leash this time so that no one would swat him. Everyone laughed, even though they knew it only encouraged him.

"I've got a ton of work to do, too." Quinn thought of Shelley and wrestled again with the idea of putting off work to spend the day with her. But any way he turned it, he was already way too far behind to take off for more than a few hours at the fireworks tonight.

"I know all of us are loaded down by our current schedules, but we've committed, so we need to make it happen." Trent consulted his watch. "How's five this afternoon at Sierra's?"

"Fine. Text me if anything changes." Ethan took off through the lobby.

"I'll be there at five," Derek said. "But then I've got to leave the island as soon as we have this all settled."

"You can't leave until we come up with a schedule that will appease Chandler," Trent reminded him. "We have some leeway with the ninety-five percent rule, but it's not like you can just disappear."

"One year, Trent," Derek said, his voice grim. "That's my commitment. I'll figure out the rest."

"Trent," Quinn said, "I hate to break this to you, but I'm also out of here soon." It was going to be like walking a tightrope between spending time on the island to appease his grandfather and running his own business. Just another heavy rock to add to the pile he was already carrying on his shoulders. And that was without even trying to factor in all the time he wanted to spend with Shelley.

"What the hell did you two think?" Trent shot at them. "That you could commit and then leave it to the rest of us to run? Hell, I have a ton of work to take care of with my law practice, but I'm not dashing out of here as soon as I can."

"Maybe you should be," Quinn shot back. "How are you going to manage that while you're here for a year? Or"—he couldn't help but add in the heat of the moment—"are you just planning to stick around the island, hoping that Reese will take you back?"

"This has nothing to do with Reese." Trent planted his legs and crossed his arms, challenging him, but Quinn had seen something flicker behind his brother's eyes when he'd said his ex-wife's name. "This is about family. Standing behind our commitments."

"We're all as loyal to the family as you are," Derek said. "So don't go there. I've got to get some work done. We'll talk more about the schedule at five."

"I'm standing behind my commitment," Quinn told his clearly frustrated older brother. "But I'm also overloaded at the moment with a merger to tend to and an employee who's being sweet-talked away from my business as we speak."

"A year's a long time, Quinn, so you'd better figure out how to deal with that stuff pretty darn quick."

"Boys, come on. This isn't going to solve a thing." Griff set a hand on each of his son's shoulders. "Your grandfather has a way of getting everyone up in arms. We're in this together, and no one expects you to give up your businesses. Like everything else, we'll figure this out. Together."

Knowing his father was right—just like always—Quinn blew out the breath it felt like he'd been holding for the past half hour. "Sorry, Trent. You're right. I'd never leave the family hanging. I'm just stressed. I'll see you both again at five."

With a nod to his father, Quinn headed back into the elevator. It was time to go back to his suite and finally get some work off his plate. But even as he left, he knew it wasn't going to be easy to hold his focus on reading through contracts when where he really wanted to be wasn't hunkered down over paperwork and in meetings, but getting to know the woman who was stealing his heart even better. He had visions of spending time on the beach with Shelley, showing her all the places on the island he'd loved when he was growing up. He wanted to share stories of their pasts while getting to know more about her hopes and dreams for her future.

He shut the door of his suite and forced himself to sit down at the desk, but even as he worked to focus his attention on the contract in front of him, he knew damn well that working around thoughts of Shelley would be like trying to avoid a tidal wave.

Chapter Sixteen

SHELLEY SPENT THE morning walking through the streets of town, watching families as they took in the sights. She noticed that Annabelle came outside when her shop was slow, and the shop owner next door stepped out to chat with her. Even when there was a steady flow of customers, the two women greeted a few of them at the door. Back home, the customers talked with Shelley, but when she had downtime and went out front, passersby were usually in too much of a hurry to stop and chat. It was lovely to see the difference between living in a suburban area and a more laid-back resort town.

After wandering through a few of the commercial streets and shops she'd missed the other day, Shelley took a walk through the residential neighborhoods. She stopped to talk to a woman who was tending to her garden and struck up a conversation with a group of teenagers heading down to the beach, who told her all about how cool the upcoming fireworks display would be.

Shelley didn't know how anyone could feel like Rockwell Island wasn't the best place on earth.

When she first set out to explore this morning, she'd wanted to see if what she was falling in love with had more to do with a certain tall, dark, and super sexy man—or the island itself. Taryn had always been great at playing devil's advocate, and when Shelley had called her this morning after having breakfast with Quinn, her cousin had suggested that she be sure of her motivations before she rented the cottage.

Now Shelley felt completely certain about what was truly drawing her to Rockwell Island: how warm and welcoming everyone was, along with the stunning location. Quinn was a nice bonus, but he'd been clear about going back to Maryland, and Shelley *still* wanted to be on the island.

She stopped in the middle of the sidewalk as it finally hit her in a big way. *I'm moving to Rockwell Island!* She couldn't stop smiling about her big life-changing decision.

And now that she'd made her decision, one hundred percent, she needed to know the name of the bakery where Quinn had bought the delicious croissants they'd had that morning, so that she could talk to the owner about possibly providing baked goods for the café when she moved there.

Realizing she was around the corner from Sierra's restaurant, she headed inside to see if she was there. Shelley spotted Sierra talking to two guys at the bar. They turned as she approached and she recognized them as Quinn's father and one of his brothers, although she couldn't remember which one.

"Hey, Shelley." Sierra pointed to a stool next to her father. "Have a seat. Quinn swept you away the other day before you had a chance to meet my father, Griffin, and my oldest brother, Trent. This is Shelley Walters, Quinn's friend."

"Hi." Shelley couldn't get over how attractive Quinn's entire family was, like they'd walked out of a Beautiful Human factory.

Griffin shook her hand, his smile warm and welcoming. "Hello, Shelley. So nice to meet you."

"It's a pleasure to meet you, too."

Trent's handshake was strong and just as warm. "Great to meet you, Shelley. Sierra was just telling us that you're thinking about bringing your coffee business to the island."

"I might have gotten a little excited about the idea," Sierra said with a grin. "I didn't say you were definitely doing it, though, just thinking about it."

"Actually," Shelley said, "I'm really excited about it, too. In fact, I wanted to ask if you might know where Quinn bought me the most delicious chocolate croissants. I'd like to talk to them about possibly providing baked goods for my café here on the island."

"Wait... Does this mean you're really doing it?" Sierra's eyes widened.

"Yes!" Shelley knew she must be beaming, but she couldn't help it. She was overjoyed with her decision, and Sierra's excitement made it that much better. "I am."

"Wow, you have guts. But, of course, I totally get why you've fallen in love with this place. I left the island for college, and I couldn't wait to get back here full-time. I honestly can't imagine ever living anywhere else." Sierra touched her father's hand. "Right, Dad?"

"You are my island girl." Griffin smiled at his daughter, then turned his attention back to Shelley. "My wife, Abby, mentioned that she'd met you and that she thought you'd looked familiar. Is your given name Rochelle, by any chance?"

Shelley felt her smile fade and her stomach lurch. She didn't use the name Rochelle except around her parents, who flatly refused to call her Shelley. Just hearing the name made her skin feel like it fit too tightly.

"Yes, it is," she admitted hesitantly.

She didn't want to be judged by her family's wealth—in a good way or a bad way. As an adult, Shelley had made her life what she wanted it to be. She didn't want to defend it, and she certainly didn't want to discuss her parents' diamond business.

Griffin glanced at Trent and Sierra. "Your mother has quite a memory." He turned back to Shelley. "Abby knew your aunt who lived in Eastham. I'm afraid I don't recall her name..."

"Marla. Aunt Marla." She felt the tension ease from her shoulders and hoped that if the Rockwells were going to judge her at all, they'd do it by her aunt and not her parents.

"Yes, that was it. Abby knew her years ago, and she said she remembered you visiting one summer when she and Marla were taking part in a charity auction together. She said it took her a few hours to put your face and name together with the feisty young girl she remembered."

"I'm sure I was a handful."

"Aren't all kids?" Griffin said. "Oh, and that bakery is called Savory Delights. It's located one block south from the town center and run by Brandi Marshall. Tell her I said hello."

"I can walk you over if you'd like," Trent offered.

Quinn's family was so kind. Had her parents been interrupted during a family discussion or asked about the name of something as small potatoes as a bakery in town, they would have snubbed their noses in the air and directed her to see their driver for directions. Griffin and Abby had obviously raised their children well, but she didn't want to drag Trent away from his family.

"Thank you, but I don't want to pull you away from everyone. I'm sure I'll be able to find it with no problem."

A few days ago she was setting out on a solo honeymoon just for the heck of it and now she was ready to change her life, and yet none of the Rockwells seemed to blink an eye at her spontaneity. They truly were a wonderful family.

Sierra came around the bar and hugged her. "I'm so happy that you're really doing this. If you need help with anything, just let me know. If I don't know the answer, I'm sure my father or brothers will."

"Thanks so much, Sierra. It was a pleasure meeting you both," she said to Trent and Griffin. "Please tell Abby I said hello."

As she left the restaurant and headed up the road toward the town center, she saw Eleanor standing outside the tourist information building talking with a woman around Shelley's age.

"Shelley, how's your vacation going?"

"Just lovely, thank you." She couldn't believe Eleanor remembered her name.

"Are you going to the fireworks tonight?"

"Yes, and I can't wait."

After Eleanor gave her a thumbs-up, Shelley headed south one block, passing the bank and Bayside Market, which had baskets of fresh fruits and vegetables out front. She could easily imagine herself stopping there in the afternoons to pick up fresh vegetables for dinner.

She found Savory Delights on the corner, one block south of the town center, just as Griffin had said she would. She walked up a slate path between two colorful gardens toward the front door. The sweet aroma of cinnamon and chocolate assaulted her senses before she even reached the porch of the yellow cottage-style bakery. She was practically salivating by the time she pulled open the screen door and took a step inside.

"Hello there!" A twentysomething brunette peeked up from where she was bent over, putting a tray of muffins into the display

BELLA ANDRE & MELISSA FOSTER

cabinet. She wore a pair of purple overalls, which were covered in flour. Her hair was thick and wavy, like Shelley's, and her smile was contagious. "It's a beauty out there today, isn't it?"

"It sure is, and it smells *heavenly* in here." Shelley marveled at the plethora of baked goods. There were cherry tarts, chocolate croissants, several types of muffins, scones, and cookies in one glass display counter, but it was the colorful arrangements of tarts and miniature pies called pie bites in the other display that caught Shelley's eyes. She'd never seen a bakery display with so many wonderful colors.

"Thank you. The aroma is my best marketing tool. Who can resist the smell of fresh baked goods, right? I'm Brandi, by the way."

"Hi, I'm Shelley...Walters." She silently chided herself for hesitating to reveal her last name. She refused to let worries about people connecting her with her family affect her excitement. "I'm working on bringing my specialty coffee shop here to the island, and I'd like to locally source baked goods, if possible. I had one of your chocolate croissants this morning, and it was delicious."

Brandi leaned her hip against the counter and smiled. "Ah, you're the reason Quinn

Rockwell was nosing around at five this morning. When he's in town, if you don't get up at the crack of dawn and catch him jogging, you usually don't see him at all. The man works like a dog. But he was here this morning, begging me to sell him croissants before I was even officially open for the day."

Shelley nibbled on her lower lip, thinking about Quinn. Clearly, it was even a big deal to Brandi that he'd skipped his morning run to be with Shelley.

"I've only known him a few days, but he seems..." *Wonderful, caring, attentive, intelligent, sweet...and sexy.* So sexy her heart beat faster just talking about him. "Really nice, and fun."

"Fun?" Brandi shook her head as she turned to wash her hands and spoke over her shoulder. "Maybe when he was a kid he was fun, but I think you'd be in the minority with that classification. Don't get me wrong. He's a great guy. A *really* great guy. He's loyal, he's honest, he's hardworking, not to mention easy on the eyes. But fun?" She dried her hands on a towel and shrugged. "Then again, maybe you've brought out a side in him that the rest of us haven't gotten to see in a really long time. If so," Brandi said with a grin, "my hat is off to you in a big way."

Shelley had certainly seen the struggle in Quinn to find that balance between workaholic and letting himself have a good time just enjoying being on the island—and with her, too. At first it had been almost as if he was afraid of giving in to his emotions. He had seemed to let go, at least somewhat, when they were clamming and watching the sunrise, but at other times it had been as if he'd catch himself having too much fun and felt like he needed to reel himself back. Either that, or his phone would ring and remind him of all the work he should be doing.

Everything seemed to have changed, though, since he'd apologized about the phone call. Now he didn't seem to be holding back his emotions with her at all. If anything, he was even more attentive than before. Shelley didn't need anyone to take their hat off to her. It would be more than enough to know that Quinn was happier now than he'd been in a very long time.

"So, you said you're going to open a coffee shop on the island?" Brandi asked. "I'm sure it's going to do really well—we definitely need a good one here—and I'd love to see if we can work something out. All of my products are organic, and I do all the baking, so we'd have to coordinate a schedule that fits both of our needs, but I think we could make it work. Once you have the details figured out, why don't you give me a call or just come by again so that we can figure everything out?" Brandi grabbed a business card from a holder by the register. "I could even make special items just for your shop that aren't sold here."

"That would be wonderful. I would love to have an exclusive menu. I'm really taken with your tarts. They're so colorful."

Brandi sighed dreamily and looked out the window, as if she were recalling a fond memory. "I took over this business from my grandmother, and she believed that colorful foods were as important as giving your child the right name or being kind to others. That's what she used to tell me, as if the three things were related."

"She sounds very special." A wave of longing passed through Shelley as memories of Aunt Marla rolled in again.

"She was. She passed away last year, but she left a legacy for me to live up to. From peach tarts to summer-berry cream pie and strawberry-lemon pastries. Thanks to my grandmother, I can't bake anything without wondering what color it should be." She reached into the display and handed Shelley a peach and blueberry tart. "Here, try this. It was her favorite."

Shelley took a bite and closed her eyes, savoring the taste of the sweet fruit, a delicious contrast to the smooth, buttery taste of shortbread. "Your grandmother would be very proud of your baking. I've never tasted anything so magical."

"Magical? That's exactly what my grandmother used to say, that because baking came from the heart, it added flavors of magic to our lives. I think you would have liked her, and she would have liked you, too. As much as Quinn Rockwell obviously does."

By the time Shelley left half an hour later, she had gotten the scoop on what to expect with on- and off-season customer traffic. Apparently the resort was a major income producer for the whole town. They held a winter ball, and hosted a fall festival and a spring carnival, bringing enough tourists in year-round to sustain the other island businesses. Shelley was confident that she could make this work, and not only that, but from what Brandi had told her, most of the tourists came back year after year, and they loved talking with the local shop owners. It sounded as if Shelley's love of getting to know people would be well received.

She walked down the road toward her cottage as she called her cousin.

"You're doing it," Taryn said when she answered the phone.

Shelley laughed. "How'd you know?"

"Because your energy comes through in your ringtone."

"You're such a goof."

"A goofy genius, you mean! So you decided that you love the island, and you're definitely not moving there just to hook up with Mr. Orgasm, right?"

"Taryn!" Shelley felt her cheeks heat up and looked around, as if anyone walking by could know what her cousin had said...or could know just how blissfully good Quinn made Shelley feel every time he kissed her, every time he touched her, every time he made her come apart for him.

"Hey, it's been a long time for you. You deserve every orgasm you can get."

"I really do, don't I?" Taryn was like the sister she'd never had, and Shelley loved her dearly. "I can't wait to get settled and have you down to show you the island."

"I want to make you a proper island dress first. I'm thinking coconut shells over your boobs and a grass skirt."

"For Halloween maybe!" Shelley said as they both laughed. "Although...I was wearing the honeymoon dress you made me when I met Quinn."

"No, you weren't. You were buck naked."

"Oh God, yes. You're right. I was completely naked when he first saw me." Heat flooded her cheeks again, even though just last night he'd stripped away her clothes and given her unbelievable pleasure. Tonight, thankfully, held promises of even more. So much more that, for a moment, she lost her breath just imagining the hard, heavy thrill of Quinn moving over her. *Into* her.

"I'm so excited that you're doing this, Shell. You're the only friend I have who's brave enough to create her own destiny. I love getting to live vicariously through you."

They continued to chat as she walked back to her cottage, where Shelley was surprised to find a note taped to her door. She untaped the folded paper and a business card fell to the ground. She picked it up as she read the handwritten note that accompanied it.

> *Shell,*
> *I was thinking of you this morning and stopped by the Realtor's office to check on the house on the dunes. I checked with her and the house is still for rent. I went to school with her, so you can mention my name if you want, although it may not carry any*

weight. I was also really hoping to see you and sneak in a kiss before I get back to slogging through contracts. But now I have no idea how I'll focus on a damn thing when what I really want is to have you in my arms. I can't wait to see you tonight.

—Quinn

She sank down to the porch step, thinking, not for the first time, about how thoughtful Quinn was. The idea that he'd reached out to the Realtor to help her make the transition to the island easier was beyond anything she'd ever expect anyone to do, much less someone as busy as him.

Quinn had been such a wonderful surprise her first two days on the island. At least, until his ignoring her for his phone call had cut her right where it hurt. But then he'd surprised her over and over, not only with countless heartfelt apologies...but also by freely giving his extremely limited time to her again and again. And by sharing himself with her, not just his kisses and the sweetest pleasure she'd ever known, but his feelings, too.

You're the first person, the only *person, who has not only obliterated thoughts of work, Shelley...but also made my heart pound like this.*

As his words from this morning resonated in her head and she looked down at his note, it felt to her that their connection had touched Quinn as deeply as it had taken root in her. And as she thought through her emotions, she was aware of the faith she had in him, faith like she'd had with only two other people in her entire life—Aunt Marla and Taryn. But this felt even stronger.

Because the truth that she could no longer deny—a truth that she no longer felt like she needed to deny for any reason, not out of wariness or to try to keep her heart safe—was that Quinn was the piece of herself she never knew was missing, too. When she was with him, she knew he accepted her for who she was, quirks and all.

Plus, she thought as she lifted her fingertips to her lips, his kisses were utterly addicting. Heck, every inch of him was addicting, with everything bursting into brilliant color every time he touched her.

"Hello? Earth to Shelley."

"Oh, sorry, Taryn. Quinn left me a note. He said he came by to give me the number for the Realtor handling the cottage I want to rent." *And for a kiss.* One she also couldn't wait to have.

Tonight couldn't come soon enough. Especially since this time she had no intention of ending the night early.

"I know I told you just to go out and have fun this week," Taryn said, "but Quinn is becoming more to you than just an island fling, isn't he?"

Shelley didn't so much as pause before telling her cousin exactly what was in her heart. "Much more, T. So much more."

Chapter Seventeen

QUINN IGNORED THE first knock on his suite door that afternoon. He should have had his feedback on the contracts for the merger in Rich's hands yesterday. Taking time to meet with his family and then meeting Shelley for fireworks at the cove would mean that he'd have to work through the night to get the information to his business partner by the morning.

Though he knew getting his work done was important, he'd missed spending the afternoon with Shelley and bantering with his siblings, even if it was only for a few minutes here and there. He realized that he might have even missed seeing his grandfather for a few minutes, strange as that was to admit to himself. The old man wasn't exactly warm or loving, but as cold as Chandler was, he'd always been a stable force in the Rockwell family. Quinn couldn't actually remember his grandfather ever *not* being there. He may have been standing stoic-faced in the background, but he was there for Quinn's graduations, for his boating races, for every meaningful event when he was growing up.

Winning races and graduating with high honors were expected by his grandfather, and Quinn respected his expectations. It had fueled Quinn to work harder, as he'd always prided himself on becoming *more* successful than Chandler, no matter what the cost.

But being back on the island and spending time with Shelley had him wondering more and more why he felt so compelled to surpass his grandfather.

Whose praise was he trying to win?

And what had he given up to do it?

Because he sure as hell didn't need Chandler to praise him. At least not anymore.

When another knock sounded on his door, he finally got up to pull it open.

Trent took in Quinn's open, wrinkled dress shirt. "You taking a nap?"

"Yeah, right." He walked back into the room, leaving Trent to follow. "I've got a ton of work to get through before meeting Shelley tonight."

"You'll have to do it later. We need to head over to Sierra's for the five o'clock meeting. And speaking of our sister's restaurant," Trent added as Quinn mumbled a curse while gathering his papers and stacking them on the table, "I saw your girlfriend there earlier today."

For a moment Quinn was taken by surprise that his brother would jump to *girlfriend* so quickly. But then he grinned. "I'm a seriously lucky bastard, aren't I? My girlfriend is gorgeous, fun, and intelligent. And for some reason, she actually likes being with me."

"She seems great," Trent said. "Really great."

But Quinn could see there was something more his brother wanted to say to him. "Spit it out."

"Look," Trent finally said, "as long as I've known you, you don't have *fun* with women. You relieve stress, then go back to work. We all do, except Sierra—at least that I know of."

Quinn gave him a sideways look. Sierra would always be their little sister, no matter how old she got or how strong she was, and he didn't want to imagine her handling relationships in the same way that he and his brothers often did. Quinn grabbed his room card and shoved it in his pocket, then pulled the door open.

"And your point is?"

"We've all got a ton on our plates right now, and despite all that, when you're at your busiest, Shelley's gotten to you. But if you're not careful..." Trent shook his head. "All I'm saying is don't make the same mistakes I did. I put my career first with Reese, but it turns out that legal briefs are pretty cold company when they're all you have left. I know you guys are still in the early stages of a relationship, but sometimes when it's right—" His brother ran a hand over his face, looking terribly uncomfortable. "Hell, you know what I'm trying to say, right?"

Quinn nodded and said, "Sure," and then mulled over his brother's comments all the way to Sierra's restaurant.

He hadn't wanted to lead Shelley on by promising her something he wasn't capable of giving, because if there was one thing he had always thought he knew about himself, it was that work came first. Except...it hadn't for the last few days. What's more, the thought of working all the time didn't seem appealing anymore. Not when he was suddenly seeing, and remembering, all the things he was missing out on by spending hour after hour, day after day, locked up in his office.

And not when every second he and Shelley spent together was bringing her deeper into his heart.

No, he definitely wasn't leading her on. His intentions were clear—in his mind, and in his heart. Now he just needed to figure out a way to make the pieces of his life fit together while keeping Shelley as his top priority.

On one hand, that was an easy task, because she was the one person who was always on his mind.

On the other hand, he instinctively knew that promising and wanting to make changes— and really making those changes—were two very different things.

But Quinn knew beyond a shadow of a doubt that he was up for the challenge.

At the Hideaway, Quinn sank into the chair beside his mother and kissed her cheek. "Hey, Mom. I haven't seen you much. How's your week been?"

"Good," Abby said with a smile as she touched his cheek. "Full of family, friends, and glassblowing, so I'm perfectly happy." Their mother had always enjoyed working with glass. She'd had a studio built on their property, and she sold the vases, bowls, and other items she made at the resort gift shop as well as at several galleries in town.

BELLA ANDRE & MELISSA FOSTER

"How about you, honey?" his mother asked. "You're working so hard, and you look tired. I was hoping that since you had to be back on the island, it might give you an excuse to take some time off."

His mother never made Quinn or his siblings feel guilty when they didn't make it home for months at a time. She was simply grateful for the time they did have together. Shelley reminded him of his mother in that way. She wasn't demanding of his time, and she took nothing for granted. Even her bucket list was filled with sentimental wishes, not grandiose endeavors.

"I've taken time off while I've been here," he assured her.

"Do you mean the afternoon you left with Shelley?"

"We went clamming."

"Clamming? Really?"

Quinn smiled at the surprise in his mother's voice and the way she was now looking at him with a new light in her eyes.

"Why, Quinn...are you smitten?"

For a moment he was surprised by his mother's question, in the same way he'd been initially surprised when Trent had called Shelley his girlfriend. But just as he had in the hotel suite with his brother, Quinn found himself enjoying the declaration.

Because if being smitten meant coming completely alive from the inside out every time he thought of Shelley—and definitely every time he touched her—then it was right on the money.

"We're planning a family dinner on Wednesday," his mother said, her grin now matching his. "Why don't you bring Shelley with you?"

Griffin leaned in closer to Abby. "I'm sorry to interrupt, but is it okay if we get started?"

"Of course." Griffin stole a quick kiss, then settled back into his chair and addressed his children.

"You kids know your mother and I are proud of you, but we want to tell you again how much it means to us that you've come together for the good of the residents of Rockwell Island." Griffin smiled at Abby, who had settled her hand over his. "Someone raised you right, and I give that credit to your mother."

"Please, Griff. Let's not get all sappy. We both raised them right, but even we can't take credit." Her warm gaze met each of theirs. "We might have provided the foundation, but each of you kids made yourselves who you are. Life is full of choices and opportunities, and we're proud of the choices you've made for yourselves."

She turned her gaze to Quinn and said, "And you'll have many more choices to make. Some imminent, some in the distant future. But as long as you always make them with your heart as much as your head, I know you'll always make the right ones."

"We'd never turn our back on the island, Mom," Sierra said. "How could we? It raised us as much as you guys did."

Boy, wasn't that the truth? From the cove being Quinn's place to unload and work through his teenage angst, to learning patience by sailing, clamming, and troubleshooting his way through fixing boats. They learned about community by assisting residents in securing their vessels before storms and fixing them afterward. After the hurricane a few years back, when some residents suffered tremendous damage to their homes, the community came together to help, opening their homes and making meals for those in need. Even Chandler had opened a wing of the resort to be used as shelter for those who had lost their homes and offered free meals at the resort's restaurant. Quinn knew Shelley would have also pitched in any way she could have if she'd lived on the island back then.

"Do you agree, Quinn?" Trent asked.

Damn, he hadn't even heard the question. "Sorry, I lost the thread for a second there."

"We're talking about positions," Ethan repeated for him. "Dad should be named as president of the resort, don't you agree?"

"Without a doubt."

Of course their father deserved the highest position at the resort. In Quinn's opinion, no better man had ever walked the earth. Griffin had taught them how to sail, how to play baseball. He'd taught Quinn how to rebuild a boat's engine alongside the deckhands. He'd given him the courage to ask out his first date and laughed with him after his prom. *You did good, son. You got your first taste of what it's like to let a woman lead you around by the nose.* Quinn smiled at the memory. His father hadn't meant it in a demeaning way. His love for Abby was evident in everything he did. It was in the way he looked at her, the way he touched her every time he passed, and when he spoke of her, adoration laced every word. He was a good man, and Quinn was proud to have been raised by him.

"As far as the other duties," Trent said, "I've been going over the current infrastructure. Chandler has directors in each division, but it doesn't appear that he's ever given them full authority. It seems like he's always had his hands in the negotiations in every department. Am I reading this information incorrectly, Dad? I reviewed the contracts from suppliers and the files. It seems he's still overseeing everything but not doing such a good job of it lately."

"As you all know, your grandfather can be quite controlling." Their father paused as they all chuckled at that understatement. "He's a shrewd negotiator, and since he lives and breathes the resort, he'd never let anything slip. But this last year, as his health worsened, so did his ability to keep up."

"Then it's time we get control of things before they start falling apart," Ethan said. "I think each of us should head up a division. Sierra and I know the staff better than everyone except Dad, so I think it makes sense to make Sierra the VP of the Restaurant and Food Service division, and I should oversee the Employee Relations and HR. Trent, obviously you should be VP of all things legal, and, Derek, you're a wiz at business and finance, so it makes sense for you to oversee those departments. And, Quinn, you're a master at corporate management and fleet."

"Does everyone agree?" Trent looked for confirmation from the others.

"It makes sense, but don't forget I'm out of here in a year," Derek reminded them.

"God, Derek," Sierra snapped. "We all know how you feel about staying here. You're giving us a year—we get it."

"Unless Didi gets to him first," Ethan said under his breath.

"She's with Chandler every single minute of every day," Derek scoffed. "You think I have a death wish?"

"What's next?" Quinn said to get them back on track since he still had a boatload of work to do before going to see Shelley tonight.

"I'll work up the corporate docs over the next few days," Trent said. "But we all still need to address the three of us going back and preparing our other businesses for our stay on the island." Trent directed this part of the conversation to Derek and Quinn, as the only others who had a business off the island to maintain.

Quinn knew that his siblings trusted them to take care of their end of the bargain, as he intended to, but he also knew it would be an uphill battle to make both businesses work without hiring someone to manage some of his responsibilities for his own business. "I'll deal with it," he assured them. Somehow, some way, he'd figure out how to make everything fit in his life. RBE, the resort, and most important, Shelley.

"Besides, it's not like he'll stay in Maryland for good," Sierra said with a little smile playing on her lips. "He'll want to come back to see Shelley now that she's decided to move her business to the island. Right, Quinn?" Before he could answer, she added, "I saw Brandi today and she said she met Shelley, too, and she loved her. I mean, how can you not? She's so easy to talk to, so smart and full of energy, and excited about moving to the island. I also heard that you picked up chocolate croissants *very* early this morning."

Quinn knew that his behavior had been completely different from the way it had been since he'd left for college, so he wasn't surprised that people noticed. He was, however, more than a little surprised by how much he *liked* the way he'd been spending his time, not working twenty-four-seven, but clamming and sailing and watching sunrises and kissing Shelley.

He gave his mother a kiss on the cheek, then stood up. "If we're done here for now, I've got to take care of a few things before heading out to the fireworks tonight." Knowing there was no point in trying to hide anything from his family—and not seeing any reason that he would want to anyway when it came to Shelley—he lifted his brows to all of his siblings' curious gazes and added, "With Shelley."

The last thing he saw before walking away were his mother's and sister's huge smiles.

Chapter Eighteen

QUINN SPENT THE next several hours in his suite with his nose buried in a thick document, trying to concentrate on the impending merger. But every time he started working through their strategy, the meeting with his family came rushing back.

How was he going to fulfill both commitments? He needed to be on the island to run the resort. If that hadn't been made clear enough by his grandfather, it certainly had been pounded home by his siblings, and he had no intention of letting them down. He didn't want to let Rich and the company they'd worked so hard to build together down, either.

And then there was Shelley...and the fact that every time Quinn thought of her, he not only heated up a good dozen degrees, but his heart also did this flippy thing in his chest.

Smitten.

He looked out the balcony door into the darkness. When had the sun gone down? Yet again, he hadn't even noticed it setting. He'd bet Shelley had not only noticed, but she'd watched the sunset and delighted in its beauty.

She had a successful business, and yet she was somehow able to push all the administrative stuff that went along with running it out of her head enough to enjoy a week's vacation. Whereas Quinn hadn't done that. *Ever.*

The alarm on his phone reminding him it was time to head down to the cove for his date with Shelley went off a second before his phone rang. *Rich.*

As soon as Quinn picked up, his business partner immediately launched into a laundry list of potential issues with the merger. By the time Rich finally paused for breath, Quinn glanced up at the clock on the wall and his stomach sank. It was five after nine.

Damn it. He was blowing it again!

"Rich, I've got to go."

He hung up before Rich could respond. Quinn wanted so badly to earn Shelley's trust, and on the boat last night she'd opened herself to him even after he'd hurt her. He shouldn't have taken Rich's call, or he should have at least paid more attention to the time.

He took the stairs two at a time, then ran out of the resort and through throngs of people waiting to watch the fireworks.

"Hey, Quinn."

He turned at the sound of Ethan's voice and spotted him standing with Derek and Sierra, with Chugger leashed at his side. Chugger whined to be set free the second he saw Quinn. Quinn reached down and loved up the pup for half a second.

"Can't talk. I'm late to meet Shelley."

Quinn spun on his heels and sprinted toward the beach. He checked his watch again—*ten after*. He sped up his pace, pushing himself to beat the start of the fireworks. Each step kicked up sand in all directions as he rounded the boulders and entered the secluded cove beach.

He saw Shelley tucked in the darkness by the trees on the other side, pulling a pretty scarf over her shoulders as she walked to the edge of the cove and let the water trickle over her toes, mesmerizing him as she had the first night he'd seen her. He quickly closed the distance between them.

"I'm so sorry." He gulped air. "I got stuck on a call. I'm so damn sorry, Shelley. I shouldn't have answered the phone and—"

"You're here now." She was smiling as she took his hand.

He'd left her waiting and she was *smiling*, holding his hand like he hadn't let her down, turning up the clarity meter once again. Forcing Quinn to see himself more clearly—and he still didn't like what he saw. Especially when his biggest fear was that he'd dim the bright light inside of her with his behavior.

"I wanted tonight to be perfect for you. I want so badly to be with you. But my work habits are ingrained, almost instinctive at this point." Damn it. It sounded like an excuse, and he didn't want to make those anymore. Not to himself. And definitely not to her. "There are so many changes I want to make. So many changes I *need* to make. Because I already care for you so much. So damn much that the last thing I want to do is to keep disappointing you."

She stepped in close and pressed her hand to his thundering heart. "You're only ten minutes late." There was no anger simmering behind her beautiful green eyes. "All that matters is that you wanted to be here and now you *are* here."

He'd never needed or wanted anyone the way he needed Shelley right here, right now. She was the light that was missing in his life. He wanted to take her acceptance at face value, the openness and trust she was offering. He wanted to take her in his arms and kiss her until she forgot his faults—until *he* forgot them, too.

But he also wanted to be the man she deserved...and that started with coming clean, laying himself on the line for her, and not allowing either of them to gloss over the things that might only end up bringing her pain.

"I will work my damnedest to be the man you deserve, and I am determined not to become just like Chandler, who hurt the people who used to love him so badly that now he has to trick them into being near him. I don't want to do that to you, Shelley. It would kill me to know that I had."

Quinn saw the blanket she'd laid out, the bottle of wine and wineglasses sitting in a wicker basket. His stomach knotted, and he scrubbed his hand down his face to try to gain control of the self-loathing eating away at him, but it was like an unstoppable force now. One that had him telling her, "You deserve a guy who will *always* put you first."

She drew her shoulders back and raised her chin. "Yes, I do. And you deserve a woman who knows that ten minutes is not a tragedy."

"I set an alarm so that I wouldn't be late by getting lost in my work—"

She touched the center of his chest as her lips curved up at the corners. "You set an alarm?"

"Yes, but then Rich called right when it went off, and I shouldn't have answered it."

She shook her head, and her voice went softer even as her smile grew bigger. "You set an *alarm*, Quinn. It's sweet and thoughtful...and so wonderfully *you.*"

"But, Shell—"

She pressed a finger over his lips. "Whatever you're going to say. Don't.

You don't get to make the call on my feelings. I do. My life, my body, my heart. My choice." He could see that she wasn't holding anything back from him now as she said, "And I choose you."

"Shelley..."

"No," she whispered, as crackles and booms sounded in the distance. Bright sparks of blue, greens, and white reflected in her eyes as fireworks exploded above the bay. "You make me feel things I've never felt before. Yes, you messed up. Twice. Well, we'll call it one and a half times, because ten minutes hardly counts. But I don't believe for one second that you're destined to hurt me, Quinn. And I've met your grandfather, so I know for a fact that even if you do share some of the same qualities, you're *not* just like him, and you never could be. But I also believe that beneath that gruff old man is a softer, kinder heart, so maybe you are alike in ways that he just hasn't shown us yet."

"Shell...how can you be so positive and so forgiving?" Forcing her to take an honest look at what he'd done was the hardest thing he'd ever done.

"Stop it. Just stop and pretend for a second that you're not Quinn Rockwell. Pretend that you're just *Quinn*. Because the Quinn that I'm getting to know, the Quinn who's seeping deeper and deeper into my thoughts and my heart, is a guy who got caught up in the whirlwind of success. He's a guy who earns the respect of everyone who meets him and built a hugely successful business. Yeah, I Googled you. I know all about your shipping empire. You should be proud of that empire, Quinn, but you're *not* the company. And you might have fallen into a pattern of work being your life..."

She reached for his hands as the lights of the fireworks showered them in hues of color. Her eyes softened, and her voice followed. "But I've seen so much of the man inside. You're funny, and caring, and I know that if you let me down, even by just ten minutes, you feel it all the way from your head to your toes. If you think I don't see that in your eyes, or feel it coming off of you in waves, you're wrong. Selfish men don't watch the sunrise or leave flowers on women's doorsteps. They don't leave hangover remedies for a woman they just met. They don't carry a woman to bed and not take advantage of her. I'm sure you left work undone to be here tonight, didn't you?"

When he nodded, she said, "Selfish men don't do that, either."

"How can you have such faith in me?" He touched his forehead to hers, wanting desperately to believe what she was saying.

"Because you're a good man, Quinn. A *wonderful* man. And you're *trying*. Trying to make changes for the better. Trying not to be consumed with work all the time. Trying to think up ways to make me smile every day. Maybe you don't recognize that. I don't know how you can't, but I see it. I see it in your eyes, feel it in your touch. I always have, right from the first moment you picked me up and carried me out of the water. Naked, I might add," she said with that wicked glint in her eyes that he loved so much.

He saw her faith in him in the trust in her eyes...and when he drew her in close, he felt it in the steady and sure beat of her heart.

"I'm falling for you, Shelley, and it scares me. Not because I'm afraid of falling. Hell, I know I'm the luckiest guy in the world to have met you. But because I don't want to ever hurt you. Even by accident."

"Then don't. You control your life, Quinn, not anyone else."

He knew she was right. And yet he sure didn't feel like he'd been in control of his life lately. It seemed like everyone wanted a piece of him, when all he wanted was Shelley. Which was why he felt compelled to add, "I don't want to change you. I don't want to turn you from the spontaneous, carefree woman you are into someone who's tied down by my life. Tied down by me."

"I'm too stubborn to let anyone ruin my fun. You've made my days better—and my nights sexier—than I ever could have imagined. I'm falling for you, too, Quinn. And," she added with a gorgeously naughty smile that heated up every place he'd ever felt cold, "there's only one way I'll ever let you tie me down. And believe me, when you do, we're *both* going to love it."

"Shelley..." Her name came in a whisper of relief. "What I want more than anything is to keep seeing you. More of you. Wherever you are and wherever I am, I want to figure out a way to make it work."

"I want that, too, but..." She paused before saying, "Maybe we shouldn't figure out all the details tonight."

"Why not?"

She was silent for a long moment before finally answering. "Because I don't want you to feel like I'm just another part of your life that's pressuring you, or something you'll feel like you need to run away from because you have way too much on your plate already."

God, she was honest. And strong.

Smitten didn't begin to describe what he felt for her.

"I don't want to run from you, Shell." He lowered his lips to hers as he said, "That's the last thing I want."

Their mouths collided, and his fingers tangled in her hair as more crackles and booms sounded in the distance. Quinn scooped her into his arms and carried her to the blanket a few feet away, lowered her onto her back, and followed her down, her body soft beneath him.

And as he gazed into her eyes, he gave her more of himself than he'd ever given anyone.

He gave her his heart.

WITH QUINN LEVERED above her, looking into her eyes, Shelley knew he was finally letting his guard down. Completely. He was opening up to her and letting her in, and in that unguarded state, she saw all of him. Not just the businessman or the brother, or the suitor or the guy who had shown up a little late with his heart on his sleeve for their date. She saw the whole of him from the inside out. She saw his big heart, his playful side—and his fierce desire to be the man she deserved.

As his lips met hers again, she closed her eyes and slid her hands beneath his shirt, desperate to feel the hard planes of his back and the warmth of his skin. His kisses were all-consuming, as if he wanted to climb into her skin and possess her.

She wanted to possess him, too. Her body pulsed with desire as his tongue trailed along her collarbone, then lower, to the arc of her breast, along the neckline of her dress. She pulled at his shirt, fighting for more of him, to feel his skin against hers.

Shelley wanted so much in that moment. She wanted *everything*. The heat of his skin against hers. His heartbeat pounding into hers. His lungs swallowing her gasps of pleasure. His groans vibrating all the way through to her soul. Hands grasping, blood rushing, mouths roaming. His talented mouth loving every inch of her body.

Only Quinn made her heart race this fast.

Only Quinn made her rib cage feel too tight to keep her heart inside.

Only Quinn made her want to leap into his arms and never let go.

An explosion of lights high in the sky brought Quinn's eyes to hers. A smile danced across his lips, but it was the liquid heat in his eyes that had her reaching for the button of his jeans. He'd bared his soul to her, and now she wanted the rest of him bared, too, so that she could pleasure him as he'd pleasured her the other night.

"Shelley…"

He slid his hand up her thigh, kissing her deeply, the heat of his hand searing into her skin. She pressed her hips to his, her anticipation mounting and a moan of need escaping her lungs. It had been a long time since she'd lost herself in a man, but that was exactly what was happening with Quinn. She had no control, couldn't stop her feelings for him if she wanted to. And she *didn't* want to. Didn't want to hold back any part of herself when she was with him. Not anymore. Never again.

She tugged at his shirt again, and he rose, eyes as black as night, tearing off his shirt with one strong arm. *My God*, he was beautiful. Masculine and perfectly formed.

She couldn't slow her roving hands as they played over his muscles. She flicked her tongue over his nipple. His skin was hot and salty, his muscles taut, and when she licked him again, the groan that came from deep within his throat made heat coil inside her. She teased him with her tongue as his hands sought her breasts, and—*Good Lord*—the man knew just how to touch her to make her whole body hum.

His hands moved from her breasts to her belly and finally to her panties.

When they were out on the boat in the moonlight, Quinn had undressed her with not just his hands, but his mouth, dropping kisses on every bare patch of skin he'd revealed. But she didn't have the patience for that kind of teasing tonight, so she quickly wiggled out of her clothes. Thankfully, he moved just as swiftly, pulling off his own clothes as the fireworks display illuminated their bodies in quick bursts of colorful lights.

When they were both naked, Shelley pushed him onto his back, empowered by the cool night air and the heat in his gaze. She never broke their connection as she ran kisses down the length of his body, earning another groan from him as he fisted his hands in the blanket. His jaw clenched and his hips rose off the blanket as she loved him with her mouth.

"Shell—"

She ignored his plea, stroking him with her hand and teasing him with her tongue.

"Shell. I need to have you. *All* of you." Reaching for her with both hands, he swept her beneath him again. "I can't wait another second," he said in a voice thick with desire.

As their mouths crashed together, she rocked against him, craving him, needing to feel him inside her. Needing him to complete her with his body the same way he had with his soul.

Her legs locked around his waist, and his hands came up to cup her hips as he pulled her even closer. So much closer than she'd ever been with anyone else. So much closer than she'd ever wanted to be with anyone else.

"Please," she begged. "I need you too, Quinn. *Now.*"

He reached for his jeans and dug protection out of his wallet, and was fully sheathed by the time he went up on his knees, looking so magnificently virile Shelley's mouth went dry. Had there ever been a man this sexy? This beautiful?

And all *hers*.

He brushed her lower lip with his thumb, and the simple touch sent waves of excitement through her. "Are you sure?"

His need to protect her only made her want him more.

"I've never been more sure about anything in my life."

That was all the invitation he needed, and then he was threading his fingers through hers and leaning forward over her so that they were only a breath apart. But even that was too far for her tonight. His gaze was dark and intense with need—and with so much emotion she nearly came apart right then and there from nothing but looking into his eyes—as he slowly began to move into her. Deeper, and then deeper still, until she was utterly lost to everything but the wonder of it all.

To the wonder of *Quinn.*

*Oh God...*There were no words for this much pleasure. For bliss that she could feel all the way down to the tips of her toes. No way to do anything but try to take it all in, the way their bodies fit so perfectly together even as emotions wrapped around them like a blanket.

"*Beautiful.*" He moved his hands to tangle one in her hair, while the other on her hip brought them even closer together. "You're so damn beautiful, Shell."

The raw emotions—and desperate need— in his voice swamped her. She moved urgently beneath him, craving more friction. More heat.

More soul-deep pleasure.

He grinned, as if he held a secret she wasn't privy to, then took her mouth in a slow, sensual kiss.

"Quinn. *Please.*" The desperation in her voice was nothing compared to the need swelling inside her.

"In a rush, sweetheart?" His voice was staggeringly rough, his kisses painfully soft.

"No. *Yes.* You're torturing me."

But he just kept moving in slow, controlled movements. Slow, sweet torture over and over again, which stole the few brain cells Shelley was relying on to remain coherent.

And when he slid both hands beneath her hips so she could take him gloriously deeper, her toes curled as every thrust hit just the right spot to make her gasp time and time again.

"*Quinn...*" Another plea.

"Patience," he whispered against her mouth. "It always pays off." One hand slid from her hips to the center of her arousal, while his hips began to move faster and faster, taking her right up to the edge before he slowed again, driving her out of her mind. "More. I just want more time with you."

No one had ever said anything so sweet— or so sexy—to her before, and his words, along with the feel of all of his hard heat over and inside of her, brought her right to the edge of a release that promised to swallow her whole.

A beat later, Quinn's entire body was corded tight as he finally gave her exactly what she needed to climb even higher and then higher still. When her insides shattered, he was right behind her, whispering her name over and over.

They lay with their bodies braided together for a long while as their jagged breathing returned to normal. Shelley reveled in the feel of Quinn's heart beating against hers. The sounds of the waves and the leaves rustling on the trees brought the world back into focus as she opened her eyes to stare up at the stars.

That first night at the cove before she'd gotten too tipsy, she'd looked up and found the brightest star to make a wish on. It was the same wish she'd made since she was a child. *Give me a guiding light. Lead me to my forever home.* Now she felt as if someone up there must have been looking out for her, because she'd found the place she wanted to put down roots.

Nestled in the safety of Quinn's arms, Shelley knew that she was finally right where she was supposed to be.

Home.

Chapter Nineteen

QUINN LAY AWAKE in Shelley's bed as dawn sneaked in through the curtains. Her cheek rested against his chest, each breath whispering across his skin.

Quinn couldn't remember the last time he'd wanted to spend the entire night with a woman. And yet here he was with Shelley, hoping never to wake up alone again—even though he knew that it was inevitable since he was going to be heading back to Maryland soon.

He had been working through logistics for the past hour, thoughts of returning to the island to see Shelley in clear focus. He figured he could probably make it happen at least once every few weeks, sneak a day in here or there between meetings. The thought of returning to his empty house in Annapolis made him feel as lonely as he had in his resort suite the night he'd screwed up and Shelley had enjoyed the bonfire by herself.

His gaze moved around the room. In the span of a few short days, she'd made the cottage feel warm and homey. She'd moved the candles from the mantel and bookshelves to the windows. She'd even moved the chair that had been in the corner of the room that first night he'd met her to beneath the window, and a paperback novel sat on the cushion with a throw blanket covering one wooden arm. He wondered what Shelley's house looked like, but could easily guess at all the simple touches that would make her house feel like *home*.

Shelley stirred beside him and pressed her lips to his chest. "How can you look so deep in thought this early in the morning?"

He shifted her beneath him, and she smiled up through sleepy eyes. "Because of you, Shell. You've jumbled my business-oriented brain and turned it into something else altogether."

She rocked her hips against his arousal. "Mm. Something naughty, perhaps?"

"Always," he said. And the truth was that it would be so easy—and so damn good—just to lose himself in making love with her again. But he didn't feel right about keeping anything from her. Not when she needed to know. "Shell, Chandler accepted our terms yesterday. We're taking over the resort. So the good news is that I'll be here pretty often."

"Of course I'm thrilled that you'll be here more, but I'm sure it's going to be really difficult to run your business and be tied to the resort at the same time." Her eyes widened as she said, "Wait... Didn't you say you were going to leave as soon as you hashed out the resort stuff? But you're still here."

He looked at her for a long moment, trying to figure out how such an easygoing person could make him feel so intensely. "I do have to head back to Annapolis, but I wanted more time with you, so I'm staying until we sign the papers."

"Quinn," she whispered. "I don't want to come between you and the work you need to get done. You'll resent me."

"No, I'll never resent you. But I do need to leave soon because there are things going on with the merger and one of our key employees that require my attention." He stroked her soft skin as he told her, "I really didn't want to disappoint you last night and cancel our date, and now I want to help you get settled in the cottage."

"But I know how much you have to—"

He pressed his lips to hers, silencing her in the most delicious way.

"Let me worry about work. I don't want you to worry, too." He paused for a moment and looked into her beautiful eyes. "How would you feel about having a long-distance relationship with me?"

"Quinn Rockwell," she said, her lips curving up at the corners, "are you asking me to go steady?"

"I know you said you didn't want to talk about details last night, but I want to be with you when I'm here."

"And know I'm not with anyone else when you're not?" She kissed his chin.

"You make me sound possessive." He caressed the curve of her bare hip. "Which I am. Especially when it comes to you, Shell. I don't want anyone else to see you like this. To feel you like this. To kiss you like this." Her mouth was warm and sweet beneath his.

"I want to be with you, too, Quinn. Only you, long distance or not."

The passion in her kiss sent a shudder of desire to his core. His hands continued to play over her waist and hips as their mouths came together. He nipped at her lower lip, her jaw, her neck, then kissed his way to her breast, grazing her sensitive skin with his teeth.

"Mm. I like your possessive side," she teased as she reached between them to touch him, too.

With a tormented groan, he drew back long enough to grab a condom from the bedside table.

"Hurry," she whispered as he tore the packet open with his teeth.

Shelley held on to his biceps, her eyes bright with heady anticipation and need. Just like last night, he had to link their hands, had to hold her close and watch her expression of bliss as he moved inside of her, one slow, hard inch at a time.

Her head fell back and her hips arched as they found their rhythm. Her hips rose to meet his again and again in a heated dance of desire. Desire and deep emotion that pounded through him with every beat of his heart. Need for Shelley coiled deep inside him, spreading with every sexy moan, every heady breath that escaped her lips. And then a mischievous smile curved her lips as she moved her hips in a circular motion, nearly dragging him over the edge.

"Holy hell, Shelley..."

"You're not the only one who can torture and tease."

But when their mouths came together again, their impatient, savage desires took over. He pulled her knee up, holding it beneath his arm as he drove in deeper.

"Oh God...Quinn..."

She was every fantasy he'd ever had rolled into one extraordinary woman. As he reached between them to drive her even wilder, her mouth latched on to his neck, and she sucked just hard enough to blow his mind.

"I'm not going to last." Heat rippled down his spine. He quickened his pace, chasing his mounting release.

A string of words fell from her mouth, words he wasn't even sure she knew she was saying. *Yes. Please. More. So good. Don't stop.*

But he couldn't stop if his life depended on it. Tingling sensations stroked down his spine just as she gave a sharp cry of pleasure, then gasped out his name, her hips bucking off the mattress. She clawed at his back as he spiraled into his own intense release.

Quinn had never felt as in sync with anyone as he was with Shelley. And as they lay with their bodies intertwined, their hearts going a little crazy in the aftermath of their lovemaking, he knew he was right where he belonged.

SHELLEY COULDN'T STOP looking at the tall, dark, intense man standing on the porch of the cottage she hoped to rent.

Last night had changed everything. The closeness she felt to him in every kiss, every caress, had deepened after he'd admitted that he was falling for her. And then this morning he'd loved her fast and hard, like he couldn't resist, as if she might run away, even though he was the one who would be leaving soon.

Quinn turned, catching her midstare. With a smile, he came through the glass doors, folded her into his arms, and lowered his mouth to hers, obviously not caring that the Realtor was standing a few feet away in the kitchen.

She loved his kisses and the way they filled her with not only such need, but also such a warm sensation of *completeness*. Even though she knew he was leaving soon, she could so easily imagine him walking through the door of this cottage at the end of a long workday and taking her in his arms. They would fall into bed together every night and then wake with their bodies tangled together every morning. If he were here, they would watch the waves roll in from the deck in the summer and share a mug of hot cider while watching the snow falling in the winter.

"My mom is having a family dinner Wednesday night. Will you come with me?"

"You want me to come to dinner at your parents' house?" She knew they'd already talked about dating exclusively, but formally meeting his parents was a big deal—and that also meant that he planned to stay at least through Wednesday, which delighted her to no end.

"I'm going to be gone a lot, Shell. And I'll feel better knowing you've got people who really know and care about you here on the island."

People who care. She'd spent so many years feeling as though the only people who cared were her aunt and Taryn, and since her aunt passed away, there was only Taryn.

"You've already met most of my family," he continued, "but dinner would be a great way for you to get to know everyone better."

"You don't have to convince me. I'd love to come."

"My mom will be thrilled." He took her hand and turned to look at the cottage again. "So, what do you think of the cottage? Still want to rent it?"

"I knew before I ever walked inside that it was right for me. But now that I've been inside?" She gave a little happy sigh as she took in the details of the beautiful, cozy cottage. "It's perfect. And it even comes furnished."

It smelled of fresh paint, which explained why the furniture was draped with tarps. The hardwood floors were scuffed and marred, which gave the cottage character. Shelley was toying with making the first-floor bedroom into an office. Across from the living room was an open kitchen, and between the kitchen and bedroom were the stairs leading up to the master bedroom.

They went upstairs to the master suite, which spanned the width of the house. It had an expansive view of the bay through French doors leading out to a deck. Shelley stood in front of the window, itching to sign the papers. Quinn wrapped his arms around her waist from behind.

"Can you see yourself living here?"

She turned to him and gazed into his blue eyes. "Yes. Definitely."

"And you don't have any reservations?"

"Not one." *Not about you and not about this adorable cottage.*

He searched her eyes, his own expression growing more intense as he said, "I can see it, too. All of it, Shell."

She didn't know if he meant just for her or for both of them, but the way he tightened his arms around her waist made her think the latter. She tried not to let her imagination run wild, but when he cupped her cheeks and pressed his lips to hers, it was hard not to.

"You're right," he said as he stroked his hand across her cheek and sent delicious shivers running through her. "It's perfect. Absolutely perfect."

"It's a lovely view, isn't it?"

Shelley whipped around at the sound of the Realtor's voice. Cara Roeden was in her early thirties, with auburn hair, misty green eyes, and apparently the ninja-like ability to sneak up on people.

"Yes, it's really beautiful. I think I'd like to rent it. If I'm approved, how quickly can I move in?"

"Are you in a hurry?"

"I was supposed to leave Friday, but I was thinking that if it won't take too long to work out the rental details, I'll delay my departure and just move right on in."

"I'm certain that the owner would be pleased with the prospect of a quick rental. It shouldn't take long to process the paperwork."

They spent the next few hours dealing with the rental agreement and the required documentation. Collecting her historical business financials took only a few clicks, thankfully. Who knew that changing her life could be so easy?

And she was surprised, in the best possible way, that Quinn stayed by her side the whole time instead of going back to his suite to tackle more of his work. He also offered to vouch for her on the rental agreement, which would have expedited the process even more, but Shelley was too independent to take him up on that.

She knew her business would stand up to the renter's background inspection.

By the time they left Cara's office they had an appointment with a commercial real estate agent to find a location for her café, and Shelley was on pins and needles with excitement.

All of her dreams were coming true on Rockwell Island. The beautiful town. A family to care for her.

And, most important of all, *love.*

Chapter Twenty

"THANKS FOR SHOWING us around, Tim," Shelley said to the commercial real estate agent a short while later, "but none of these spaces are speaking to me."

"Those are the only three prime business locations currently available to rent that have the kind of foot traffic you need." Tim Clarey, the commercial agent Cara had connected them with, was short, stout, and patient. "I'll let you know right away if anything new pops up," Tim promised her as they walked back outside.

"I still believe fate brought me here to put down roots," Shelley said to Quinn as they headed away from the storefront, hand in hand. He made little circles with his thumb on her palm, loving the way she always got a little breathless when he teased her this way. Hell, when he teased them both. "But all these spaces have been horrible."

Fate wasn't something Quinn normally bought into, but how could he deny that he and Shelley were destined to meet? They lived minutes apart from each other in Maryland, he'd been to her coffee shop, and out of all the places she could have chosen for her solo honeymoon, she'd chosen his island.

It was as if their worlds were destined to collide.

Was it fate that brought them both to Mill Cove last Friday night? Was it fate that put him on the sailboat the day of her lesson? And if it was, what else did fate have in store for them?

As if beckoned, the answer to her café location problem suddenly popped into his head.

"I've got something to show you." He spun them around so that they were heading north on Main Street toward the old gristmill.

"Where are we going?" She hurried to keep pace with him. "You heard what Tim said. There aren't any other places available right now that would offer foot traffic, and without foot traffic, a café would sink. Even a really good one."

He heard the disappointment in her voice and stopped walking. But he had no chance of restraining the smile that stretched across his cheeks, and he was too excited to even try to temper it. "Do you trust me?"

She didn't hesitate for even a second. "I do."

After giving her a quick—and very hot— kiss to let her know how much having her trust meant to him, he led her up the block, then turned down the next street. The shops on Mill Row were unlike the other commercial streets in town. They set up sidewalk displays and were more geared toward the arts. Together they weaved through the busy sidewalk, past a photography gallery where Shelley slowed to look over a few of the pictures.

"Quinn! I haven't seen you in months." Todd MacGuire owned the gallery, and they had gone to school together.

"Todd, this is my girlfriend, Shelley Walters." The look in her eyes told him that she liked hearing him say the word *girlfriend* as much as he liked saying it.

"It's nice to meet you, Shelley. Do you live in Maryland, too?"

"I do, but I'm moving to the island soon." They chatted for a few minutes about the island and her coffee shop, until they were interrupted by a customer and Todd excused himself.

They passed the Whalers Museum and the Little Shop of Sweaters, and then Shelley stopped in front of Trent's ex-wife, Reese

Nicholson's, place—a gallery called Dandelion—to take it all in.

"This whole street is so full of life. I love the brightly colored shutters on the shops and the sidewalk displays. It feels very artsy."

"Locals call this Mill Row." He took her gently by the shoulders and turned her so that she could see why he'd brought her here. "And this is the old gristmill. It's been vacant for as long as I can remember."

Shelley drew in a deep breath as she looked at the old gristmill across the street, sitting stately beyond a line of tall bushes. She took a step forward, as if she couldn't resist its pull. "Is it for rent?"

"I'll have to check into it to be positive, but I'm pretty sure it is."

They hurried up the grassy hill, and her excitement was contagious as they slipped between two overgrown bushes and the property came into view. The building was larger than most of the shops in town and resembled a two-story house rather than a business, with four windows upstairs and two big picture windows on either side of the front door. The cedar siding was gray with age, and the white trim brought it to life. Overgrown gardens swallowed most of the large front yard. An iron railing spanned the length of the side yard and overlooked Mill Brook. The gardens and the babbling brook were enough to make anyone realize the appeal of the property, but what set the mill even farther apart from any other location in the area was the enormous historic waterwheel attached to the side of the building, powered by the brook. Quinn knew that the inside of the building would need renovations, but there were plenty of capable hands on the island—heck, in his family alone!—that could easily bring the mill back to life.

"I can see it so clearly." Shelley swept her hand out, indicating the rough wooden deck that covered the area in front of the front door. "Tables with beautiful umbrellas overlooking the brook. Listen to the water, Quinn. Isn't it soothing?"

He was so busy watching her fall in love with the property that he barely heard the question, and before he could answer, she added, "And even if the mill doesn't work, we could probably get it functioning enough to catch water. If the property actually is available, it's going to be amazing."

Nodding his agreement, Quinn joined her by the railing. Beyond the front bushes, there was a breathtaking view of Mill Row and residential streets peppered with homes that led to the glorious blue bay. "The town acquired it about three years ago, after Charley Mill passed away. He had family off the island, but he left the mill to the town."

"Charley *Mill*? *Mill* Row? *Mill* Cove?" She gripped his shirt and gazed up at him. "Are they all connected?"

"Yes, they are. See? You really *are* fated to be here."

Shelley threw her arms around Quinn's waist. "This feels like what I've been searching for my whole life."

Quinn wanted to tell her that *she* was what he'd been searching for, but the truth was that he hadn't been searching. Instead, Shelley had come unexpectedly into his life on the island right when he was looking to get off of it.

And now, just as unexpectedly, he didn't want to leave anymore.

SHELLEY SAT WITH Quinn, her feet tucked beneath her on the sofa in the honeymoon cottage, feeling as though her life had finally shifted into place. After finding the gristmill and falling in love with it, Quinn had made a call to his mother, who sat on the town planning committee. Abby used her connections to get the scoop on the property, and within two hours she had tracked down the town officials who would need to approve the sale and arranged to have the property opened for Shelley and Quinn to look inside.

But Shelley hadn't much cared what the inside looked like. The feeling she'd had the first time she'd set her eyes on the gristmill was the same one she'd felt when she'd first seen Mill Cove and had decided to go skinny-dipping. She was drawn to it like metal to magnet.

It was, she thought with a smile, the same way she felt every time she looked at Quinn.

The interior of the mill had been dusty with the scent of old wood hanging in the air. Wide-planked and scarred wooden floors told of years of millwork, and in the center of the first floor was a big grinding stone with the bed and runner stones still in place. The gears in Shelley's mind were already turning. She'd keep that beautiful grinding stone in place for customers to enjoy, maybe even put up a little information piece about it with the history of the mill.

A narrow stairwell led to a second floor, which could be perfect as living space or rented out as a separate shop for a local artist. She'd learned that until the mid-1960s, when most of the Mill family moved to the mainland, the mill had been used to grind cornmeal for the island, and it had remained empty ever since. With a little airing out, a lot of cleaning up, and the addition of shelves and work space, she knew it would be perfect for the café. Intimate and filled with character.

BELLA ANDRE & MELISSA FOSTER

She stretched her legs across the couch and tucked her toes beneath Quinn's thigh. They'd spent the late afternoon working side by side. He read through reports while Shelley worked on logistics for moving her business—and, of course, they kissed each other constantly. Long-distance relationships had never sounded very good to her, but if it meant being with Quinn, then she was up for anything. Especially, she thought with a wicked grin, a little break. One that involved a heck of a lot less clothes...

As if he could read her mind, Quinn slid his hand up her calf and smiled. "Your planning going well over there?"

"I'm a little excited," she said, for more than one reason now as he set his document down on the coffee table and pulled her onto his lap. "Can you tell?"

"You've been writing ideas down like crazy in that notebook in your lap." He lowered his mouth to the curve of her neck and nipped at the sensitive skin there. "There's nothing sexier than seeing you so happy."

And there was nothing sexier to Shelley than this moment right here, right now, with Quinn. Wrapped in his arms, filled with the heady anticipation of pleasure soon to come. "I could get used to this."

She thought she saw a flash of worry in his eyes, but it disappeared as quickly as it had come.

"Making out with me on the couch...or us?"

"Both."

He cupped her face in his hands and kissed her again. "Good answer. Now, about all these pretty clothes you've got on..."

Each of them already had a fistful of fabric in their hands, hurrying to strip her dress away, when her phone vibrated on the coffee table. From the corner of her eye, Shelley saw *Mother* on the screen, and her stomach clenched. She purposely didn't put the word *Mom* on her mother's contact information because the word *Mom* felt soft to Shelley, and her mother was anything but soft.

Quinn stopped undressing her to ask, "Do you want to get that?"

She grimaced. "Not really."

But both of them obviously knew she wasn't going to ignore it. He gathered her hair over one shoulder and kissed her cheek as the phone vibrated again. "Maybe she'll surprise you this time and be supportive."

"I wish that were the case, but since it isn't going to be, I'm not sure I want her to burst my bubble yet."

"Don't you think old dogs can sometimes learn new tricks? Take me, for instance, blowing off work to clam and sail and help my girl rent a cottage."

My girl. His words were so sweet it melted her enough that she foolishly reached for the phone and reluctantly moved off of his lap.

"I'll take it on the porch so just in case there aren't any new dogs on the line, you won't be tortured with the conversation."

She answered the call on her way outside.

"Rochelle, it's Mother. I spoke to Taryn's mother today, who said you are entertaining some silly notion of moving to Rockwell Island?"

Damn it, Taryn. Her cousin knew better than to say anything to her mother, but must have been caught off guard. Just like that, Shelley's happy, blissfully contented mood started to go down the tubes.

"Yes," she said with a stubborn tilt of her chin that her mother couldn't see. "I'm moving to Rockwell Island."

"Rochelle." Her mother exhaled loudly. "You're twenty-seven years old and getting a little long in the tooth for finding a suitable man. It's time you gave up your childish whims and focused on the important things in life."

Shelley lowered the phone from her ear and looked out over the bay. She didn't need to hear another diatribe about finding a suitable man or a life filled with snooty social gatherings and bragging about meaningless material luxuries. She closed her eyes and breathed deeply, extremely thankful that she was here on the island and not anywhere near Greenwich. When she lifted the phone back up to her ear, she caught the tail end of her mother rambling about the Lavingtons. When her mother finally paused to inhale, Shelley cut her off.

"Thanks for your call," she made herself say. "But I really have to go. I have a lot of planning to do."

"Planning? You're not taking my advice, then?"

The disappointment in her mother's voice hurt, not only because she knew she had let her mother down, but because she couldn't believe her mother *still* refused to accept her for who she was and support the things *she* wanted in her life.

Another call beeped through. Immensely glad for the interruption, Shelley said, "Hold on one sec. I need to answer this call." She quickly clicked to the other call. "Hello?"

"Shelley? This is Cara. Good news. We were able to reach the bank and expedite your paperwork and credit check. The cottage on the dunes is yours as soon as you'd like to move in. We just need to agree on a date and sign the final lease."

Shelley's eyes filled with tears of joy. "Thank you. Your call couldn't have come at a better time. Can I move in tomorrow?"

"That's when they have a cleaning crew coming in. How about the following day?"

After they agreed to meet, Shelley switched back over to her mother's call.

"Finally," her mother said in a voice threaded with deep irritation. "I was beginning to think you had hung up on me."

"No. I was just confirming the details of my rental cottage."

"Rental cottage? Rochelle, truly, all of this nonsense has got to stop. When will you learn that you're wasting your time? You've been this way your whole life, belligerent and bullheaded. Frankly, it's an embarrassment to me and your father."

Her mother's words should have cut right through Shelley. But she refused to let anyone or anything ruin what had been one of the best days of her life. "If you can find a way to be happy for me one day, I'd love to hear from you again. But until then, I think it's best if we say goodbye, Mother."

Quinn's arms came around her from behind a moment after she hung up the phone. She turned to him, and even though she was intent on staying strong, she buried her face in his chest.

"Shell, what happened?"

She hated that her mother still affected her this way. "My parents will never understand me. It doesn't matter what I do, or how hard I try..." She knew she sounded petulant and angry, and that upset her even more.

"You don't deserve to be discounted by them or anyone else. You know I'm all for family, but honestly, if they can't adore you for the incredibly talented and giving person you are, then they don't deserve the energy you expend on them. They're fools. Fools that I wish I could lay into right now for ever hurting you." His voice was full of empathy, but in his embrace she felt tethered anger.

She gazed up at him, blinking away tears. "You're angry."

"You bet I'm angry. It breaks my heart to see anyone hurt you this way. I've never met anyone like you, who could look at something and immediately see beyond the masks and facades that the rest of the world sees. Whether it's a dusty old building or..." His gaze softened and the tension around his mouth eased. "Or a workaholic like me."

He sealed his lips over hers and lifted her into his arms. Her legs naturally circled his waist, and her arms wrapped around his neck as he kissed her salty tears away.

"You're perfect, Shell, just the way you are. Don't change a damn thing about yourself."

And then he carried her into the bedroom and loved away the pain and sadness until her heart was so full of him that she didn't have room for anything else.

Chapter Twenty-one

WEDNESDAY MORNING, QUINN and Shelley had breakfast on the terrace of the resort. Shelley had been quiet most of the morning, and Quinn wondered if she was still upset about the things her mother had said to her.

Last night, when he'd found her trying to hold back tears on the front porch, his protective urges had barreled forward, urging him to pick up the phone and give her parents hell. All along he'd held out hope that her parents would relent in their pursuit to make Shelley into the woman *they* wanted her to be, but last night had wiped that wish out. It broke his heart to know how much she'd struggled to be loved by the people who should love her most.

He was so glad his family seemed eager to embrace Shelley being a part of both his life and theirs.

"Are you excited about moving into the cottage tomorrow?"

She'd been looking out at the water with her chin resting on her palm and a thoughtful look in her eyes. "Super excited."

She reached for his hand just as his phone vibrated in his pocket. He knew it had to be Rich but debated letting his partner's call go to voicemail.

"It's okay, Quinn. Take it."

She must have seen the struggle on his face. "Are you sure?" The phone vibrated again.

"It's fine. We both have to live our lives, and you'll be going back soon, so I need to get used to it. We both do."

He hated having her get used to anything other than waking up in his arms, but she was right. "I'll make it quick." He answered the call on his way across the terrace.

"Quinn," Rich said in a harried voice, "things are getting out of hand. I've met everything they're offering Joseph, but he hasn't accepted yet. He wants more responsibility, a higher position. Short of giving him one of our jobs, we're stuck."

"Isn't there anything else we can offer him? He's been with us since the inception of the business. He's the best at what he does. He deserves more. What are *they* offering him that's more than what we are?"

While Rich explained what Joseph was being offered, Quinn walked back to Shelley and settled a hand on her shoulder, giving it a gentle squeeze. He wanted her to know he hadn't forgotten about her.

It's okay, she mouthed.

He blew her a kiss, then walked a few feet away to finish his call.

"I've got this covered for now," Rich said, "but your presence is key here. Joseph trusts you more than he trusts anyone else."

"Do what you can there and I'll try to get things wrapped up here. And let me know if it looks like the lid is going to blow with either Joseph or the merger."

By the time Quinn hung up, his mind was going a hundred miles an hour. He had faith in Rich's ability to handle whatever came up with the business, but Rich was right when he said that Joseph's trust and respect for Quinn was greater than his trust in anyone else. He rubbed the knot that was quickly forming in the back of his neck.

Shelley walked toward him and wrapped her arms around him. "Everything okay?"

"Some parts yes, some parts no." But he didn't like grumbling to her, especially when

BELLA ANDRE & MELISSA FOSTER

their time together was counting down way too fast. "Tell me something, Shell. When you're away from work and you let yourself relax, if you're not being productive, what are you doing? Do you ever feel like you're just wasting time when you could be making more, doing more, working toward a bigger goal?"

She gave him a look so full of understanding that it made his heart turn over in his chest.

"No," she said softly, "I don't feel like that. But that's because when I'm not working, when I'm not being productive or working toward a goal, I'm living. Enjoying. Exploring. Laughing. Hopefully I can do all of that when I'm working, too, but it's so nice just to let go sometimes and be totally free to take in the joy and the beauty that's all around us."

He pulled her even closer, wondering how she made things seem so reasonable and easy when something as simple as taking in joy and beauty seemed easy to him only when he was with her.

"I wish I could harness your spirit and carry it with me all the time."

She rested her head on his shoulder as they made their way down to the beach. "That'll be hard to do from Annapolis."

Therein lay the problem.

"Once I'm gone," he said in a raw voice, "you might decide there are better, easier fish in the sea."

"Yeah, you know me. Always looking for easy. Oh, and dumb, too, because a man who thinks for himself is such a bore. And..." She flashed a playful grin. "While we're at it, how about a guy who *doesn't* get me. That would make me feel right at home."

Quinn was amazed at how she was always able to get him to laugh. "You have no idea what you're getting into with me. I'm moody."

"Yes," she said with a nod. "I know that already."

"I'm intense."

Her eyes darkened with desire. "And I love it."

He had to kiss her deep and long before saying, "I've also developed a really bad habit over the years of being married to my work. But I'm working on that."

"What successful person isn't married to their work to some degree? Especially if they love what they do. It seems to me that you've been able to fit in work and time for us over this past week. Or does that not count?"

He pulled her closer as they walked through the dense sand. "It counts. But," he added as a kind of warning, "it's also a first for me. A good first. A *great* first. And like I know I keep saying, I'm working on changing."

"Change can be good sometimes," she said slowly, "but I'm not sure why you are so convinced that you can't have a wonderful, happy life just being the person you already are. I *like* who you are. Why can't you like him a little more, too?"

When he didn't answer right away, she pulled them to a stop on the sand and pressed her palms to his chest. He loved when she did that. Those two spots, one over his heart, the other over his muscles, were *hers*. She totally owned him.

"Let me ask you this," she said. "What if I decide to go back to Maryland instead of moving my business here to the island?"

"Then I'll find a way to spend most of my time there."

"Okay, bad example. What if I go to dinner tonight at your parents' house and fall madly in love with your brother Ethan and decide to sail away to live on his boat with him?"

His gut churned and a scowl replaced his grin.

"See?" She smiled up at him. "You know it's a silly thought, something that would never happen in a million years, but you still can't help reacting to it. Your face is all frowny, and you look dejected. It's really quite cute. Like an angry toddler."

"Toddler?" He grabbed her ribs, and she squealed.

"Don't tickle me. I'm making a point."

"Then make it already, and let's leave Ethan out of it." Especially since jealousy was still clawing at his nerves at even the mere *thought* of his brother touching Shelley.

"Okay, but you're so cute when you're jealous." But then she stopped laughing and grew serious again. "All I'm saying is that if you allow yourself to be seeded with doubt, it weighs you down. Shoulda, coulda, woulda does no good. The only thing that ever works is to believe in yourself. And if that feels too difficult sometimes, then you can believe in me, because I have total faith in you. I have never lived my life afraid of what-ifs, and I'm not going to start now."

Shelley's faith in him moved Quinn in a way nothing else ever had. No big deal, no big payout, no big award had ever brought him such pleasure.

Or such happiness.

"I love you, Shelley."

The words came directly from his heart. It didn't matter that they'd met less than a week ago or that the logistics of having a relationship both on and off the island were messy.

All that mattered was what he felt for the beautiful woman standing in front of him.

And when she looked at him with her entire heart and soul open to him on her beautiful face and said, "I love you, too," then kissed him without holding any of her passion—or joy—back, it was difficult to remember why he'd ever had any doubts at all.

Chapter Twenty-two

QUINN AND SHELLEY spent the afternoon exploring the island. Quinn took her to see the lighthouse, and they had lunch at a little café overlooking the water. They drove by the aquarium, and he showed her the rocky cliff where he, his brothers, and their friends used to hang out as teenagers. And the whole time, there were kisses, caresses, and whispered promises of all the wonderful ways he was planning to give her pleasure tonight.

After the call from Rich, she'd expected him to tell her that he was going to head back to Maryland early, but what he had said was a million times better.

He loves me.

And she loved him, too. With all her heart.

While Quinn was with his family, signing papers for the resort, Shelley took a walk to see the cottage she'd rented one more time before finalizing the rental agreement and moving in the next day. It was a beautiful, sunny afternoon, and there was a gentle breeze coming off the water. Up on the dunes, the breeze was stronger. She couldn't wait to move in, open all the windows, and feel that breeze in every room.

As she headed back down the beach with her heart beating a little faster, she thought about how angry Quinn had been over the things her mother had said. He cared so much, so fast, and it meant everything to her that he did. Especially because she cared just as much about him and his happiness.

On the beach there were a bevy of flat rocks by her feet. Aunt Marla had tried to teach her to skip rocks every summer, but she'd never been able to master the flick of her wrist. Shelley picked up a flat rock, turned her hand sideways and tried to skip it. It splashed into the water a few feet away and sank.

Picking up a handful of pebbles, she simply tossed them into the water, smiling as they plunked like raindrops.

"Now, that's more like it," Shelley said, laughing as she did it again.

A short while later, she was surprised to turn and find she wasn't alone on the beach anymore. Didi crouched beside Chandler Rockwell's wheelchair, and he was leaning over the side, watching his nurse clear the sand around the wheel. He was grumbling something Shelley couldn't hear.

"Is everything okay?"

Didi shaded her eyes from the sun and squinted up at her. "Shelley, hi. Nice to see you again. I seem to have hit a rock beneath the sand." Didi clapped her hands together and shook off the sand. "There, that should do it."

Shelley smiled at Chandler. "Hello, Mr. Rockwell. How are you today?"

He squinted against the sun. "You're that Walters girl. You've been spending time with my grandson Quinn, haven't you?"

Shelley wondered if he knew her parents or had heard about her from Quinn's family. She decided to err on the side of caution.

"Yes, I am, and yes, I have. But please don't judge me by my family."

His long fingers curled around the arms of the wheelchair. Shelley imagined his large bony hands had once been as strong and agile as Quinn's. He set a steady dark gaze on Shelley. She shifted her footing under his scrutiny.

"Then how should I judge you?"

His words were slightly cutting, and Shelley got the impression that they were supposed to sound like that. Shelley felt sorry for Didi, having to stand by while he made such sharp comments. But the look in Didi's eyes wasn't one of cowering to the old man's harshness. It was one of obvious support aimed at Shelley.

Shelley met his steely gaze again. "By my actions. And by how much I care for your amazing grandson."

Shelley held her breath for a beat, unsure of what to expect. But in the space of a breath, the muscles in Chandler's jaw softened and his grip on the wheelchair eased slightly. He *harrumphed* and motioned for Didi to wheel him away...but for a split second, Shelley swore she saw appreciation in his eyes.

"I hope to see you again soon, Shelley," Didi said with a smile, before heading back up the beach with Chandler.

Maybe the old man didn't have a heart of stone after all.

Maybe, like the gristmill, and even Quinn, all Chandler Rockwell needed was the right kind of affection to reveal a kinder side of him. Or maybe he really was a curmudgeonly old bastard. But even in the brief interaction she'd had with Griffin, she believed in her heart that the fruit couldn't fall far from the tree.

Somewhere beneath Chandler's gruff exterior *had* to be a nicer man.

In any case, Chandler's body might be failing, but his mind was clearly still very sharp. And it didn't evade her that Quinn's careful consideration before speaking mirrored Chandler's, much more so than Griffin's easy nature, which she'd witnessed at Sierra's restaurant.

The longer she thought about it, the more Quinn seemed like a mix of the two men. She'd seen Quinn's carefree side, and she'd definitely noticed that he was his own worst critic, always worrying that he'd hurt her.

Once she was back inside her cottage, she picked up the champagne bottle with the candle he'd made for her and set it beside the flowers he'd left on her doorstep. They'd started to wilt, but she knew she'd keep them until the petals fell off.

You're the perfect mix of sexy, fun boyfriend and powerful businessman, Quinn Rockwell. I hope one day you can see that, too.

There were myriad details she needed to take care of to get her life in order. Starting with a call to Taryn to let her know she'd changed her flight.

"Hey there, girlfriend."

Shelley smiled at the sound of Taryn's voice. "I wanted to let you know that I delayed my flight for two weeks. I'm still waiting to hear if the property I want to buy for the café is going to come through, but I should know within a week, and I've rented a cute cottage that overlooks the bay. I can't wait for you to come visit."

"You can count on it, and soon, since I'm already halfway done with the island dress I promised you. Did you talk to your monster...I mean mother about it?"

"Yes, and she was perfectly rotten."

"Aw, Shell. I'm sorry, but you didn't really expect anything different, did you?"

"No, I didn't." But the little girl in her apparently had still held out hope for a miracle. "I'm not going to let her ruin my excitement, though. I *know* I'm doing the right thing. Oh, and thanks for telling your mom, who then told mine. What were you thinking?"

"Yikes. I forgot that slipped when we were talking. I'm really sorry, Shell. I should have been more careful."

"It's okay. I probably would have put it off for weeks. You just tore the Band-Aid off all at once, most likely saving me weeks of stressing over doing it."

"I hate that your mother can make you feel so bad," Taryn said, "but then again, we both know my mother went to the same school of snooty behavior as yours. And just so I know if I need to keep my mouth shut again, have you told Casey yet? Is she okay continuing to manage your coffee shop for another two weeks and then closing up shop when you move the business to Rockwell Island?"

"I'm actually going to call her next. It'll take a little while to get the shop set up here, so she'll have some time to get used to the idea and find another job. Who knows? Maybe she'll want to come to the island, too."

"Especially if you can find her a hot guy to fall for. How is Mr. Sexy, by the way?"

A dreamy sigh escaped before Shelley could stop it.

"Did you just do one of those swoony sighs that we always make fun of?"

Shelley didn't even feel the least bit bad about it as she said, "I sure did."

"Who are you, and what have you done with my best friend?"

"I know it seems crazy, Taryn, but...I love him. So much. From the tippy top of my head to the ends of my toes. I love the way he looks at me. I love the way he kisses me. I love the passion he has for his work. I love the careful way he makes decisions. His family is here and I really like them, too. Everything just feels so right."

"Wow." Taryn was silent for a long moment. "I've never heard you say any of those things about anyone."

"I know it hit fast, but now I think that must be what true love does. Just hits you from out of the blue and leaves you breathless."

"I don't know if true love will ever come my way, but breathless sounds pretty fun," Taryn said, a hint of longing in her voice. "How many brothers did you say he has?"

"Three, all gorgeous, of course, and lots of cousins, too."

"Well, hopefully you two will leave a little of that Rockwell *love* magic for the rest of us."

Right then Shelley felt so happy that she was not only positive there was more than enough love for everyone...she was also sure that *magic* was exactly the right word for it.

Chapter Twenty-three

WHEN SHELLEY AND Quinn arrived at his parents' house for dinner that night, his cell phone dinged with an incoming text and he immediately reached into his pocket for it.

"Do you ever take a break from answering your phone?" She knew this might be a touchy subject, but she really did wonder if he ever took a complete mental break from it all.

His brows knitted together as he paused with his hand still in his pocket. "Not usually, no." He turned to look her in the eye. "Do you even have a phone with you?"

She smiled as she repeated his answer. "Not usually, no."

He was laughing as he walked around to Shelley's door and helped her from the car. "Thank you."

"You're welcome," she said before asking, "For what?"

"For reminding me to live my life." He took her in a kiss that started gentle and sweet, but quickly turned wild and desperate.

"If that's how you always thank me, maybe I should remind you more often."

His phone forgotten, at least for the moment, they walked hand in hand up the stone walkway, kissing every few steps. Shelley had expected the Rockwells to live in an opulent mansion overlooking the bay. She was right about the waterfront location, but their modest Cape Cod–style home was nothing like the lavish estate she'd imagined. It was cedar sided, with beautiful gardens in the front and side yards. The house sat up high on a bluff overlooking the water, with woods bordering both sides of a lush green lawn.

"What a wonderful house! I wish my parents' house was like this one. Growing up, our house always felt like a museum, even from the outside."

"That sounds just like my grandfather's wing of the resort," Quinn told her. "But my parents have never lived like that. When we were growing up, I shared a room with Trent. Derek and Ethan shared a room, and only Sierra had her own room. My brothers and I had bunk beds, because two twin beds took up the whole bedroom. If we ever got too big for our britches and complained about wanting our own space, my mom would point to the backyard and say, *Pup tents are really easy to set up. Have at it.*"

"I think I like your mom even more now."

Shelley was delighted with these new discoveries. She never imagined that a family as wealthy as the Rockwells would be content living in such a moderately sized home. Yet again she chided herself for lumping all wealthy people together. Especially since that was the stereotype she'd spent her life trying to avoid.

Quinn held tightly to Shelley's hand, looking handsome in a pair of jeans and a collared shirt. "Are you nervous?"

"Not really nervous, just..." She trapped her lower lip between her teeth. She'd anguished over what to wear and had changed her clothes several times before finally deciding on a colorful halter dress and a cute pair of strappy sandals. "Okay, maybe I am a little nervous."

He nipped at her lower lip that she'd been biting, sending heat pouring through her as he said, "My mom and dad and Sierra and Trent already met and really like you. Dinner tonight will give you a chance to get to know everyone better and for them to fall for you just like I have."

Fall for you. She'd never tire of hearing that. Just like she knew she'd never grow tired of his kisses, or holding his hand.

Shelley yelped at the feel of a cold, wet nose against the back of her thigh.

"Chugger!" One of Quinn's brothers came around the back of the house and knelt to call the rambunctious pup. "Hey, guys. Glad you made it." He rose to his feet and eyed his dog. "Sit." Chugger sat beside him, wagging his tail excitedly.

"Hi. I'm Ethan. It's great to meet you." He was as broad and tall as Quinn, with wavier hair and thick scruff covering his strong chin. Ethan's eyes were as dark brown as Quinn's were piercing blue, and while Ethan had a naturally relaxed gaze, Quinn's was darker, more serious.

Seriously sexier.

Still, Shelley understood why Quinn had reacted so strongly to her joke about being interested in Ethan. He was a very good-looking guy, but Quinn needn't worry. There wasn't a man alive who could draw her attention away from him.

"I'm Shelley, and it's great to meet you, too. Although I already met Chugger the other day."

Ethan looked surprised. "You did? Where?"

"He was on the beach with your grandfather and Didi." She crouched to pet

Chugger, and the pup licked her cheek. "Aren't you adorable?" She'd always loved dogs, although they'd traveled too much for her to have one when she was a kid, and as an adult she'd been too busy to make the time for one. Maybe once she was settled on the island she'd consider adopting one.

"You met our grandfather?" Ethan asked. "That must have been a joy." He turned to Quinn. "You didn't rescue her from the old man's bite?"

"I didn't need rescuing, actually." Shelley rose to her feet. "Your grandfather seems stern, but..." She looked at Quinn, remembering the softening around Chandler's eyes when she'd said she was falling for his grandson. "I think below his gruff exterior there's a warm heart. It's just buried deep."

"Really?" Ethan didn't look particularly convinced. "Well, I suppose it's good that someone thinks that." The brother Sierra had called the "strong and silent" one gestured to the backyard. "Everyone's outside. Sierra and Mom have been talking about you all week, Shelley, so I know everyone's dying to spend some time getting to know you better."

White lights were strung from tall iron poles around the stone patio, giving the gorgeous evening a festive glow. Sierra was leaning over a table set for eight, fiddling with a vase, when she noticed Quinn and Shelley.

"You're here!" She ran over and hugged Shelley.

Shelley couldn't hide her smile as she wrapped her arms around Quinn's sister. Maybe it was crazy, but even though they hadn't known each other very long, she felt like they had already become close friends. Then again, that wasn't any crazier than falling head over heels in love with Quinn so quickly, was it?

"Hey, sis," Quinn said to Sierra as he gave her a warm hug.

Ethan called out to Quinn to come take a look at something, and as soon as Sierra and Shelley were alone, Sierra said, "I heard you're thinking of buying the gristmill."

"News travels fast," Shelley said with a smile. "I'm just waiting to hear from the town, actually."

Over her shoulder, she could see Quinn asking her the silent question: *Are you okay?* She nodded, smiled, and turned her attention back to Sierra just as Griffin and Abby headed their way.

"Shelley, welcome." Abby opened her arms and embraced her.

Shelley was struck once again by how different Abby was from her own mother.

Quinn's mother had a warmth about her that put Shelley instantly at ease.

"Abby, thank you so much for allowing me to crash your family dinner."

"Crash all you'd like. The more the merrier in this house. Especially when I can see how smitten my son is with you."

Smitten.

Shelley could feel her cheeks flush at the lovely comment. Even lovelier because it had come from Quinn's mother, who would only want the very best for her children.

Abby turned as Griffin draped an arm over her shoulder and kissed her cheek, magnifying another difference between her parents and Quinn's. Shelley's parents' idea of open affection was *air* kissing each other's cheeks.

"Shelley," Griff said, "we're all so glad you could join us tonight."

"Thank you. You have a lovely home"— Quinn's laughter at something his brothers were saying on the other side of the patio turned her head—"with a spectacular view."

Sierra chuckled. "I know you think Quinn is the best view on the island, but this one is way better." She pointed behind them to the bay.

Shelley laughed to try to hide her embarrassment. "I didn't mean..."

"It's okay if you did." Griff leaned in close and lowered his voice. "Quinn's a good-looking guy. He gets it from his old man."

"Yes, he does. Now, leave the poor girl alone before you make her blush." Abby dragged Griff away.

"Are you uncomfortable yet?" Sierra teased.

"Oh my gosh." Shelley lowered her voice and said, "You and your parents just caught me drooling over your brother."

Sierra shrugged. "We didn't mean to embarrass you. Especially since we're all really excited that Quinn brought you along. My dad was just telling me how he'd never seen Quinn look happier than he's been this past week."

"Really? I mean, he seems happy, and I know how happy *I* am."

"Really," Sierra said. "Look at him."

Quinn stood between Trent and Ethan, across from Derek. The others were intent on hearing whatever Derek was saying, but Quinn's attention was locked on Shelley. The heat and adoration in his eyes were both impossible to miss.

To her he stood out from his brothers. Though they were all tall and broad, none of the others made her insides flutter like Quinn did. Even the look he gave her now was as caring and thoughtful as it was longing and possessive.

"I better take you over there or he might pounce." Sierra guided her across the lawn while Shelley secretly thought just how much she loved it whenever Quinn *did* pounce.

"There's my girl." Quinn tucked Shelley beneath his arm, and her stomach did that fluttery thing again.

My girl. She loved that.

"Derek, this is Shelley."

"It's great to meet you." Derek's voice was as deep as Quinn's, but he had the look of a troublemaker about him. Shelley liked Derek instantly for that alone.

"You're the custom builder and stonemason, right? Quinn said you made this gorgeous patio." He had filled her in on each of his siblings on the way over.

Derek flashed a crooked smile. "Yup, that's me. The stone guy." Without missing a beat, he said, "I hear you're interested in the gristmill."

Word really did travel fast, at least between the Rockwells. "It would be perfect for my café. If I'm lucky enough to get the property, I want to keep its rustic charm. I'm thinking about lowering the height of the bushes out front so customers can sit on the deck and enjoy the view of the town—and the bay, of course." She simply couldn't temper her enthusiasm, even if she knew she was rambling. "The brook is just so beautiful that Quinn and I thought it would be nice to put a patio out back. Derek, if I get the property, would you consider designing and building a stone patio?"

"See?" Sierra said before Derek could respond. "Shelley is the perfect café owner for the island. She already loves it as much as I do, and she's been here less than a week."

"I'd be happy to consider the stonework," Derek said. "As long as it's done within the next year."

Sierra groaned. "Derek's planning on hightailing it out of here just as soon as his one-year contract is up with the resort. But my money's on him staying on the island. I've seen how he looks at Chandler's nurse."

"I'm not saying she's not gorgeous," he said, "but my biggest question right now is whether she's qualified to take out my latest round of stitches so that I can skip a trip to the island's clinic."

Quinn pulled Shelley against him. "Derek is the adventurer in the family. An adventurer who is always getting hurt. Although," he added with a sly look at his brother, "I'm not buying that your stitches are the reason you couldn't stop looking at her the other day...or that she couldn't stop looking right back."

"Are you talking about Didi, your grandfather's nurse?" Shelley asked.

"That's her," Ethan confirmed as he reached down to pet Chugger. "Now that I think about it, since she's gorgeous *and* has a thing for Chugger, maybe *I* should ask her out."

Derek gave him a shove. "Stitches outplay dogs." But for all his playfulness, there was a hint of possession in both his words and in his expression.

Abby held up a long wooden stick. "Hey, boys, how about we get out some of your aggression while dinner finishes cooking?"

"Stickball! I'm in." Sierra took the stick from Abby and grabbed Shelley's hand, dragging her across the yard.

"What's that building?" Shelley pointed to a small cottage near the woods.

"My mom's studio. She blows glass."

"Wow. I'd love to see her stuff sometime."

Sierra glanced at her mother with a thoughtful look in her eyes. "She'd love that. She's really talented. I hope she can keep blowing glass for a very long time."

Ethan dashed around the yard, pointing out trees and bushes. Chugger stole the rubber ball from where Abby had set it on the ground, and everyone laughed while watching Ethan chase the pup. Quinn, Shelley, Griff, and Ethan were on one team, while Trent, Derek, Sierra, and Abby were on the opposing team.

BELLA ANDRE & MELISSA FOSTER

"My mom would never play anything like this," Shelley said to Abby. "Your kids are so lucky to have you."

"Oh, honey. It's the other way around. I'm lucky to have them. Besides," Abby added with a grin, "you can't let these boys get one up on you. I learned that really quickly as a young mother surrounded by testosterone." Abby walked up to the plate, and Griff, as the pitcher, took aim.

"Looking good up there, Mama," Quinn's dad called out.

"Sweet-talking will get you nowhere in this game of stickball, Griffin Rockwell." Abby choked up on the stick. "Pitch the ball."

He lobbed the first pitch over the plate and Abby swung—and missed. The boys all clapped and cheered her on.

"You can do it, Mom," Quinn yelled.

"Keep your eye on the ball," Trent directed.

"You've got this, Mom." Ethan stood on first base and clapped his hands. "Hit it right here."

Abby leaned in to reach the next pitch and hit a grounder that slid past Griffin and was intercepted by Chugger, causing chaos and laughter to ensue as Abby jogged around the bases while Ethan chased his wildly happy puppy some more.

Trent ran alongside Abby, cheering her on the whole way. "Great job, Mom. You're almost there."

Shelley felt as though she'd been plunked down in the middle of the best family in the world. They laughed hard and played hard, but the thing that really stood out was how supportive they were of one another. Shelley had once thought there were no couples where the husband and wife loved each other more than they loved material things and appearances. But now that she'd met Quinn's parents, Shelley knew differently. Abby and Griff clearly loved each other—and their kids—more than anything else on the planet.

During the game, she overheard Quinn and Trent talking about the resort. Trent said he would cover for Quinn when needed, and Quinn agreed to reciprocate. At one point, Sierra twisted her ankle and Derek ran to get her a chair, but she promptly limped back into the game, unwilling to be left out.

When it was Shelley's turn, Quinn came up behind her and wrapped his arms around her, showing her how to hold the stick. During the summers when she'd visited her aunt, Shelley had often played Wiffle ball with the other kids on the beach. But she wasn't about to give up the feel of Quinn's big, hard body wrapped around her to clue him in to her experience.

"When you hold the stick, choke up a little higher. It'll give you more control." He threaded one hand into her hair and turned her face to his for a kiss.

"Come on, lovebirds," Ethan hollered.

But Quinn wasn't about to be rushed as he finished what he'd started. Finally, after he drew back from her mouth, he said, "You good to go?"

She had to work really hard to form words after that kiss. "I think so."

A few moments later, Trent pitched the ball, and Shelley whacked it into the side yard. Quinn's jaw dropped open, and everyone cheered as she ran the bases with Chugger at her side. When she crossed the plate, Quinn swept her into his arms and spun her around.

"I'm going to have to call you *slugger* now." Quinn kissed her again, fast and hot enough to make the night feel far warmer than it actually was. "I never knew you could play ball."

"Much to my parents' chagrin, I've got a pretty good arm, too. It's not exactly feminine to be athletic in the Walters family."

She thought about the summer she'd come home from visiting her aunt after learning to play baseball. She'd been bubbling over with excitement, and when she told her parents, her father had said, *Walters women do not play ball.*

No one had celebrated her athletic achievements, that was for certain.

As Quinn set her feet back on the ground, she could see that hint of anger lighting his eyes, the same way it had when she'd gotten off the phone with her mother.

"It kills me that they'd make you feel bad about anything, but playing ball? All kids should learn how to play ball."

Shelley wasn't about to let thoughts of her parents ruin her night—or Quinn's. She forced the memories away and said, "Don't worry. *My* children will learn to play ball, get muddy and sticky clamming in the bay, and maybe even have to contend with puppy fur. I'll do everything I can to help them follow their dreams, find true love, and be happy, because in the end, those are the things that matter."

Quinn opened his mouth to say something, but they were interrupted by Abby calling them in for dinner. Quinn lagged behind, talking privately with his mother as the rest of them headed for the table.

Shelley wondered what was being said and why Quinn looked so serious again. The two of them hadn't talked about kids before now, and Shelley was left wondering—was he scared off by the thought? Or did he want children of his own someday, the way she did?

Griffin settled a hand on her shoulder as she helped bring food to the table and said, "Nice arm. We need you on our team next time," which made her feel warm and fuzzy all over again despite her questions about what had turned Quinn so suddenly pensive.

Quinn kept one hand on Shelley's leg throughout the meal. She loved that his parents didn't sit at opposite ends of the table, as many parents would. They sat beside each other on one side of the table with Sierra and Ethan, while she, Quinn, Derek, and Trent sat across from them.

"I'd like to make a toast." Griffin rose, holding up his wineglass. "To the Rockwell family coming together tonight without a single cell phone interruption!" Griffin winked at Quinn, then turned his attention to Shelley. "And to Shelley moving to the island. May you love it here as much as we do."

Her heart overflowing, she dug into the delicious dinner. Ethan told her about his fishing business, which he'd started right after college, and Sierra talked about what it had been like to open a restaurant on the island. But it seemed to Shelley that Ethan's and Sierra's love of the island was only part of what kept them there. Their love for their family was clearly the overriding factor.

While Derek and Trent talked with Griffin about the resort, Shelley imagined what it would be like to sit at the Rockwells' dinner table every week, catching up with people who cared.

But she already knew what it would be like: simply *amazing.*

All of them were so excited about her move, and with Griffin's lovely toast, Shelley felt like she was already part of the family. She had a pang of longing over the difference between Quinn's warm and inclusive family and her cold, distant parents. But instead of wallowing in what she didn't have, she silently reveled in the way it felt to be with the Rockwells.

And, best of all, with the man she loved.

IT HAD BEEN a long time since Quinn had spent such a relaxing and fun evening with his family. While he always enjoyed their time together, he was usually rushing to get back to work, or taking business calls and juggling the two. He was glad Shelley had asked him about his phone before they joined the others, because for the first time in his adult life he'd felt completely untethered and was able to enjoy his family without the distraction of work.

As they drove away from his parents' house, he thought about what his mother had said when she'd pulled him aside before dinner.

Remember why Eloise walked away from your grandfather's marriage proposal?

He'd heard the story enough times to remember it clearly. Chandler had always been a workaholic, even as a young man, and Eloise had refused to play second fiddle to any man's business.

His mother had gently reminded him how much Quinn had hated seeing Grandma Caroline treated like she was third best to both Chandler's workload and Eloise, the woman who had turned down his grandfather's proposal. But it was what his mother added next that had his gut twisting into knots.

Work isn't everything, honey. You've made it, and we're all very proud of you. Maybe now it's time to let your heart have a turn at living.

And even though he'd been worried that he was too much like his grandfather, wasn't it true that his parents had been the ones who'd taught him how to love—not Chandler? He could definitely make this work. It might not be easy to balance all the different parts of his life, but he'd never backed down from a challenge and he wouldn't back down now.

Especially not when a future with Shelley was on the line.

"Thank you for taking me home with you tonight."

Shelley's voice brought him back to the present. She sat in the passenger seat looking more beautiful than ever. Everything about her seemed brighter tonight, from the happiness in her eyes to her smile. Even the way she held his hand felt warmer, better than before—and before had been damn good.

He wanted to keep making her happy and was really glad he'd planned a surprise for her.

"It wouldn't have been nearly as much fun without you. But was my family overwhelming? I know we can be a rowdy bunch."

"Are you kidding? They're great! I've spent my whole life wishing for a family like yours. I can't imagine how you and Trent and Derek moved away. Your family is so full of love and support. They're warm and wonderful, and...I know I'm gushing, but I can't help it."

"I love when you gush." He turned onto the street and made a sharp right onto a narrow dirt road that led up into the woods.

"Where are we going?" Shelley peered into the darkness. "Is this even a road?"

"Sort of." He parked the car and went to the trunk, shouldered two duffel bags he'd packed before picking up Shelley, and helped her from the car.

"Is this the part where you kill me and bury my body?" she teased as they followed a dark trail deeper into the woods.

"Only if it's really possible to love someone to death. But even then, I'd give you a proper burial," he teased right back. "These are my old stomping grounds," he said as he snaked his arm around her waist and led her up a big hill. "My brothers and Sierra and I used to run around these woods like wild banshees. We'd build forts and chase each other around."

"That sounds like fun."

"There are so many places like this that I haven't even thought of for years. Tonight, Shell, this is all for you."

He let go of her hand and bent down in the dark to fiddle with something. A few seconds later, strings of white lights illuminated an enormous tree trunk that grew up from the ground at a slight angle.

The trunk bloomed wide, horizontal to the ground, like a giant hand, palm up, with gnarled branches like long, thick fingers that reached up toward the sky. Lights followed the thick trunk, guiding a path up roughly built steps that led to a platform in the palm of the tree.

There, in the center of the platform, was a tree house—just like the one she'd told Quinn she'd always dreamed of having as a little girl.

Chapter Twenty-four

"QUINN..." SHELLEY WHISPERED into the night. "I've never seen anything like this! It's *amazing.*"

This was no ordinary tree house. It was built with plywood walls that had been whitewashed. A hole was cut as a window, and there were shadows cast inside from what she imagined were more lights. A railing of tangled branches bound together with rope surrounded the structure.

He pulled her in close. "Welcome to your night in a tree house. One item off your bucket list."

Shelley swallowed against the lump thickening in her throat as he continued speaking.

"I can't promise to be with you every day, but I hope to make the days—and the nights—we're together ones that you'll never forget."

He sealed his lips over hers, and Shelley melted against him, wishing he'd never leave but knowing it was inevitable. They'd discussed a long-distance relationship and had agreed to it. So even though she couldn't imagine a day without him, loving Quinn meant loving *all* of him.

Shelley was a strong woman. She knew she could do anything. She'd never needed a man, not for one stinking thing.

But as Quinn pulled her in even closer to him and deepened the kiss—his heart beating fast against hers—she finally realized that when you loved someone, *need* had nothing to do with the ache of *wanting* that person with you every minute of the day.

QUINN LAY BESIDE Shelley on the blankets in the love nest he'd created just for them, complete with pillows and a bottle of wine.

"I can't believe you went to all this trouble to decorate your childhood tree house for me," Shelley said. "How old were you when you built it? And whose idea was it? Derek, since he's so into building things?"

"I was thirteen, but it was actually my mom's idea. We were tearing around the house with way too much energy, so she not only suggested that we try to build a tree house, but she brought us to this tree, too." Quinn smiled as he remembered the sunny April morning they'd followed their parents and traipsed through the woods. "She called this Inspiration Point, because she said it looked like a giant hand that held all our dreams. When we had a problem to work out or we were just out of sorts, she'd say, *Head up to Inspiration Point. You'll sort it out.*" Quinn looked around the small room, taking in each of the boards they'd pounded together with hammers and old nails. "She was right. I came up here a lot over the years. This is where I slept the night before I left for college. This is where I made the decision to leave the island and start my business in Annapolis. It was like my big goodbye to the island." And now, he thought, he was here with Shelley...about to say goodbye again. Knowing it was going to be only a week or two before he was back on the island didn't make it any easier to go.

"I still can't imagine ever wanting to leave. You have so much here. Don't you ever miss it?" He could tell she wasn't asking to try to convince him to stay, but because she was truly curious. "I think I'd miss it, and I've only been here a few days."

"The island has that effect on a lot of people," he agreed. "I see it in Trent's eyes now that we're back, actually. It might not have been his initial choice to come back here, but now that he's been back a little while, I can tell he's fully committed to being here again. Excited about it, actually. Whereas Derek can't wait for the handcuffs to come off so that he can leave again. Then again, Derek has never been the kind of guy who's ever been happy settling down in one place."

When Shelley settled her hand over his after he said the word *handcuffs*, and her eyes went serious, Quinn easily guessed that she must be thinking about how vehement he had been about leaving when they'd first met.

"You're a careful thinker, Quinn, and this has all happened so fast. The speed of our relationship doesn't faze me, but I can't help wondering if in your mind you're still processing it. *Us*." She rubbed her thumb across his palm. "I just want you to know that I get it, because I never saw you coming, either. After all," she said with a laugh, "this was supposed to be my *solo* honeymoon. I never expected to meet you in the cove at midnight and fall head over heels in love with you, practically at first sight."

Not for the first time—or, he was certain, the last—Quinn wondered what he'd done to deserve her. He'd never met a woman who understood his need to overthink things. Nor had he ever met one who was so honest in every moment, even when honesty wasn't the easiest path.

Most women, he knew, would either be giving him an ultimatum about staying on the island or they'd be offering to move to Annapolis with him. But as much as Shelley loved him—and he knew without one single doubt that she loved him as much as he loved her—she had way too much self-respect to ever give up her own dreams to follow a man. Especially not when she'd been searching her whole life for a place that felt like home, and there was no doubt that Rockwell Island was that place.

He'd known she belonged here from the moment he'd seen her in the cove that first night. She'd bonded with the elements, both tangible and intangible, and had become one with the island in the same way most of his family was. And the truth was, seeing the island through her eyes had him also now feeling the pull of the bay, the draw of the close-knit residents, and the love and support that his family doled out effortlessly and consistently.

But more than anything, he knew he'd be drawn back to the island again and again by Shelley. "You make me want so much," he told her as he laid her gently on her back and kissed the ridge of her shoulder. "You make me think about my future in such a different way than I ever have before." He kissed a heated path down her arm. "You make me feel like the island is home again, when it hasn't been that way for a very long time." He pressed a kiss to the pulse point at her neck, then licked out against her deliciously soft skin. "And tonight, when you talked about having kids, you made me realize how great that would be...and that I want to be there for my kids the same way my parents were there for me."

"You're a loving, caring son and brother, Quinn," she said softly, her breath hitching from his mouth playing over her skin. "So I know you're going to be a protective, loving father one day, too."

He lifted his head to look into her eyes. "You have so much faith in me, don't you?"

Because even though he now wanted all these new things, he also still needed to figure out how to balance this powerful love he felt with his crazy schedule and propensity to overwork. He wanted to be there for her when she needed him and not let her down by canceling trips to see her at the last minute because of a meeting about the resort or an issue at the shipyard.

"Always," she said against his lips before pressing a kiss to them. "I'll always have faith in you. Just like I know you'll always have faith in me."

"How did I get so lucky to find you, Shell? You're sweet, you're beautiful, and you're *mine.*"

"*Yours,*" she agreed in a whisper as he ran his hands over her, from her shoulders to her waist and then over her hips. "Love me, Quinn."

"Always," he said as he untied her halter top and drew down her dress, loving how she always vibrated with pure pleasure as he ran his mouth and hands over her. He stroked, caressed, teased, and tempted until she was writhing beneath him and tearing his clothes off.

He gazed into her beautiful eyes, hazy with desire. "Do you know how much I love you? Your heart. Your honesty. Your passion."

"Show me how much, Quinn. And let me show you, too."

He wanted desperately to be a generous lover, to make this night more memorable than any other. But when she began to kiss and touch him the same way he'd been touching her, he knew if he had any hope of pleasuring her, he had to get control of his desires...and fast.

Lacing their fingers together, he brought her hands to the sides of her hips and held them there as he took her in another needful kiss before slowly licking and nipping and kissing his way down from her mouth to the swell of her breasts, then down over her rib cage and past her belly button. By the time he scraped his teeth lightly over one hip bone, she was lifting her hips closer to his mouth and he was beyond desperate to taste her.

Finally, he brought his mouth to the center of her arousal, teasing her with his tongue as she panted out his name. She tasted sweet as honey, and the sexy moans escaping from her lips as he let one of her hands go to slide his between her legs made it even harder for him to hold back. Within seconds of thrusting his fingers deep inside of her, her inner muscles clenched, pulsing as she rode the wave of her climax.

He didn't let her come back down to earth before moving back up her body and taking her in a greedy kiss. Her mouth was warm and sweet as she met every stroke of his tongue with an eager slick of her own. Watching her come was the most erotic, sensual experience of his life, and he wanted to do it again and again and again. Shelley had come into his life from out of the blue and turned everything he thought he knew upside down, and every kiss, every soft sigh she gave him was a gift. Ones he'd treasure forever.

He sheathed himself and came down over her, lacing their fingers together again and holding them beside her head as he said, "I love you, Shell. So damn much."

"Oh God, Quinn..." She closed her eyes as he brought them as close as two people could be, then opened them again to gaze up at him in wonder as she whispered, "I love you, too."

Their hips moved in exquisite harmony as her breasts brushed against his chest and her hips rocked off the blankets. His hands were shaking with need as he explored the soft lines of her ribs, her waist, and the swell of her hips, where he held on tight. Wrapping her legs around his waist, he couldn't wait one more second to angle her hips and drive in deeper. So deep that they both groaned at the soul searing pleasure of it.

He could feel her heart beating hard against his, her damp skin sliding against his as she took him inside again and again, her breath sobbing out as he greedily ran his tongue, his teeth, his lips over her soft skin, from the wild pulse beating in her throat to the swell of her breasts. He felt her shudder, felt her clench hot and perfect against him, and he needed to give her even more. Needed to give her *everything,*

every last part of him, with nothing held back—
just the same way she was giving herself to him.

From their very first kiss out on the sand
with the stars shining above them, with every
smile, every laugh, every single breath, he'd
been helplessly falling deeper and deeper in
love with her.

And every single day he would be thankful
that he'd come back to the island and found
Shelley in his cove. His girl. His *love.*

"Oh God..." She closed her eyes again.

"Look at me, sweetheart. Let me see you
come apart for me."

And when her eyes fluttered open and their
gazes connected for a split second and she let
him see all the way into her very soul, for a few
blissful moments Quinn was able to forget his
past and stop worrying about his future.

Everything he needed, everything he
wanted, was right here in Shelley's arms.

Chapter Twenty-five

LATE THE NEXT morning, Shelley turned the key in the lock of the cottage she'd just signed papers to rent for the next two years.

"This is it," she said to Quinn as they stood together on the front porch. "My new beginning officially starts now."

She pushed the door open and inhaled the scent of furniture polish—and the huge vase of flowers she knew Quinn must have put inside the cottage for her to welcome her to her new home.

She laughed with delighted surprised as he lifted her into his arms and carried her over the threshold with a beaming smile.

"I'm so proud of you, Shell. You saw what you wanted and you went for it. I've said it a million times and I'll say it a million more.

You're a remarkable woman." He kissed her again before her toes touched the hardwood floor.

She crossed the room and opened the doors to the balcony. Fresh sea air brought the sheer curtains to life.

He moved behind her, wrapped his arms around her, and nibbled on the curve of her neck. "What do you say we christen every single room?"

After enjoying such a romantic evening at the tree house, Quinn had spent an hour and a half this morning catching up on phone calls he'd missed while Shelley had made a to-do list for moving her café. They'd had breakfast with his parents at Sierra's restaurant, stopped by Quinn's suite to pick up work he had to take care of for his partner, and then met the real estate agent.

She'd planned to unpack right away...but making love with Quinn in every room was the *perfect* way to celebrate what was already one of the best mornings of her life.

She turned toward the man who had appeared the first night she'd set foot on the island and had effortlessly wound his way into her heart. He'd accepted her for who she was, supported what surely looked like a whim, and had given her the best week of her entire life.

She hadn't even been looking for a boyfriend. Who knew she would find love here on Rockwell Island?

Every ounce of her believed in Quinn's love for her, and as much as she knew he worried about hurting her, she also knew he'd always do everything in his power to keep it from happening.

"Now that you've mentioned it," she said in a husky voice as she turned in his arms, wonderfully aware of his hard wall of muscle beneath her hands and against her curves, "unpacking can definitely wait."

His kiss was demanding and loving at once, sending a quiver through her. His hands explored her back, her hips, then moved back up to tangle in her hair. With a gentle tug, Shelley's head tipped back as his lips traveled over her jaw, down her neck, and settled on her bare shoulder.

"Bedroom," she whispered.

In one forward motion she was in his arms again as he took them up the stairs. They were nearly at her bedroom, and she was already reeling with need from the kisses he'd given her as he mounted each step, when his phone rang.

Quinn's body immediately went rigid and Shelley held her breath. He'd spent a long time already on business calls that morning, and even though he'd tried to act like everything was okay, she'd seen restrained frustration written in every tight muscle for about an hour after the calls.

But he didn't reach for the phone, clearly trying to ignore it as he laid her on the bed and came down over her. But when the phone sounded off again in his pocket, he cursed, two hundred plus pounds of tension levered above her on his forearms.

"Answer it," she said softly.

"It can wait," he nearly barked. His eyes were dark with the private war going off in his mind.

She caressed his cheek. "Quinn, we can wait."

He looked down at the phone still ringing in his pocket and scowled as he moved to the side of the bed and rested his elbows on his knees. A moment later, the ringing stopped.

Shelley came up on her knees behind him and rubbed the knots from his shoulders. "You have to take care of your work, just like I'll have to take care of mine, but I have faith we'll figure out how to strike a balance that works for both of us."

But instead of agreeing with her, he simply brushed his hand lovingly once over her hair, then pushed to his feet and paced. Every step carried the weight of the storm brewing inside him. A storm that she could now see was even bigger than she'd thought.

His phone rang again, and they both froze. After a long minute of staring at each other with the phone ringing insistently between them, she stepped from the bed and put her arms around him.

"Take your call. And whatever it is you're afraid to tell me, I can take it. It won't change my moving to the island or my feelings for you."

QUINN DIDN'T WANT to answer the phone. He knew what was coming, and he wanted to buy more time with Shelley, but when the ringing began for a third time, he had no choice. He'd learned earlier that morning that the merger was on the line because of potential fair trade issues—and they needed him in Maryland to negotiate.

"Yeah." He couldn't even muster a cordial greeting for Rich.

"It's on, Quinn. You've got to get on the next flight out if you want this merger to happen."

He'd worked his ass off to bring the merger to this point. He'd thought the legal teams had handled any issues revolving around the Sherman Antitrust Act, but now that monster was rearing its ugly head again. If he wanted the merger to take place, he had to be on-site, elbow deep in the legal issues. It would take weeks to work through the legal channels.

He peered into the empty hall. Shelley must have gone downstairs. So then why did it feel like she'd gone a million miles away?

They'd agreed to the long-distance relationship. They knew it wasn't going to be easy—he just never imagined it would be this hard. And he hadn't even left yet.

But, damn it, he'd built this business from the ground up. He couldn't just let it falter, could he?

"I'll be there. I've just got to wrap up a few things first."

Wrap up a few things. His gut twisted as the words echoed in his head. Because how was he supposed to tell the woman he loved that he needed to leave for what was, at the very least, a few weeks? But probably even longer.

"Hey, look at the bright side," Rich said. "Now you have a legitimate excuse to get off the island."

Rich was right that if Quinn could have turned around and walked back onto the plane last Friday, he would have done it without as much as a look back.

But that was before Shelley. Before he'd fallen so deeply in love with her that nothing else seemed to matter anymore.

He ended the call and pressed his fist against his breastbone, but it did nothing for the tightening in his chest. He wished he could grab Shelley, head back to the big stable tree and see the gorgeous afterglow of their lovemaking in the pink of her cheeks and the sweet, sultry gaze of her green eyes one more time before he left.

But there wasn't time for that right now. Wasn't time for anything but saying goodbye.

He found her out on the deck, standing at the railing. Her thick dark hair tumbled down her back in carefree waves. She turned as he approached, her eyes full of love as she reached for him and pressed her cheek to his chest.

He gathered her in his arms, opened his mouth to speak, and hesitated, riding the wave of conflicting emotions that surged through him. He'd worried that he'd dim her light if he got involved with her, and here he was, about to throw sand on her flame.

Shelley took a deep breath, then hooked her fingers in the waist of his pants and smiled up at him. Someone else might not notice the sadness hovering in her eyes, but he'd always noticed—and loved—every single thing about her.

"Okay, I'm ready for you to tell me you need to go back to Annapolis."

She might have been ready for it, but he wasn't.

He'd faced down fierce competitors, gone head-to-head with the savviest of businessmen in boardrooms across the country. He'd crushed his classmates on the curve at college and graduated top of the class. And yet now that he'd found the one person on earth he never wanted to hurt, he was powerless to keep from hurting her.

He'd never felt powerless before, and it sucked.

"I need to leave right away," he confirmed in a raw voice as he held her gaze.

"Don't worry about me, Quinn. Take care of what you need to take care of."

She was the person he most wanted to take care of. He wanted to stay here longer, so that he could laugh with her and love her while holding her in his arms, instead of doing all of that from a distance.

But since he couldn't stay, he knew he needed to explain the whole situation. "I'm afraid this isn't going to be a quick trip. We've got legal issues to deal with pertaining to the merger, and I've also got to deal with an employee who's threatening to leave. I've been putting it off, but...it will be weeks. Probably several."

She swallowed hard. "Several weeks." She paused and dropped her eyes to his chest. "Well, that'll give me time to get things ironed out with my business." She shifted her feet a little wider, as if she were trying to ground herself again. "We'll both be busy."

"Shell." He lifted her chin and nearly broke at the depth of sadness in her eyes. "We'll Skype, and text..." But they were all poor substitutes for holding her in his arms.

"Of course." She pulled her shoulders back as he'd seen her do so many times before, and he watched as she forced herself to smile up at him. "So...can I help you pack?"

How many times in her life had she been forced to do that? Pick herself up from heartache and carry on? How many times had her parents berated her or made her feel unloved?

The reality of why she was able to morph so quickly from heartbroken to strong sliced through him.

Quinn wasn't used to this, having never allowed his emotions to rule his life, but Shelley was guided by passion like others were guided by their GPS systems.

"I'd love your help packing, but I have to say goodbye to my family, too."

"I can wait here if you'd rather do that alone."

He drew her in close, memorizing the feel of her against him. These memories of holding her in his arms were all that would keep him going for quite some time.

"No way, sweetheart. I want you with me until the second I have to board the plane."

Chapter Twenty-six

"ARE YOU SURE you're okay with me leaving my bags at your cottage?" Quinn asked as Shelley helped him pack the last of his clothes in his suite.

God, she'd miss him while he was gone. Every time he left the island, she'd miss his passion, and the way he looked at her with pure, unconditional love.

"I'm *way* more than okay with it," she said in a deliberately light voice. "I'm thrilled that you've just given me permission to rifle through your clothes and find the comfiest shirt that smells like you to sleep in."

He lifted her by the waist and set her on the dresser, parting her knees with his, and slid her close. Shelley closed her eyes and breathed him in, borrowing his strength to call her own.

"I like thinking about you sleeping in my shirt."

"I'd rather sleep in your arms"—she smiled up at him—"but this'll have to do for a little while."

Their lips brushed as a knock sounded at the door. Quinn touched his forehead to hers.

"The universe really doesn't want us to get naked today, does it?"

"It's probably better that way," she said with another smile she could barely force. "It would be even harder to let you go if you'd just loved me silly."

"Quinn?" Trent called through the door.

Quinn gave Shelley another deeply passionate and emotional kiss before she hopped off the dresser. He pulled open the door, and Trent barreled in.

"I got your text. You're taking off?" Trent didn't look surprised to see her. "Hi, Shelley. It's nice to see you again."

"Hi." She wanted to tell him it was nice to see him again, too, but her throat was too tight right now to say more than hello.

"I'll cover you here while you're gone," Trent said to Quinn, his expression understanding. "But when you come back, you should probably set up meetings with your staff at the resort to establish your authority and to figure out what Grandfather didn't get done."

"I already planned on having my secretary set up a virtual conference early next week so I can establish my position while I'm in Annapolis."

"Good to know you're always one step ahead of me." Trent glanced at Shelley and then stepped closer to Quinn and lowered his voice.

Shelley tried not to eavesdrop, but it was such a small room that even if she hadn't been tempted she would have overheard.

"I was young and stupid," Trent said to Quinn. "What's your excuse?"

What is that supposed to mean? Shelley wondered as Quinn made a strangled noise in his throat.

Shelley's phone vibrated with a text. She moved to the side, allowing the men to say their goodbyes while she read the message from Sierra.

Quinn said he's leaving. Want to have lunch tomorrow? I have some ideas for your café, and I'd love to spend more time with you.

She looked at the text for a long moment, feeling that it underscored just how caring the Rockwell family was to innately understand just how much she'd miss Quinn after he left.

After his brother left, Quinn picked up his bag, looking grim. "We've got to get going or I'll miss my flight. Especially since I need to have a word with Chandler before I go."

He shouldered his bags and they headed for the elevators.

"I'm proud of you, Quinn," Shelley said as they stepped inside.

"Proud?"

"I know it isn't easy to leave your family, or us. But even if I'm sad to be apart, it's an impressive quality that you don't shirk your responsibilities."

The elevator doors opened on his grandfather's floor, and they stepped into the hall as the doors to the second elevator, beside them, opened and Didi pushed Chandler's wheelchair into the hallway.

Quinn and Shelley both pulled their shoulders back and stood up straighter. He wasn't even Shelley's grandfather and she felt the need to straighten up in Chandler's presence.

Didi smiled and placed a hand on Chandler's shoulder. Shelley liked the way she did that. It made her believe the softening she'd seen in Chandler's face must have been real for Didi to act so protective of him.

Or...perhaps that touch was a warning, a reminder to Chandler to behave?

The thought gave her pause as Quinn and his grandfather had a brief stare down. She imagined years of tension filling the space between them, much like the air shift that occurred when she visited her parents.

Chandler raised an imperious eyebrow in his grandson's direction. "Quinn."

"I have an emergency with my company and have to leave the island for a few weeks." Quinn spoke with certitude and without a hint of defiance, something Shelley had rarely been able to pull off with her parents.

"We'll soon know where your priorities lie." Chandler's eyes skittered over Shelley. "Didi." He motioned for her to wheel him to his office.

Didi flashed an apologetic smile, then turned Chandler's wheelchair around and began to push him away.

Quinn's hands fisted at his sides. "Grandfather."

Chandler said something to Didi, and she turned the wheelchair around but didn't advance toward them.

Shelley stiffened at Chandler's challenging stare, but Quinn reached for Shelley's hand with cool confidence. "I can only assume that you failed to notice Shelley was here with me. Otherwise I'm sure you would have acknowledged her with a greeting."

Chandler's eyes shifted to her, and she was beyond shocked when his lips suddenly curved up in a half smile, softening many of his sharp edges. He nodded slowly, never breaking their connection.

"I do apologize, Ms. Walters. I'm afraid I'm not having one of my better days. But it is a pleasure to see you again." With a final nod, he said, "Good day," then gestured for Didi to wheel him away.

Once his door closed, Shelley let out the breath she'd been holding and wrapped her arms around the amazing man beside her. "I love you, Quinn Rockwell."

She could read the love in his eyes as he gazed down at her even before he said, "I love you, too, Shell. More than you can even imagine."

But she didn't need to imagine anything at all, because he'd just proved it to her yet again.

THIRTY MINUTES LATER they were standing inside the small island airport. It was the size of a fast-food restaurant, with one long counter off to the left and a glass-walled room to the right, where passengers waited to board the plane after going through a brief security check.

Standing within the confines of Quinn's embrace for what would be the last time until he returned in a few long weeks, Shelley was determined not to make their parting any more difficult than it already was. He had been nearly silent since they'd arrived at the airport, and every time he looked at her his eyes became hooded and he rubbed the back of his neck as if a winter chill had settled into his bones.

She had to be strong. She refused to be one of those clingy, weak women who made her man feel guilty for doing what he had to do.

Quinn touched her shoulders, keeping her at arm's length, his handsome features downturned as if he were readying them both for his departure. Shelley nuzzled against his chest again. She didn't want space between them. Not yet. Not until they were about to close the airplane doors and she had no other choice. They stood off to the side as passengers filed through the security gate, and somehow it still felt like they were the only two people in the room.

"Shell, before we saw my grandfather you said you were proud of me for not shirking my responsibilities and that it must not be easy to leave the island. The truth is, before meeting you, it *was* easy to leave the island. You've changed everything, and…"

He paused, and she took in the pained look in his beautiful blue eyes. Knowing that he was fighting the same devastation she was tugged even harder at her heart.

"I just want you to know I meant everything I've said to you." His hoarse whisper nearly broke the dam and set her emotions free. "I love you. I'm not leaving *you*. I'm just fulfilling my obligations and then I'm coming back." Determination radiated from him as he repeated, "I'm coming back."

As the last call for passengers on his flight came through, Quinn pulled her in close again, and with one last tender kiss turned to walk through security. He glanced over his shoulder and blew her a kiss as he passed into the room where others were already lining up to board the plane.

Shelley pressed her palm against the glass wall. In three determined steps, his palms met hers through the glass. Quinn mouthed, *I love you,* then disappeared into the small plane.

Chapter Twenty-seven

THE FLIGHT FROM the island to Boston was less than thirty minutes. Quinn had thought that by the time they touched down, the longing that clutched his chest would have eased and the guilt that lay buried deep inside his heart would have subsided. After all, he'd left his family dozens of times without feeling as though he'd left a piece of himself behind, hadn't he?

He followed the other passengers off the plane and rushed to the standby desk to check in for his connecting flight. Maybe he just needed to get back to work to get his mind back on track.

"Sir?"

The woman behind the counter held his driver's license out toward him a handful of minutes later. He had forgotten he'd given it to her. He felt as though he was moving on autopilot.

"You're all set. Your flight is boarding now." She pointed to a line of people standing off to the side.

He put his license away and walked mindlessly into line, still thinking of Shelley. He glanced out at the setting sun and wondered if she was watching the sunset from the deck of the cottage.

Was she already missing him as much as he was missing her?

His phone buzzed as he walked down the Jetway and onto the plane. Shelley's smiling face filled the screen with the caption, *I got the gristmill!*

He typed in a response on his phone as he took his seat. *Congratulations, sweetheart! We'll have to celebrate.*

But before sending, Quinn hesitated with his finger over the screen. Celebrate? When would they get a chance to do that? Six or eight weeks from now?

He deleted the second half of his message, wishing she'd received the call hours earlier so he could have held her in his arms and felt her enthusiasm with his whole body.

I'll call you tonight and we'll make plans for the renovations.

Before sending this second text, he also worked it over in his mind. She'd need time to get her licensing figured out, and plans needed to be drawn up. Drawing up plans was tricky, even if Derek agreed to help her. And the contracts with subs would need overseeing. He knew his family would help her with all of those things. His brothers would never leave her hanging, but damn it, he should be the one helping her.

"Sir, you'll need to put your cell phone away," the flight attendant said as she walked past.

He hesitated again, his fingers hovering over the screen as he tried to figure out what to say to Shelley that wouldn't only highlight the distance between them.

"I'm sorry. Now, sir," she said with a polite but firm tone.

He powered down his phone without sending a text back, then shoved it in his pocket. But even as he flung open the document on his lap, he knew his enormous workload wouldn't do a damn thing to help mask the dull ache of loneliness gnawing at his gut.

SHELLEY CLOSED HER fingers around the broom handle and took a few quiet moments to look at the interior of the gristmill, which was soon to be hers. With Abby's help, a little finesse, and the charm of doing business on an island, the verbal agreement to purchase the gristmill was as solid as the ground Shelley stood on *and* she was granted access to the property to begin cleaning even though they still had to go through the formal closing.

It was the perfect way to work off the ache of missing Quinn.

Sierra and Abby had come by her cottage shortly after he had left to give her the good news about the gristmill and to bring her a housewarming gift for her newly rented cottage. Now they were here with her, scrubbing and mopping, helping to clean up the amazing building that she couldn't wait to make her own.

"I think it'll take you a week just to get the dust out of this place," Sierra said as she wrung out the mop.

"I don't care if it takes a month. Look at how incredible it looks after just two hours! I swear this place was put here just for me."

Abby stopped scrubbing the counter she was cleaning and wiped her hands on a towel. "I think you're right, Shelley. And," she said with a soft smile, "I think Quinn has been waiting his whole life to meet you, too."

Shelley had been working hard to keep from pining over him, but at the mention of his name, loneliness crept back in. "Is it silly that I miss him already?"

"Not at all," Abby said as she began scrubbing again. "If I know Quinn, he's missing you just as much."

Sierra set the mop on the floor again. "I miss him, too. It's funny, when Quinn, Trent, and Derek are gone for months at a time, I'm pretty much okay. I miss them, but I get used to it and I get busy. But when I've spent a bunch of time with them, I miss them *more* after they leave."

With every scratch of the broom on the aged hardwood, Shelley wished Quinn were there with her. But short of that impossibility, she couldn't have asked for a more enjoyable evening than spending time with, and being supported by, Abby and Sierra as they helped prepare the gristmill for her café.

QUINN BECAME MORE agitated by the second as he walked behind what had to be the slowest family in the world while trying to get off the plane.

He'd tried to bury himself in work on the flight, but his mind was drenched in thoughts of Shelley's smile, her laugh, the way she touched him, inside and out. She was everywhere. Every thought, every scent sparked memories of something they'd done together or something she'd said.

He'd gone into the bathroom and splashed cold water on his face in an effort to center his focus on the work that he needed to be completely on top of, but when he'd looked at himself in the mirror, it was as if he was finally seeing himself—and what he *really* wanted—for the very first time in his life.

Yes, he'd worked his ass off to build his corporate empire, but what good was it if he couldn't be with Shelley? He already knew he didn't want to be like Chandler, a resentful old man whose true love turned him away because he was a workaholic. And he'd vowed to never put disappointment in Shelley's eyes again, either.

Damn it, there was no way in hell that she was going to play second fiddle to his job. She deserved to come first, and she was going to come first.

Starting *now*.

When he finally broke free from behind the other passengers, the first thing he did was make a quick call to his fleet manager to arrange for a private plane back to the island—one that he found out was closing its doors in a matter of minutes. Quinn ran through the airport, weaving through the crowd. He reached the gate with less than a minute to spare, the door closing behind him as soon as he took his seat.

All it had taken was one short trip off the island for him to realize that he was done putting work ahead of starting his life with Shelley. He knew how much he loved her. And he knew he was capable of changing whatever he needed to in order to keep from hurting her and to give her the fulfilled and happy future she deserved. He didn't need to be stuck in Annapolis, missing her every single second, to prove to himself that she was what really mattered. He already knew that.

Stuck in Annapolis. A week ago he'd felt *stuck* on the island. Shelley had not only opened his eyes to the beauty of the island he had once found too confining, but she'd also made him realize he needed something more than a shipping empire to fill his soul. Shelley had also reminded him of the importance of family.

Trent's parting words came back to Quinn as the staff did their final preparation for takeoff: *I was young and stupid. What's your excuse?*

Even though Trent's marriage had failed, his brother clearly seemed to recognize that it wasn't because love was fundamentally flawed, but because Trent and Reese had been barely more than kids when they'd gotten married. Which also meant that Trent had seen Quinn's leaving the island, and Shelley, as a mistake before Quinn had. Everyone had probably seen it, but they respected him enough not to rush or push him.

Maybe now it's time to let your heart have a turn at living, was what his mother had said before dinner. Abby Rockwell had always been wise. But never more than when she was gently counseling him on finding—and keeping—true love.

Before the flight staff made everyone turn off their devices, Quinn dialed Rich's number and drew in a deep breath, mentally preparing for his business partner's anger.

"Where are you?" Rich barked. "The driver said he can't find you."

"He's not going to find me. I'm on a flight back to the island."

"Quinn, you can't be serious."

"Dead serious."

"What about Joseph? We'll lose him."

Quinn still loved the company he'd started from little more than an idea and the gumption to succeed. He'd given years of his life to building the shipping empire that he and Rich now treasured. But Quinn had only so many hours in the day to give—and now he wanted to give lots of those hours to Shelley. What's more, he also now knew that he *needed* to be on the island as much as he *wanted* to be there.

How could he have thought it was fair to leave when his family was doing exactly what they'd committed to doing? And who knew he'd learn the most important life lessons of all from the naked beauty he'd seen flitting about in the cove the night he'd arrived on the island?

Quinn hadn't known if he believed in fate before he met Shelley, but now he believed that things *did* happen for a reason. In this case—his leaving the company was actually the perfect way to get Joseph to stay.

"Let's promote Joseph and give him most of my current responsibilities, including negotiating the fair trade issues I was coming back to deal with. He's been a loyal employee for years, and right now, with the way my life has changed course, he's exactly what our company needs—a gung-ho employee who wants to take it to the next level." *While I focus on creating a life with Shelley. A life she deserves with a man who is there for her. A life both of us deserve.*

The flight attendant motioned for him to turn his phone off as they taxied out on the runway.

"I'll have a remote office set up next week. From here on out, all of my conferences will be virtual. I've got to hang up because we're taxiing out on the runway, but I have faith that Joseph is the right man for the job. Oh, and I'm taking the weekend off, but we'll talk Monday about the merger."

Quinn ended the call feeling like the luckiest guy on earth—and also the biggest fool. He gazed out into the dark sky as they flew toward Rockwell Island and wondered how he could have been so blind, so stupid, to have left the woman he loved?

Anyone with half a brain would have grabbed at this type of true love with both hands and done everything within their power to nurture it and keep it strong. Which was exactly what he was going back to do.

To nurture Shelley's love and keep it strong. *Forever.*

AFTER GRABBING A bite to eat with Abby and Sierra, Shelley hadn't wanted to go back to her empty cottage. Sierra'd had to go back to the restaurant, and Abby had gone home to Griffin, though, so she'd come back to the gristmill and worked until her arms felt like wet noodles. At least the windows on the first level were clean and she no longer kicked up dust with every step.

It was already after ten o'clock and she hoped Quinn was okay. But she was worried that the reason he hadn't called yet was because he was so horribly overloaded with all the work and pressure waiting for him in

Annapolis. She only wished she could be there with him at the end of his stressful day to hold him in her arms and help him relax.

She'd never been in love before, and she'd questioned the validity of people saying their hearts ached or they felt empty when they weren't with the one they loved. She'd never imagined feeling any of those things because she'd been so sure that true love would never hurt. But now she realized that this complexity of emotions—feeling hollow and full at the same time, strong and weak, like she could make the world spin on its axis or just as easily fall into a well of tears—was the beauty of love.

How could she treasure the incredible highs if she didn't accept the depths of missing Quinn when he was gone?

Shelley had begun mopping again with renewed vengeance, when she heard the sound of the bushes at the edge of the property rustling. Through the window she could see a figure illuminated by the faint moonlight emerging from between the two tallest bushes.

She was wondering who the heck could be out there at this time of night when Quinn's face suddenly came into focus amid the dim light.

"Quinn!" Her breath caught in her throat as she dropped the mop and ran outside to leap into his arms. She kissed his lips, his forehead, his cheeks. Everywhere she could. "You're here." She could hardly believe it. "You're really here."

"Yes, I'm really here." His smile shot straight to the center of her chest. "And I've never been happier to see anyone in my life."

Their hearts hammered in time with the other's, and they were both grinning like the lovesick fools that they were, when it finally occurred to her to ask, "*Why* are you here?"

"Because you're here, Shell. While you were falling in love with the island, I was falling in love with you. I realized on the way back to Maryland that it wasn't signing the takeover papers that had the power to change my life, Shell. It was *you*. The whole flight back, I was planning to stop to buy you a ring and get champagne, and then I was going to take you out on one of my boats filled with roses to profess my love for you and show you how much you mean to me. But, Shell..." He stroked her cheek and held her emotional gaze. "Once I touched down on the island, I couldn't wait another second to be with you. And then I realized what you've known all along. *Things* can't prove my love for you. There's only one way to do that, by being with you. I'm here, Shell. And I have faith in us, too. Because when I'm with you, I'm home. It doesn't matter where we are or what we're doing as long as we're together. This is where I belong. With you. Every day. And every single night."

Shelley wanted to tell him how much she loved him and that he was right—the only thing she cared about was that they were together—but when she opened her mouth, emotions swallowed her voice. Which was just as well, because he had more he needed to say.

"I knew you'd be here working late to try to drown out the voices in your head that said we shouldn't be apart, just like I was. But I don't want you to ever have to work to drive away pain again. I want to give you more joy, more happiness than you've ever known before. More than you ever thought was possible."

"You already have." Each word was drenched with love. So much love she was bursting with it. "You already do."

"No, sweetheart. This is only the beginning. You told me that I held your heart in my hands. What kind of a man would I be if I didn't cherish your heart with everything I had? From the first night we met in the cove, you made everything brighter, everything better. You're the light of my life, Shelley."

Give me a guiding light, had been her wish. *Lead me to my forever home.*

Her wish—all of her wishes—had come true. But who would have ever thought that *she* would be *his* guiding light, too?

Shelley couldn't stop smiling as she told the man she loved, "I've wished for true love my whole life. And now here you are. Giving me Cape Cod kisses in the moonlight."

"I want to make all your wishes come true, Shell. Let me teach you how to skip rocks, and you can teach me how to keep making the most out of every precious moment, especially the ones when we sneak out to *our* cove and go skinny-dipping together." She had to kiss him, had to let him know how happy he made her, even as he continued to say, "I want us to have rebellious children with minds of their own. We'll teach them to enjoy all the little things in life, and they'll grow up with more love than any children have ever known. I want to drink in every single gasp of pleasure as I make love to you each night...and then be the luckiest guy in the world when I get to love every inch of you again each morning." He gazed deeply into her eyes. "Say you'll marry me, Shell, and be mine forever."

"Forever," she echoed breathlessly, before laughing out loud in amazement at the realization that her solo honeymoon was going to end with her saying, "Once upon a time I thought dating was a bore and husbands were overrated"—both of them were laughing now—"but now there's nothing I want more than to be yours. *Forever.*"

Epilogue

Six weeks later...

TRENT ROCKWELL HAMMERED in the last few nails on the shelves he and his brothers were building inside the old gristmill that Shelley had purchased for her new coffee shop.

The renovations were really coming together. Quinn, Shelley, and Derek had come up with impressive plans to maintain the integrity and character of the old building while using materials that would enhance the rustic charm of the historical structure.

Trent set the hammer down on the old millstone and took stock of what was left to do. *A little sanding, some painting, staining.* In a few weeks, the coffee shop would be up and running. He'd forgotten how much he enjoyed working with his hands and how great it was to come together with his family on a project that was separate from running the resort—which was also shaping up, though not quite as quickly or as simply as Shelley's café.

It was after ten p.m. and his siblings had already called it a night. He pulled his shirt over his head and tossed it aside, trying for the hundredth time since he'd gone outside an hour ago to retrieve tools from his truck to distract himself from thinking about the light he'd seen on at Reese's gallery. He knew Reese was still away, helping her sister with her new baby, which meant her assistant, Jocelyn, was probably working late.

Working late had become the bane of Trent's existence. He thought of how much Quinn had changed since meeting Shelley. His brother had finally begun to take some time off work and enjoy life. Trent had learned the hard way what being a workaholic earned a person—and other than the income and prestige, which in his view were highly overrated, he didn't have much to gain by continuing on that path.

Which only sent his mind drifting back to Reese.

Was she ever far from his mind?

A little more than ten years ago, they'd shared both a wild passion for each other *and* big hopes and dreams of building a life together in New York. They had thought he'd establish his career as an attorney and she'd grow to love city life and would eventually open her own gallery. But she was an island girl at heart, and he...

Well, he'd taken after his grandfather—perhaps a little too much—and those seventy-hour work weeks had destroyed their relationship. He could hardly believe Reese had only been nineteen when they'd wed. He smiled, thinking about how young they'd both been, even though it hurt sometimes to remember how beautiful she'd looked standing on the beach beneath the moonlight in her wedding gown. So beautiful, and so sexy, that they hadn't slept one single moment of their wedding night.

Had it really been a decade since he'd found the *Dear Trent* note that had ended their marriage?

He rubbed the knot at the back of his neck, reminding himself that it was better to leave the past in the past.

But as he glanced at the front door again, he suddenly couldn't keep from wondering about second chances with the woman he'd once promised to love forever...

—The End—

LOVE ON ROCKWELL ISLAND

SIGN UP FOR BELLA & MELISSA'S NEWSLETTER TO BE NOTIFIED OF THE NEXT LOVE ON ROCKWELL ISLAND RELEASE!

http://www.LoveonRockwellIsland.com/Newsletter

* * *

Love Bella's and Melissa's writing?

Find more of **Bella's books** at your favorite retailer, including **THE LOOK OF LOVE**, the first book in her *NYT* bestselling series about the Sullivans.

Find more of **Melissa's books** at your favorite retailer, including **LOVERS AT HEART** (currently free), the first book in her bestselling series about the Bradens.

More about Bella and Melissa
BELLA ANDRE

Bella Andre is the New York Times, USA Today, and Publishers Weekly bestselling author of "The Sullivans" and "The Morrisons" series.

Having sold more than 4 million books, Bella Andre's novels have been #1 bestsellers around the world and have appeared on the *New York Times* and *USA Today* bestseller lists 23 times. She has been the #1 Ranked Author at Amazon (on a top 10 list that included Nora Roberts, J. K. Rowling, James Patterson, and Steven King), and *Publishers Weekly* named Oak Press (the publishing company she created to publish her own books) the Fastest-Growing Independent Publisher in the US. Known for "sensual, empowered stories enveloped in heady romance" (*Publishers Weekly*), her books have been *Cosmopolitan Magazine* "Red Hot Reads" twice and have been translated into ten languages. Winner of the Award of Excellence, *The Washington Post* called her "One of the top writers in America" and she has been featured by NPR, *Entertainment Weekly*, *USA Today*, *Forbes*, *The Wall Street Journal*, and *TIME Magazine*. Bella also writes the *New York Times* bestselling "Four Weddings and a Fiasco" series as Lucy Kevin.

MELISSA FOSTER

Melissa Foster is a New York Times and USA Today bestselling and award-winning author of the Love in Bloom series which includes the "Snow Sisters," "The Bradens," "The Remingtons," and the "Seaside Summers" series.

Melissa writes sexy and heartwarming, award-winning contemporary romance novels with emotionally compelling characters that stay with you long after you turn the last page. Her books have been recommended by *USA Today's* book blog, *Hagerstown* magazine, *The Patriot*, and *Mensa Bulletin*. Melissa is the founder of the World Literary Café and Fostering Success. When she's not writing, Melissa helps authors navigate the publishing industry through her author training programs on Fostering Success. Melissa is also the author of the *New York Times* and *USA Today* bestselling, and award-winning historical fiction novel Have No Shame, as well as several other award-winning suspense and women's fiction titles. Melissa enjoys discussing her books with book clubs and reader groups and welcomes an invitation to your event.

Made in the USA
San Bernardino, CA
10 July 2015